MORE PRAISE FOR CHARLES SHEFFIELD

"*Putting Up Roots* is to the '90s what Robert Heinlein's *Farmer in the Sky* was to the '50s. . . . It's yarns like *Putting Up Roots* which built science fiction and Sheffield is one of today's writers keeping the tradition alive."

—*Starlog*

"Versatile and excellent . . . he must be ranked as a leading heir to the mantle of Arthur C. Clarke."

—*Booklist*

"Sheffield's writing is literate and clean."

—*Minneapolis Star-Tribune*

"Sheffield, a physicist, proves to be one of the most imaginative, exciting talents to appear on the SF scene in recent years."

—*Publishers Weekly*

"Far and away the most believable and interesting near-space milieu I've seen in years."

—Orson Scott Card on *Higher Education*

"Adventure that echoes Robert Heinlein's best coming-of-age novels."

—*Booklist* on *Higher Education*

THE
CYBORG
FROM
EARTH

A JUPITER™ NOVEL

CHARLES SHEFFIELD

A TOM DOHERTY ASSOCIATES BOOK · NEW YORK

This is a work of fiction. All the characters and events portrayed
in this novel are either fictitious or are used fictitiously.

THE CYBORG FROM EARTH

Copyright © 1998 by Charles Sheffield

A Tor Book
Published by Tom Doherty Associates, Inc.
175 Fifth Avenue
New York, NY 10010

Tor Books on the World Wide Web:
http://www.tor.com

Tor® is a registered trademark of Tom Doherty Associates, Inc.

ISBN: 0-812-57184-3
Library of Congress Card Catalog Number: 97-29846

First edition: March 1998
First mass market edition: January 1999

Printed in the United States of America

0 9 8 7 6 5 4 3 2 1

To Rose and Toria

THE CYBORG FROM EARTH

CHAPTER ONE

JEFFERSON *Kopal is a coward. He knows it, and if he doesn't do something about it soon, so will everyone else.* Jeff wrote the words on the yellowing sheet of paper that he had found folded in the back of one of the old books. He read the note aloud, three times. Finally he crumpled the sheet into a ball and looked around for a good way to dispose of it.

Logically, the end of an exorcism ought to be by fire. He should burn the page. But how? The library fireplace was wide and deep, but it was too early in the year for anyone to think of lighting a fire there. No one would anyway, since Jeff seemed to be the only person who ever came to browse through the shelves of old books, with their leather and cloth covers and their look of having been here forever. Everyone else preferred the new library, with its instant and flexible services. It was centrally heated, and the regular array of terminals would never see a naked flame.

What about his rooms, or one of the never-used upper suites?

There were matches in his bedside table; but with fire monitors scattered everywhere through the vast old house, it was difficult to know where something might be burned without setting off alarms.

Outside, then.

Jeff walked over to the library window. The weather was clear and calm, with distant trees showing the first tinge of a fall change of color. He looked across the broad lawn toward the pasture and felt a twinge of nervousness, like a sudden cramp in the belly. It was ideal conditions. There was not the slightest chance that the competition would be postponed.

He put the ball of paper into his trouser pocket and left the old library that occupied part of the second floor's west wing. It was Jeff's favorite haunt and hideaway. His private suite of rooms was one floor higher. To reach them he had to head over to the house's central atrium, then ascend the wide, curving staircase.

He hurried that way, thankful that he didn't meet anyone. It was bad enough to have the framed portraits of the Kopal family staring at him accusingly from the walls. At the very top, the full-length painting of Rollo Kopal had been there to terrify Jeff for as long as he could remember. Rollo had died long before he was born, but Jeff's earliest memories included the frowning picture of his great-grandfather in full uniform, hand on sword pommel. The hard, pebble eyes of the Space Navy admiral and founder of Kopal Transportation stared right at you, no matter where you stood on the staircase.

When Jeff reached his rooms the attention light was flashing on the monitor inside the entrance. He called for messages and was surprised to hear Midgeley's voice. The senior servant of the Kopal household sent routine information over the house's public-address system. That meant this message must be personal—or Midgeley had some other reason why he would not send it to Jeff in public.

"I have important information, sir, regarding your mother." There was no picture, and the voice was totally impartial. No one listening to it—or seeing the man himself—would ever know what Midgeley's own opinions might be of anything that he conveyed to the members of the household.

It was the subject, not the tone, that brought Jeff to instant attention. He at once forgot his own worries. He waited, fearing the worst, until Midgeley went on, "It is good news."

Before Jeff could decide that the old man maybe had feelings after all, Midgeley was continuing: "Three days ago, Lady Florence was judged well enough to be shipped down to Earth for continued treatment. Given the uncertainty of her condition, she did not wish to arouse advance expectations that might not be fulfilled. Therefore, she instructed me to inform no one of her arrival at the manor until it actually took place. She is resting in her rooms and would welcome your visit. She would prefer that word of her appearance here not be generally known."

Jeff hardly heard the last sentence. Mother was *here*—after three whole months, in which her survival was doubtful and visitors to the low-orbit hospital facility were utterly prohibited! Without a thought of matches or anything else he went running down the hallway to the east wing.

Somehow, Midgeley's message had translated itself in Jeff's mind to the idea that his mother was close to being her old, vigorous self. It was only as he charged without knocking into her rooms, to find them dimly lit and quiet, that he realized how wrong he was. The slight figure lolling in the armchair by the window was unrecognizable.

He knew there had been bad burns in the accident, but

after that he had heard optimistic talk of skin grafts and skin regrowth.

Enough to save his mother's life, perhaps—but not enough to restore her appearance. She had lost weight, and the skin of her gaunt cheeks and forehead was rough and scarred. A thin tube extended from a blue cylinder on the wheeled metal structure at her side and ran up to enter her nose.

"Not a pretty sight, eh?" The voice was hoarse and breathy, but it convinced Jeff that that was really his mother in the chair.

"I'm improving, Jeff," she went on. "I really am. You should have seen me a month ago."

She looked so frail, he didn't dare hug her. Instead he walked over and took one of her thin hands in his. He couldn't tell her the truth, that he was horrified by her appearance. And he couldn't possibly talk about his father. All he could think of to say was, "It's great to have you back."

"It's good to be here. Even if it's just for a few hours." And, before he could react to that, she continued: "Later today I'll be leaving. I'm scheduled for lung replacement surgery in the next few days. About time, too." She gestured to the cylinder at her side. "I've been on oxygen long enough. They told me to go straight to the hospital, but I wanted to see this place again. And I had to talk to you."

She paused, closed her mouth, and breathed hard through her nose as though so much speech had taken all her strength. But then she was talking again, compulsively, her hand patting and squeezing his.

"I'm sure you read all about the accident. Maybe you wondered. Well, it *was* an accident—I wasn't sure for a while, but now I am. A piece of bad luck. We ran into a small space boulder, right when we were set for node entry and the detectors were neutralized. The *Nautilus* was disintegrating when it entered the node, at the wrong speed and attitude. I was fortunate. I was in a section with a sealed bulkhead, and it stayed sealed through the fire."

"What—" Jeff wanted to ask, What about Father? but he couldn't say it.

The words had frozen in his throat, but somehow she knew his question.

"That's what I wanted to talk to you about. Jeff, I've never told another soul, and I don't propose to." She gripped his hand, harder than he thought she could. "Your father is dead. I'm sorry, Jeff, but I'm absolutely sure of that. I saw Nelson's body on the screens. It was after we left the node, and before the fire started. He had been blown clear of the ship. He wasn't wearing a suit. By that time he was already dead."

"But the reports said—all the reports said that you said— and your messages—" The dreadful uncertain feeling he had felt right after the accident came flooding back.

"I know. I wasn't misquoted." Florence Kopal's voice dropped in volume, as though the hardest task was over and she could now relax. "I didn't want to lie to you. I wished I'd dared to tell you the truth about your father, but there was no way to get a message from the Belt or the hospital without danger it would be heard by others. This is the only place where I feel absolutely secure."

"But *why?*"

"Why did I say I thought your father had survived the accident, when I knew he hadn't? It's very simple. While Nelson is believed to be alive—or at least, not legally pronounced dead—he still has the controlling interest in Kopal Transportation. Your uncle Giles and the others can't do much damage. They *daren't* do too much damage. They're afraid of your father, every one of them."

Not only them. Jeff loved his father, but he had always felt overwhelmed by him. Nelson Kopal was infinitely brave, infinitely competent, infinitely confident. While Jeff—the thought of the afternoon's competition passed through his mind—was none of those.

"You can't keep this up forever, Mother." Jeff couldn't say it, but along with shock and sorrow at the certain knowledge of

Nelson Kopal's death came a strange relief. Now his father would never be forced to stand by and watch as his only son failed at everything that the Kopal family felt important. "Even without a body, won't there be a time when Father has to be declared dead?"

Florence nodded slowly. "There will. It will happen two years from the time of his disappearance. If I keep insisting that I believe Nelson was thrown somewhere through the node and is still alive, we'll have time. You'll have Space Navy training, and you will be of age. You can take over your father's position on the board of Kopal Transportation. But if your father were declared dead now, before you've served and come of age, there would be a royal battle over control. And I think you would lose."

Florence Kopal wasn't telling the whole story. The laws of Kopal behavior had been laid down by the iron hand of Great-grandfather Rollo Kopal. First, you proved yourself by service in the Space Navy. Success in military matters would be followed, as a matter of course, by success in business affairs. A Kopal was expected to perform outstandingly in both areas.

And if you didn't? Since no Kopal admitted such a word as *failure*, anyone who proved inadequate for space service would be disowned and disinherited, or at the very least play no part in company affairs.

Florence Kopal didn't need to explain that to Jeff, any more than he could possibly explain how he felt to her. Military ideas and attitudes did not come naturally to him. Business matters bored him. He wasn't sure which he disliked more.

He nodded. "I understand. I'll do my—my best."

"I'm sure you will." The machine at his mother's side suddenly clicked and whirred. A pale green tentacle crept forward from it and touched her below the left ear. She stared at it disapprovingly.

"You know what that means? It means I've used up my breath allowance. I have to shut up, or it will shut me up. Three minutes more, you stupid machine. Then you can take me away." She turned to Jeff. "It won't take any notice, you know. No wonder we hate machines. It's going to get me ready for travel. Talk to me, Jeff, tell me how things are going for you. I'll keep quiet. And open the curtains, so I can really see you."

Jeff didn't hate machines, not at all. He found them fascinating. As for how things were going—he pulled the curtains aside, and the room was flooded with fall sunlight—the bulge created by the crumpled ball of paper in his trouser pocket said exactly how things were going. It felt enormous. If his dead father were to read the words written by Jeff less than an hour ago, Nelson Kopal would turn in his deep-space grave under the silent stars.

"Things are fine, Mother. I have a competition coming up this afternoon, so I have to leave here soon and get into uniform. Myron will be in the competition, too. Looks like we'll have perfect weather."

He was babbling. Better if she didn't know that this was the final piece of navy entrance requirements, and that only a few hours ago he had been praying for heavy rain. Fortunately, his mother didn't seem to notice his nervousness. She was leaning back with her eyes closed to slits. In the brighter light he could see the lines on her mouth, nose, cheeks, and forehead where the skin grafts had been made.

He tried to keep talking. He wanted to say he was sorry if he was not what she and his father had hoped. He couldn't do that. Instead he found himself describing the old aircar that he had found in one of the barns, over on the edge of the Kopal estate. There were no manuals, but he had studied the machine and felt sure that he was close to making it work. In another week or two he would have it flying again.

He thought she wasn't listening, until suddenly her eyes opened and focused on him.

"Jeff, Jeff," she said. Her voice was so faint that he had to lean over to hear her. "My Jeff. Aircars, motors, engines, spacecraft. I always thought it, and now I'm sure. I hear Uncle Drake's voice in yours. You've got his genes."

Her mouth closed, and a moment later her eyelids. He leaned nearer in alarm, until he realized that she was breathing faintly but evenly. The machine at her side buzzed its reassurance.

Jeff tiptoed away, though he doubted that silence was necessary. His thoughts were accusing—self-accusing. He had been worrying about the stupid riding competition, while his mother calmly faced an operation to replace both of her lungs. She was only a Kopal by marriage, yet she was more of a Kopal than he would ever be.

He hurried back to his rooms. He could blame himself as much as he liked, do anything he liked to try to summon courage. It wouldn't help. As he changed into his uniform and struggled with the ornamental straps and buckles, he felt nervousness like an electric current making his muscles twitch and his fingers tremble.

He tried to cheer himself with one inarguable fact: No matter what happened, no matter how badly he performed, in three hours the competition would be over.

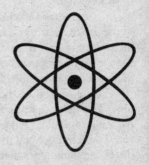

CHAPTER TWO

HE still had the stupid note that he had written. What was he going to do with it? When he wrote the message to himself he had never thought there might be a problem disposing of the thing.

Swallow the page? The paper looked indigestible, but if all else failed. . . .

Divide it into little pieces and let the wind blow them wherever it chose? That was better. He tore the sheet into tiny squares, each no bigger than a fingernail, and carried them downstairs squashed in his fist. His bright idea seemed a lot less inspired when he went outside and found that the warm autumn day was flat calm. Anything thrown away would not blow anywhere.

The stables and riding rings were beyond the boundaries of the estate, nearly two miles away. Instead of taking one of the little electric go-carts used for general runabout, Jeff went on foot. Every few yards he scattered a few bits of paper. He felt like an idiot, an escapee from a children's fairy story.

As he walked he thought about what his mother had told him. The news that his father was dead was no surprise at all. As the months had passed, the chance of Nelson Kopal's survival had felt more and more remote. What was disturbing were the other statements that she had made. Apparently he, Jefferson Kopal, was all that stood between his uncles and aunts and their control of Kopal Transportation.

Nelson Kopal owned a majority of the stock. Jeff had always assumed that was all that mattered. But if Nelson were declared dead, and Jeff were to be disinherited, then the biggest block would belong to Jeff's uncle, Giles Lazenby. Mother's unstated plea was clear: Qualify for navy service, no matter how you do it. Don't give your father's cousin a reason to challenge your fitness to inherit.

She didn't realize that the afternoon's competition was the final qualifying requirement for Space Navy entrance. The entry rules made no sense to Jeff. The navy operated far off in space, where the only animals were small pets, and weapons were controlled by computers. But the training for the navy included marksmanship and horsemanship!

He had scraped through the first with the lowest acceptable marks. As for horse riding, how many horses were in low Earth orbit, in the E-K Belt, or out in the node network territories? Jeff didn't know the answer, but he was willing to make a bet: zero.

On the other hand, maybe he was trying to justify his own feelings. When he had been given his first lesson, ten years ago, he had been frightened by the huge animal in front of him.

Compared to his own size it had loomed enormous. When he was on its back, he felt miles off the ground.

Since then he had grown a lot. The trouble was, horses *still* seemed amazingly big. The idea that he could control such a large animal sounded implausible, and, perhaps because the horses sensed his nervousness, much of the time it was.

He was approaching the stands and the riding ring. Even from a hundred yards away he fancied he could see the flies and smell the dung, sun-warmed leather, and pungent liniment.

He had no watch on him, but he glanced up at the sun. He had taught himself to estimate the time from its position in the sky.

Close to noon; half an hour, then came the draw for first contestant; less than an hour to the first round. He had inspected the eight-fence jump course earlier in the day, and it didn't look too bad.

Predictably, Myron was already over by the horses. He was tightening girths and talking softly to his white-speckled stallion, Lysander. He saw Jeff approaching, stopped work, and strode in his direction.

"I'm almost done. Do you need a hand with Domino?"

Jeff shook his head, not sure of his voice. His problem wouldn't be with the saddling and grooming, he rather enjoyed doing that. As for Myron, as usual he was picture-perfect. His tunic was spotless and creaseless, its silver buttons and epaulets shining in the midday sun. His breeches fitted perfectly, and his knee-high riding boots were highly polished and free of scuff marks. Jeff's cousin was tall, blond, and decisive, every inch the Space Navy recruit most likely to succeed. His older sister, Myra, was already in the navy and doing marvelously.

Myron held out his hand. "Good luck. Though I'm sure neither of us will need it."

Jeff took the outstretched hand and mumbled his own words of encouragement. As usual with Myron, Jeff couldn't tell how much of what his cousin said was genuine, and how much was for appearances. It was certainly as important a day for Myron as it was for Jeff.

As for not needing luck, that was a joke. Myron had seen Jeff in the past. While Myron responded well to pressure and in a stress situation did better than usual, Jeff couldn't help imagining what might go wrong—and as a result, many times it did. He wished that, just once, Myron would miss a jump, or finish *his* round sprawled over the horse's neck.

As soon as he could, he escaped to prepare Domino. The brown mare turned her head as Jeff approached and nuzzled at his shoulder in a friendly way. When Jeff walked to where the saddles were draped over the saddle rack, Domino calmly followed. The horse cooperated as Jeff lifted her hooves to examine them. If anything does go wrong today, Jeff thought gloomily, it won't be *her* fault.

And what had his mother meant, when she said that Jeff had Drake's genes? Although Uncle Drake had been dead and gone for years and years, most of the family were still reluctant to talk about him. When they did talk, they didn't agree. His father had been the kindest.

"There was no holding Drake." Nelson Kopal's eyes took on a strange little smile when he spoke of his brother. "He had the oddest mind you can imagine, a new wild idea a minute. I could never keep up with him, even though I was three years older. If he had lived, and grown a bit more mature, he might have. . . ." The smile faded and was replaced with a look of sad reminiscence. "But he didn't. Didn't grow up when he was young, and he never had time after that. The idea that killed him, node-hopping without a defined destination—that was so typical, and so crazy. I tried to talk him out of it. I'd have managed to persuade most people." Nelson shook his head. "But not your uncle."

Except for Uncle Lory Lazenby, who was nice about everything, Jeff's other relatives had not been nearly as charitable. Aunt Willow, Father's cousin and a board member of Kopal Transportation, was the most direct.

"I'm not one to speak ill of the dead, Jefferson, but your uncle Drake was *totally irresponsible*, from the day that he was born. Irresponsible, and *totally obstinate*. All the family traditions, everything that your Great-grandfather Rollo"—you could hear the reverent capitals in Aunt Willow's voice—"worked so hard to establish, Drake ignored. He had no respect for family or military standards. He took no interest in our business, or in the company's finances. We could have gone bankrupt and all ended in the Pool for what he cared. He was worse than poor Lory! I tell you, Jefferson, I'm not one to speak ill of anyone." Aunt Willow drew in breath through her nose, and her nostrils pinched. "Not of *anyone*. But in my humble opinion it was a *blessing* in many ways when Drake was lost. That foolish space game he *insisted* on playing! Ridiculous, for a grown man. It's his own fault that he isn't around anymore to bring shame on his family."

Just as I'm bringing shame on the family, Jeff thought as he stood at Domino's side, cinching a girth. *"You've got Drake's genes, Jeff."* Sure. Not much doubt what that means. But I wish I'd been older when Uncle Drake had his accident, so I'd understand what they're all getting at.

Then there was Uncle Giles. He was always smiling, and he smiled when he spoke of Drake. But his words didn't match his grin. "Drake had everything a man could wish for, Jefferson—money, power, position, family. He was missing just one thing. *Character*, the big one, that's what he lacked. And without that, a man or woman has nothing. Drake would not get serious. He wanted to fiddle his life away, nothing but playing with machines and computers and those queer gadgets he'd build."

But did that mean you didn't have character? If it did, then Jeff had no character, either. What was so wrong with trying to make an old aircar fly again, without the tools and the manuals? Did the whole world have to be either military tradition or running a transportation company?

A shadow fell across Jeff's hands. He turned, half expecting to see Uncle Giles's white-toothed smile or Aunt Willow's tight-faced glower. Instead it was Myron again.

"I thought you might like to know the draw," he said. "Since you weren't there for it."

"Already?" Jeff wondered how long he had been day-dreaming.

"Five minutes ago. You're fifth up—next to last. I go first." Myron grimaced. "If anything's wrong with the setup that we didn't notice on the walk-through, I'll be the one who finds out. But at least I'll get mine out of the way early, and that's a blessing."

Jeff nodded. He didn't believe for a moment that Myron was suffering from nerves. He was just saying that for Jeff's benefit, rubbing it in. Myron knew from past experience how twitchy Jeff became when it was close to contest time.

Like now.

Jeff glanced down and saw that the rein he held was shaking from the tremor in his hands. He stood up, placing it behind his back so that Myron couldn't see.

"How long before you do your round?"

"Ten minutes." Myron glanced toward the circuit. "I'd better get over there."

"Sure. I'll come watch you, as soon as I'm done here." And then—he couldn't help it—he asked, "Who's there?"

He didn't need to explain. His cousin was being judged, as well as Jeff himself.

"Pretty much the whole family." Myron grinned. "Plus, of course, the three navy representatives. Cross your fingers, Jeff. This is the big one. Think 'clear round.' "

He turned and walked away. Jeff looked after him, sure that Myron didn't need crossed fingers. Like his older sister, Myron was totally poised and assured.

Instinctively, Jeff looked down to see if he had mud on the knees of his breeches. He didn't—for a change. And the presence of representatives from the navy had one advantage. Since he was not supposed to try to influence their judgment, he wouldn't be allowed to go into the stand where they and senior members of the family were seated. His own awkwardness and lack of confidence would not be revealed.

He led Domino to a position where he could see all the jumps without being in sight of the judges' stand. The weather was changing. The sun was still bright, but the day was hotter and more humid. There was the weight of an afternoon thunderstorm in the air, and he could feel perspiration dampening the armpits of his tight uniform. He wiped a trickle of sweat from his forehead with his sleeve. He should have brought a handkerchief.

Myron was ready and waiting. Jeff didn't see the signal, but suddenly his cousin was trotting Lysander in a circle, then cantering toward the first jump. They took it cleanly, and the next three. They turned, and Lysander changed lead leg smoothly for the second half of the course. The fifth fence offered no problem, but at the sixth Myron's horse clipped and dislodged the top rail. He recovered well, and they took the other two jumps rapidly and without a problem. There was hearty applause from the stand as Lysander walked past it. Myron removed his riding helmet and inclined his blond head to the judges. He had an excellent time, and he knew it.

Competitors were not supposed to speak to each other, but as Myron continued out of the ring and passed the waiting Jeff, he muttered out of the side of his mouth, "That sixth fence, it's a bitch. Doesn't look it, but it's out of alignment for a straight approach."

Jeff stared at the jump. From his angle it looked fine. There would be no adjustment unless Myron made a formal complaint, and from the look of him he was not about to do that. His round was not clean, but it was close.

The next competitor's effort didn't give Jeff any useful information. Her horse, a rawboned gelding three sizes too big for her, decided what it would jump and when. It meandered around the course and never went near the troublesome sixth fence. The rider was red-faced and would not look at the judges' stand when the round ended, but the spectators gave her a good round of applause. She was only eleven or twelve, and it was her first contest.

The third rider had problems with four fences, including the troublesome sixth, but struggled through. The one who came after him had obviously been watching closely. She turned unusually wide after the fifth fence, so that her mare could add a stride and pick up a little extra pace on the approach to the sixth. They went over cleanly, then finished the rest of the course smoothly and easily.

A clear round. But Jeff was hardly aware of the applause. If the previous rider could do it, why couldn't he? He had their experience of the course to build on.

He moved into position, waiting for the signal, concentrating all his attention on the first jump. His stomach was churning, and he could feel the sweat on his forehead.

Domino caught the start signal almost before he did. The mare trotted through the preliminary circle, then accelerated smoothly forward and glided over the first fence with almost no guidance from Jeff. He settled back in the saddle, shortened the reins, and took Domino through the second, third, and fourth jumps without a problem. The mare changed lead leg smoothly, and they began the second half of the course.

The fifth fence was easy, everyone had cleared it without trouble. As Domino approached the jump Jeff could see the hoof marks of other horses in the soft, powdery earth. He did not pay much attention to them. Already he was thinking ahead, to the difficult sixth. For a clean round it would be necessary to take it without an error.

Thinking beyond the present was a mistake. Jeff had pressed Domino a little too hard, so that the jump over the fifth fence was made too close to it. The mare went high but not far, catching the heavy top rail with her left hind leg. She landed off balance, and Jeff—never a great horseman—tilted far forward in the saddle instead of settling back. The change in weight distribution affected Domino, who came awkwardly to the sixth fence. At the last moment, knowing there was no chance of clearance, the mare refused.

Jeff went over Domino's neck and crashed headfirst into the heavy timber of the top rail. The helmet he was wearing saved his skull, but the blow was hard enough to knock him dizzy. He couldn't protect himself with his hands as he fell over the fence and tumbled down the other side.

His left shoulder hit the ground, then his head. He did not lose consciousness, not quite, but he was far enough gone that when he tried to stand up he had no idea where he was.

Domino, having refused the jump, had walked quietly around the fence and was standing head-down just a few feet away. Jeff had fallen off enough in past practices for his instincts to take over. He rose unsteadily, placed a foot in the stirrup, and climbed without thinking onto the mare's back.

He sat swaying, not sure what had happened. When Domino started forward it took all Jeff's strength to hold on. The horse went easily over the last two fences, then cantered to a halt by the judges' stand.

Jeff, head buzzing and stomach rolling, tried to dismount. He would have fallen flat on his face, but other people were suddenly there to help him. He was grabbed and lowered, until his feet met the ground. And finally he could obey the urge that had grown stronger and stronger as he lurched and rocked over those final fences. He leaned forward and threw up breakfast and lunch onto three pairs of polished riding boots.

When his swimming eyes at last cleared, he saw that the boots all bore at their top a little embossed pattern of silver stars. He peered at them.

Riding boots? No. Not riding boots at all. They were Space Navy boots.

Jeff decided that he was as far from a clean round as you could ever get.

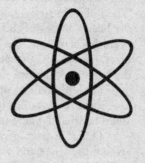

CHAPTER THREE

IT should have marked the end of his misery, to be hauled
off in an electric cart, prodded by a doctor, scanned, ques-
tioned, and put to bed.

It didn't, of course. He had been told to sleep, but when
he closed his eyes he saw again the faces of his aunts and uncles,
clustered around the vomit-spattered navy representatives.
Uncle Giles wore a fixed and ghastly smile, as though his perfect teeth had locked into position like a row of piano keys.
Uncle Terence and Aunt Willow had their mouths open, gasp-
ing for air like landed fish. Aunt Delia was green and looked
ready to throw up herself. Even Uncle Fairborn's attention was

distracted from the exotic young woman he had brought with him to the meet.

Only Uncle Lory, hovering on the edge of the group, appeared unaffected. But that was Lory for you, never quite all there. Maybe that's why Jeff liked him.

It was past ten o'clock, but he knew he wouldn't be able to sleep, no matter what the doctor had advised. He eased out of bed, dressed, and examined his monitor. The single message was from his mother. *I'm at the hospital now. The operation will be late tomorrow. I'll call you after it. Good luck.*

Good luck. They all wished him luck, but it hadn't done any good. He headed for the corridor and wandered along it. He didn't want to talk to anyone, didn't want to see anyone. What he needed was a long walk, by himself. The promised thunderstorm had arrived, and he could see through the corridor windows that it was raining like mad. He didn't mind that. It would feel good to walk alone under the dark night sky, even to get soaked through.

The air outside was cool. As he walked toward the pasture the driving rain lashed his exposed face. He didn't try to use his hood. Maybe the rain could wash away the feeling of failure. It couldn't wash away the worry. What was he going to do now? No one in the Kopal and Lazenby families ever asked the terrible question: What if you are not accepted into the navy?

Would he be abandoned, thrown into the great pool of the unemployed and the unemployable? Surely his mother would not let that happen—if she were alive and able to stop it.

Water was inside his raincoat and trickling into his shoes. Myra, on one of her leaves from navy duties, had told him and Myron that water was plentiful through the outer solar system—but almost never as a liquid. Earth, and the interior of Jupiter's moon Europa, were the only water worlds.

He turned and retraced his steps, squelching across the sodden ground. By the front doors of the house he paused. He didn't want to go in. He wanted to turn, and walk, and never stop walking.

No. Get it over with. He could almost hear his mother saying that into his ear.

He went inside, took off his raincoat and shoes, and dried himself as much as he could. His shirt was soaked around the collar, and his socks left damp patches on the floor wherever he walked. He needed a complete change of clothes.

He walked from the hall toward the rear of the house. Uncle Lory was sitting by a flight of stairs that descended to the first basement level, his back resting against the end post of the banister. He did not move as Jeff slowly approached.

"Feeling better?" he said, when Jeff was a few feet away.

"I'm not sick anymore." *Better* was not the right word for the way he felt. "Thanks, Uncle Lory, I'm all right."

"Good." Lory said not a word about Jeff's sodden appearance. "They're in there."

He nodded his head toward a door on the left side of the ground-floor rear corridor. Two antechambers and the big conference room lay beyond them.

"Who?" Maybe Jeff wasn't as recovered as he thought. In spite of the cool drenching, the inside of his head felt woolly and unfocused.

"Oh, you know. The board. Everyone was here for the meet, so Uncle Giles scheduled a board meeting."

That ought to have been a sore point with Lory Lazenby. He, a grandchild of Rollo Kopal, had not been invited to serve on the board of Kopal Transportation. But he didn't mind at all—or if he did, it never showed.

When Jeff was smaller he had not understood. Uncle Lory was the nicest of the whole bunch, the only one of the Lazenby aunts and uncles with whom he felt totally comfortable. Why shouldn't Lory be on the board with the rest? But now he knew why. Uncle Lory was out of step with the rest of the world. He was always pleasant and kind. He just wasn't smart, and he had trouble understanding things. No one had ever considered *him* a candidate for Space Navy service.

Jeff sat down with a bump on the bottom step. If he were more like Uncle Lory, none of today's horrors would have been necessary.

"So if you feel all right," Uncle Lory was saying, "then you ought to go in."

"Go in?" Jeff wondered if he had missed something.

"To the board meeting." Lory frowned. "You will go in, won't you? Giles told me to wait here, and he said if you came by I was to tell you to go into the meeting. So that's what I'm doing."

"I'm to go into the board meeting?" It sounded clear enough, but sometimes Uncle Lory got things mixed up. And surely there was no possible reason why he should go in—

Jeff froze where he sat. There was a very good reason. After his disastrous performance today, the navy must have rejected him for service. They would have told Uncle Giles, informally, and official word would arrive later. But now Uncle Giles and the other board members had to inform Jeff of the decision.

"Go in anytime," Uncle Lory said. He was tapping on the banister rail, an odd and complex rhythm, as though accompanying a silent song. He was in his midforties, but his face was as smooth and unlined as a child's. "That's what Giles said. Giles told me to wait here, and he said if you came down I was to tell you to go into the meeting. So—"

"Thanks, Uncle Lory." Jeff stood up abruptly. His mother had told him a hundred times, if you had to go through a bad experience, get it over with as soon as you could. It was a lesson he still had trouble applying. He had always been the one who stood shaking on the edge of the pool, putting off the shock of cold water as long as he could, while Myron had already plunged in and was swimming laps.

"Go into the meeting, Giles said. Go in anytime." Uncle

Lory was helping Jeff, though he didn't know it. If Jeff didn't do what he was told, his uncle would go on repeating the message until they both went crazy.

"I'm going, Uncle Lory. Right away." Jeff opened the door, walked slowly through the first and second antechambers, and paused before the double doors of the conference room itself. *Get it over with.* He took a deep breath, swung the doors open, and strode in.

The five Lazenby board members were all present. They sat close together at a table big enough for thirty. Uncle Terence and Aunt Willow were on the left. Aunt Delia was on the right, next to Uncle Fairborn. Uncle Giles occupied the head of the table at the far end.

They gazed in disapproval at his sodden and bedraggled appearance. Finally Giles, smiling as always (Jeff wondered, Did he grin like that in his sleep?), waved him into the room.

"Come in, Jefferson, come in. We were just talking about you."

Jeff could believe that. Except for Giles, everyone in the room looked unbelievably gloomy. Not just gloomy—*angry*. That was odd.

"The navy representatives have gone," Uncle Giles continued, "but your aunt Delia and I had the opportunity of a few private words with them before they left. Some of those words, naturally, pertain to you and your future."

Jeff didn't doubt that for a moment. He felt his chest tighten, and he tried a trick that had worked for him in the past. When you are in a situation that is too frightening or disturbing, you look at it as though you are outside the action and not personally involved at all. So here we have a person—a stranger, certainly not Jeff Kopal—standing at one end of the long table. Down at the other end are five people.

Strangers. Study them. What are they like?

On the left we have one man and one woman. Their names are Terence and Willow. The man is in his fifties, and he looks fat and red-faced enough to burst. Maybe one day he will.

He won't admit it, but he gobbles down food like a starved pig. Very different from the woman next to him. She is thin, and from her face she has been sucking on a lemon for the past half hour.

Another man and woman are sitting on the right side of the table. He is called Fairborn, but it's a poor name for someone so ugly. See those piggy little eyes, and the low forehead, and the mouth like a rattrap. He's usually with some flashily dressed woman, though it's hard to guess what they see in him. They are all a great contrast to the woman next to Fairborn, who has a cool and elegant beauty. No one would ever realize that Delia is the oldest person at the table. With top-priced cosmetic surgery, the marks never show.

And at the end—but Giles is talking, and his words drag you back into the scene.

"For you, and for Myron." The smile never stops. "As we expected, in the case of Myron there was never any doubt. The navy representatives confirmed that he performed outstandingly, as always."

Don't mention the fact that he is your own child, Jeff thought. I wonder if you told the navy people that.

"Like his sister, he has been accepted into the Space Navy," Giles went on. "Effective at once. His initial assignment will be to the Central Command."

He didn't have to say more. Jeff knew, as well as anyone at the table, that the Central Command was the navy's elite. Nine out of ten future captains and admirals were CenCom trained. Acceptance as a CenCom recruit meant you were being groomed for the top. *All* Kopals and Lazenbys went into CenCom. Like his cousins and his older sister, Myron Lazenby was on the way up.

"He has already received our congratulations," added Giles. "I am sure that when you see him you will want to add yours. Your own case, however, was rather more . . . shall we say, complex."

Here it comes, Jeff thought. He tried to distance himself

again, but it didn't work. His mouth was dry and his pulse was racing. The atmosphere in the big room felt charged with something—anger? hatred?—larger than any thunderhead. He moved his feet and felt his toes squelch inside his socks. He must be leaving a trail on the conference-room floor.

"You are of a family with a long and distinguished navy record," Uncle Giles said slowly. "That fact certainly counts in your favor. However, your test scores in the past have not been good. On abstract subjects, such as mathematics and physics, you have done well." Giles continued to smile, but his added frown showed his own low opinion of the value of such useless time-wasters. Jeff wondered how he could do that, smile and scowl at the same time. "However, in the practical manual skills so important to Space Navy training you have been borderline at best."

Practical manual skills—like fencing and swimming and shooting. Useful in the navy maybe five hundred years ago. As for riding horses, had it *ever* been relevant to any navy?

"Did you wish to say something, Jefferson?" Giles was staring at Jeff, his eyebrows raised.

Jeff shook his head and stared down at the tabletop. If he had muttered something of his thoughts, it had been from sheer frustration.

"Very well. To continue, everything came down to today's competition. I do not need to tell you, Jefferson, that your score was a poor one. In fact, it was the lowest of anyone in the meet."

Which includes an eleven-year-old first-timer, whose horse took charge and carried her wherever it felt like. Brilliant. Get it over with. Jeff wasn't sure how much more of this he could stand.

"That, coupled with your mediocre previous perfor-mances, added up to an overall negative prospect. All of us were forced to that assessment. *However. . . ."*

On that final word, the voice changed. Jeff looked up. Uncle Giles was still showing his teeth, but it seemed more like a grimace of agony. His uncle was swallowing, as though some-thing had stuck in his throat.

"However," Giles went on at last, "the navy representatives observed that after you were thrown from your horse and suffered a bruising impact and descent, you somehow managed to remount. And you then completed the course. They noted all this in their report, saying you persisted although you were clearly nauseated and must have been in pain and physical distress. They consider this an act of considerable valor."

Jeff stared at his uncle. Considerable valor! He had been panic-stricken from the start. He hadn't known where he was or what he was doing. After he had been thrown he had climbed back on the horse out of pure reflex—and *Domino* had completed the course, while Jeff sat on top of the mare like a stuffed rag doll. As for throwing up on the boots of the navy people. . . .

From the strained look on his face, Uncle Giles was going to smile if it killed him. "The representatives felt," he continued, "that the Space Navy cannot afford to risk losing such a resolute individual, regardless of certain other deficiencies. They have therefore approved your induction, effective at once. They offer you their congratulations." He paused and took a deep breath. "As do I, Jefferson. Speaking for myself, I believe that the decision of the navy representatives will prove to have long-term benefits. We are all very happy for you."

Happy? Except for the smiling Giles, they looked as happy as a group of pallbearers. Jeff was in a daze as his aunts and uncles came forward one by one to give him a ritual handshake or a formal hug. All he could think was that, in spite of everything he had done wrong, he would have good news for his mother. He hadn't flunked out of the navy.

"Do you know where I will be assigned?" He pulled free of Aunt Willow's cold embrace.

"As a matter of fact, we do. We had the opportunity to make suggestions to the navy personnel." Uncle Giles and Aunt Delia exchanged quick glances. "We agreed that at this time, the Central Command would not be . . . appropriate for you. The pressures of that environment might be too great. We are proposing, and they will approve, assignment to Border

Command. That should give you an opportunity to, shall we say, hone your skills."

"Border Command?" Jeff didn't even know the name.

"BorCom is very new. Its activities are confined to the more distant regions."

"You mean out in the Belt?" Jeff thought that the E-K Belt still came under CenCom's charter.

"Beyond that. BorCom is concerned with those territories accessible only through the node network."

In other words, way beyond the solar system and out to the stars and the great dust clouds. Once you went through a node, you couldn't even communicate with Earth until you came back. No wonder Jeff hadn't heard of BorCom.

"Where will I be going?"

"That will be up to the navy to decide. Although we, of course, hope to have some say in the matter." Uncle Giles had regained his perfect smile. "But now, Jefferson, the board has other important business to discuss. Why don't you run along and enjoy the evening?"

In other words, go away. Jeff was glad to leave. He had a million things to think about. But he wasn't quite fast enough. He was still inside the room when the comment came from Uncle Terence: "Do him good to go way out there. Know what I mean? Get some experience, stiffen his backbone."

As the double doors closed, Jeff heard—or felt—the knife of Aunt Willow's reply: "Stiffen his backbone? Terence, my dear, I don't really think so. For that to happen, you need a spine to start with."

Jeff stood by the double doors and closed his eyes. Was he pleased? Yes, of course; he was in the navy. Was he upset? You bet he was. The first Kopal to fail to be assigned to Central Command. As for BorCom, it might be anything—except high in prestige.

He went back to the dark, stone-tiled corridor. Uncle Lory was still lounging at the foot of the staircase. He might be curious to learn what had happened inside, but Jeff doubted it. Lory just had nothing to do and nowhere special to go.

But regardless of his uncle's interest, Jeff couldn't help blurting out the news. "I've passed. I've been accepted into the navy."

"That's wonderful," Lory said—and meant it, unlike Jeff's other uncles and aunts.

"Myron, too. We'll both be leaving in a few days."

"You will?" Lory Lazenby did not know how to hide his emotions, and the change in his expression could not be missed. "I wish I could go with you. Into space, I mean. I've always wanted to go, wanted to see what it's like. Out there." He waved a hand vaguely upward and shook his head sadly. "But it was the tests, you see. I couldn't pass the tests. I tried and tried and tried. I tried so hard. But I never could pass."

Jeff knew that he had really *failed* his test, but he couldn't tell that to Uncle Lory. It would only make things worse. He had never realized before that Lory yearned for space, never known that his uncle had his own tragedies and longings and heartaches.

It must be like Jeff's own awareness of incompetence and inadequacy when he compared himself with Myron, except amplified a thousand times. He suddenly felt like the biggest fraud in the world. He couldn't stand it any longer. Lory deserved to go to space, far more than Jeff did.

He turned and fled up the stairs. As he went he heard Lory saying softly—but not to Jeff—"I wonder if I ought to try again. Maybe I could pass, if I tried again. If only I didn't get so flustered when they ask me questions. . . ."

The meek—like Uncle Lory—will inherit the Earth. The fakes like me get to go to the stars.

Jeff ran into his room, threw himself on the bed, and wondered why, on this the luckiest day of his life, he felt like crying.

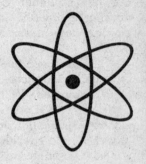

CHAPTER FOUR

JEFF awakened wishing he hadn't. Yesterday's painkillers were no longer working, and he was a mass of aching bones and throbbing bruises. He felt exhausted and emotionally drained by all that had happened the previous day, but more than anything he was worried about his mother. His first act when he rolled out of bed was to limp over to the query link in his room and say, "Give me a status report on Florence Kopal."

If the query link needed more information, it would ask for it. But apparently his request was clear enough, because the answering voice said only, *"Do you want a written or a spoken response?"*

"Spoken, of course." The link wasn't very smart.

"Florence Kopal is in Midvale Hospital, awaiting lung replacement. Her condition is stable, and she is scheduled for surgery late today. Communication with Florence Kopal prior to the operation is prohibited."

It wasn't much, but at the moment it was all that he would get. Jeff had been itching to tell his mother about the navy acceptance, but that would not be possible. He left a message for her—leaving out the embarrassing circumstances of *how* he had passed—then said, "Tell me about Border Command."

"Do you want a written or a spoken response?"

"Do it both ways. I'd like to hear it now, but maybe I'll want to read it later. Give me a summary in spoken form and write out the details."

A twenty-second silence followed. Jeff waited impatiently, although he knew that nothing was wrong. It was just the house equipment making its slow contact with the appropriate databases and sorting out what it needed. The query server was ancient; it hadn't seen an update in thirty years. On the other hand, its out-of-date electronics fitted in with the antique furniture and fixed social habits of the house. Sometimes Jeff thought that he had been born to an environment frozen in time. Everything matched the Kopal family lifestyle, its rules laid down (of course!) by Rollo Kopal: Duty is sacred. Courage is a requirement, not an elective. Superior performance is assumed. What's good for Kopal Transportation is good for the Space Navy. Old is better than new. Tradition is more important than innovation. Human services are superior to machine services.

All very fine—provided that humans were available to provide the service. But then who did the work for *those* people? Jeff had asked that question once, when he was very young, and quickly learned never to mention it again. The assumption by the Kopals and Lazenbys—even by Jeff's own father—was that the family *deserved* to have human servants rather than machines.

Didn't the Kopal and Lazenby families contribute more to the world than almost anyone? Not only this world—as ship-builders to the Space Navy, the families served every world. And were there not large numbers of idle unemployed in the Pool who were fortunate to be offered a position of service in the Kopal household?

Maybe. But what would it be like if there were no Pool? Or suppose *you* were born a member of the Pool, without money, without a job, and in most cases with no prospects of a job?

You were not allowed to ask such things, not in this house; but if you were Jeff, you certainly wondered.

"*Are you in a position to receive information?*"

The query link's sensors must have noticed that he was starting to wander. Jeff blinked and nodded to show that he was ready.

"*The Border Command, usually abbreviated both in speech and writing to BorCom, was established seven years ago as an independent unit of the Space Navy. The head of BorCom reports directly to the head of Central Command. BorCom's official charter is to identify, and if possible to solve, problems that arise beyond the boundaries of the solar system.*"

"*Continue?*"

"Yes, but first I have a question." Jeff had been forced by Kopal family tradition to learn more than he would ever wish to know about the territories of the old Roman and British and Chinese empires. He could describe the strategies employed in ancient naval battles like Salamis and Trafalgar and Midway. He had learned the features of all the moons and planets of the solar system important to Space Navy operations; but of the universe outside the boundaries of the solar system he knew next to nothing.

"What do you mean when you say that BorCom works *beyond* the solar system? List some of the places for me. And what sorts of problems do BorCom ships have to solve? Do they fight battles? If they do, who do they fight against?"

There was again a few seconds' pause. *"You are asking several questions at once. Taking them in order, BorCom vessels operate in all regions of space accessible through the node network. However, any ship assigned to BorCom duties leaves the solar system through just one of two nodes. The first is located between the orbits of Mars and Jupiter. The second, most commonly used by BorCom ships, is situated in the E-K Belt beyond the orbits of Pluto and Neptune.*

"BorCom vessels are prohibited from operating within the solar system, except under the direct command of Central Command.

"Continue?"

Jeff was beginning to see the picture, and he didn't like it. BorCom ships never operated within the solar system. So Uncle Giles, by suggesting to the navy representatives that Border Command was right for Jeff, was in effect banishing him. In particular, he was putting Jeff far from Central Command—which was where all the rapid promotions took place. But where would Jeff be going?

"Continue."

"Forty-three extrasolar nodes are currently in operation, with seven more scheduled for completion in the next five years. Do you want a complete list?"

"Print the whole thing. But tell me the ones where most of today's BorCom action is."

"There are currently four trouble spots on which BorCom attention is focused. They are, in order of estimated urgency: Node 23, which threatens a secession from Sol control. Node 35, in whose vicinity both commercial and navy vessels have been vanishing without trace. Node 14, where the Lastrealis colony is endangered by indigenous parasitic life-forms. And Node 09, where disputes over mining claims have led to violence. BorCom is being asked to serve as arbitrator."

Jeff tried to recall if any of those nodes or subjects had been mentioned last night by Uncle Giles. He couldn't remember. He could scarcely remember the meeting itself. The painkillers had put him far more out of it than he had realized. He made a mental note: Nodes 09, 14, 23, 35. He would have to find out more about each of them—and his own future assignment.

He was about to ask, but the query link was continuing: *"Unlike Central Command vessels, BorCom ships are not equipped to fight major battles. If and when superior firepower is needed, BorCom calls on the Central Command fleet for assistance. The Central Command vessels possess—"*

"Skip that. I know about the weapons of Central Command ships. Do you have information about my own assignment to BorCom?"

He hadn't expected an answer, and it was a surprise when after a few seconds the query link buzzed and answered: *"Your assignment will be to the patrol vessel* Aurora."

Someone had been moving superfast in the twelve hours since Jeff had received the news that he would be accepted into the navy. It was a safe bet that Uncle Giles and his other uncles and aunts were involved. They wanted Jeff far off in space, leaving the road to promotion clear for Myron and the other Lazenby children. Jeff knew why. He might not be much, himself, but the rest were all aware how long a shadow his father, grandfather, and great-grandfather still cast on navy affairs.

"Where is the *Aurora* now?"

"The ship is in Earth orbit. The Aurora *is scheduled to make a node transition in fifteen days from the E-K Belt node, and will jump to Node 23. You are expected to be on board at that time."*

Someone not only wanted Jeff far away, they wanted him away *fast.* Even at maximum acceleration, it would take a few days to reach the E-K Belt. Jeff's suspicions were growing.

"If I'm to be on board the *Aurora* when the ship makes its node transition, when will I have to leave here?"

"You are scheduled for an evening ascent to orbit from Point Merrick."

"Which evening?"

"This evening. Following arrival in low Earth orbit, you will transfer to the Aurora *and proceed in a high-acceleration mode to Node 02, in the E-K Belt. From there to Node 23—"*

The query link stopped. It might not be very smart, but it could tell when no one was listening. Its sensors showed Jeff, bruises, aching head and all, dashing at high speed out of the room.

Jeff knew what was happening. He was being run out of town—out of the solar system—as fast as his relatives could arrange it. Before his mother's operation, still less her recovery, he would leave Earth. In days, he would make the jump to Node 23. According to the query link, that node represented Border Command's number-one hot spot.

Secession from Sol control. Someone was trying to set up their own government. Who, and why? He didn't know, but he didn't like the sound of it. In fact, he didn't like the sound of anything that was happening. Particularly the things happening to *him.*

Why was all this being done? Uncle Giles Lazenby and Aunt Delia Lazenby never, in Jeff's experience, acted without a reason. They had surely expected him to be refused navy entrance. At that point, according to Rollo Kopal's inflexible rules, he would have been on the path to disinheritance.

Except that he had passed. They couldn't force him out now. But they could do other things.

Did they hope that he wouldn't return from his BorCom assignment? That he would perish or vanish in some accident of the node network, like Uncle Drake many years ago?

Jeff ran down the long, curved rear staircase, slowing toward the bottom as his bruised left leg threatened to buckle under him. The conference room was empty—numerous scattered cups and plates, still awaiting collection by the serving staff, showed that the board had been in session late into the night.

How much had Jeff's fate been an item on their agenda?

He kept moving. No one in the great hall, but in the vaulted sunroom he found Uncle Lory, staring vacantly at a picture of Jupiter's big moon, Ganymede. Jeff knew that it was ancient, one of the first images returned to Earth centuries ago by unmanned planetary probes. Now a thriving human settlement existed on that moon. Did Lory know, and did he long to go there?

No time to worry about it now. Jeff nodded to his uncle, called "Good morning," and kept going. He wanted to find Giles or Delia and ask some direct questions.

No one in the parlor, no one in the communications room, no one in any of the four studies. No one *anywhere*. Could they all be still in bed? At last, in the sunny breakfast room at the very end of the ground-floor east wing, he came across Myron.

His cousin stared at him coldly. With good reason. Jeff hadn't washed, hadn't combed his hair, and was still in his pajamas. He could guess how he looked, with his bruised face and hobbling walk. Myron didn't look too good himself. He was neat and clean, but oddly pale. Probably from celebrating too late into the night his success and acceptance by Central Command.

Jeff nodded—a mistake. His head pounded. "Congratulations on the ride yesterday. You did really well."

Myron did not speak. Jeff dropped into a chair opposite his cousin. He saw the filled dishes of scrambled eggs, waffles, rice, and sausage, and suddenly he was starving. He had eaten nothing since noon the previous day.

He piled a plate full and was beginning to eat when he realized that Myron had not, so far, said a word—not even "Good morning."

"Are you feeling all right?" He spoke through a mouthful of pancakes and syrup.

Myron nodded. "I am. I saw your ride yesterday."

"Not too great, was it? I thought I was going to break my neck when I hit that top rail."

"Your round ought to have been ruled as over and done with at that point. It was totally wrong for you to be allowed to remount and continue—even if you knew what was going on, and I don't think you did. I saw your face. I think you were semiconscious."

Jeff stopped eating. "Hey, don't blame me for the way the people from the navy reacted. I had nothing to do with that. I agree with you; I thought I was dead meat the second that Domino refused the sixth jump."

It was no good, his cousin was not looking at him. Myron was staring out of the window, presenting to Jeff his clean, strong-jawed profile.

"You are a Kopal," he said coldly. "Do you think that fact had no bearing on the way that you were treated? That it did not affect the navy representatives' reaction? If I had fallen off Lysander, do you think I would have been permitted to continue my round?" Myron swung around to glare at Jeff. "I'm sure you know the answer. My round would have been judged over. And then this morning I heard that you volunteered for the Border Command."

"I didn't volunteer! They told me—"

"Border Command, where the hottest action is. We all know that. While I will be stuck with CenCom."

Jeff stared at his cousin in disbelief. Myron really meant what he was saying. He was *jealous*—although everyone knew that CenCom was the place to be if you wanted to get ahead. Jeff had never beaten Myron at anything; his cousin had wiped the floor with him in every activity that they had ever tried, from swimming to hang gliding. It was no different in this case.

"I tell you that I didn't volunteer. I had nothing—"

Jeff saw the look in Myron's eyes and gave up. It wouldn't matter what he said, the other would assume that he had been granted special privileges. And—Jeff didn't like this idea any better than Myron—maybe he had.

He tried to change the subject. "I've been looking all over for your father. I can't find him, or any of our aunts and uncles."

Myron at last stopped scowling. "I'm not surprised. They've flown up to the capital for a court hearing."

"What about?"

"They are seeking to have a change approved in the by-laws of Kopal Transportation. It concerns in absentia voting rights." Myron stopped abruptly and walked over to the sideboard. "What sorts of juices have they put out for us? I need something cold."

As a deliberate attempt to change the subject it didn't fool Jeff for a moment. In absentia voting rights could only concern his own father. All the other board members had been present the previous night. They must have been discussing his father's situation, questioning the ruling that he was still legally alive. Had his mother spoken to one of the others yesterday and inadvertently let slip something that suggested she knew differently?

"What sort of change?"

But Myron apparently felt that he had said too much already. He looked vague. "Oh, I don't know." He poured and sipped a glass of apple juice. "My father never tells me what he's doing."

Jeff was willing to believe that. Uncle Giles probably didn't give his feelings away to Myron, any more than he did to Jeff. On that subject at least, Jeff felt full sympathy for Myron and his sister, Myra. Of all the Lazenbys, Uncle Giles would be his own last choice for a parent.

Still trying to avoid an argument, he said, "Anyway, you probably know as much about my BorCom assignment as I do. All I know is that I'll be on a ship called the *Aurora*. And we'll be making a jump to Node 23."

That, finally, was news to Myron. The shocked expression showed that Jeff's last remark came as a complete surprise.

"Node 23? Are you sure?"

"That's what I was told. You've heard of it?"

"I have." Myron waved his arm excitedly, and apple juice spilled from his glass onto the polished hardwood floor. "Last year, I did a review of all the nodes beyond the solar system for a test elective. Node 23 is close to the edge of a dust cloud, twenty-seven light-years from Sol. It's officially known as the Messina Dust Cloud, but no one ever calls it that." Myron's face filled with satisfaction. "They call it Cyborg Territory."

Myron was suddenly willing to tell Jeff what he knew. That was a bad sign. Jeff, nervous, settled back to listen.

"I heard Cyborg Territory stories, when I was small," Myron said, "but I thought they were just like bogeymen, told to scare us."

"So did I. Aren't they? I'm not even sure what a cyborg is."

"None of the normal references give a definition." The color had returned to Myron's face. "I had to look that up in the general databases. A cyborg is part human, part machine. It's against the law to try that on Earth or anywhere in the solar system, because of the humanity statutes."

Though not in Cyborg Territory? Humans were humans, machines were machines. They were nothing like each other. Jeff could not imagine a mixture of the two.

Myron was continuing. "On the other hand, there's lots of information about the Messina Dust Cloud. It was discovered a couple of centuries ago. As soon as a node was placed there, people began to explore and exploit it. There are harvesters collecting stable transuranics—the Messina Cloud is the main source of those, apart from Solferino. And there are rakehells, looking for Cauthen starfires and shwartzgeld—those are found nowhere else—and then there's something weird called *space sounders*. Nobody knows quite what they are, or even whether they are alive. They distort space in some weird way, so it's dangerous to go near one."

"But cyborgs?" Jeff prompted. He felt sure he could look up the Messina Dust Cloud for himself. He would probably be required to do so, if the *Aurora* were headed there. "Why is it called Cyborg Territory?"

"Out beyond the solar system, they have machines much smarter than anything allowed here on Earth. The humanity statutes are being violated. Apparently in the Messina Dust Cloud they are really short of people, so they allow machines to do things we would never permit. Even to merge with humans. Their cyborgs are supposed to be combinations of parts of humans and smart machines."

That conjured up in Jeff's mind an unpleasant vision of a human torso with spindly metal arms and legs, topped by the silver head and glittering crystal eyes of a food service robot. Apparently Myron had the same thought, because he smiled and said, "They wouldn't be human, would they?"

"But it might explain why they're trying to secede from Sol control." Jeff didn't care to think too much about the cyborgs themselves. "Maybe they don't believe they have anything in common with us."

"I bet they don't," Myron said. "But what do you mean, secede?"

Apparently this was something new, something that had occurred since Myron had written his paper. Jeff explained what he had been told by the query link about Node 23 threatening secession. "It can't mean that the *node* is seceding," he said. "A node is only a transportation link point, a place in space. The data item has to mean that the people living in the Messina Dust Cloud—"

"If they are people."

"Whatever they are, they want to secede and have their independence. But why?"

"I told you," Myron said. "If they're really cyborgs, then they're not human. *Not human.*" He repeated the last two words with a fair amount of satisfaction. "They won't feel sympathy with humans. Probably they'll hate us. But the *Aurora* has to go there. . . ."

Myron was no longer complaining about Jeff's good fortune. He left the sentence hanging, and it was easy for Jeff to guess how his cousin might have finished it. *But the* Aurora *has to go there . . . and persuade the human-hating cyborgs to give up their plans to break away from humanity.*

How do you persuade nonhuman beings to do anything?

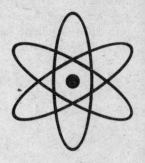

CHAPTER FIVE

HOW do you persuade nonhuman beings to do anything?

Jeff pondered that question from the moment he left the breakfast room. He didn't find an answer.

Not that he was offered much thinking time in the first days. Uncle Giles set the schedule, and he made sure there was no slack. Jeff lost track of the number of things he was obliged to get through in a matter of hours: the frantic packing and farewells, the short flight to Navy Base, and then—almost before he was off the plane—the navy induction ceremony. The induction process itself was easy: Sign your name in a hundred places, salute a thousand uniforms, and don't ask questions.

There was no time for that, anyway, because a suborbital flier was already waiting to carry him and half a dozen other recruits to the equatorial spaceport.

No pause there—the lasers were pumping when Jeff arrived. He and thirty other navy personnel were hurled within hours to low Earth orbit. He was left in free fall long enough to learn that he was emphatically not one of the lucky few immune to space sickness. When he felt a little better he was given the luxury of one call back to Earth. He learned that his mother had survived the operation and was now in the first stage of recovery. He left a message, sending his love and telling her where he was going.

And then it was another rapid transfer, this one to the *Aurora*. The two-G flight to the node began an hour later. Two Gs didn't sound like much—until you had to live with it. At twice your normal weight, eating, walking, and especially sleeping were difficult.

His cabin on the *Aurora* didn't help. It was small and cramped, nothing like his mental image of the facilities of a proud navy starship. He had less living space than in any single one of the rooms of his suite at Kopal Manor. Worst of all, his quarters were not particularly clean. On the third day he left his cabin, situated right amidships at the fattest part of the ship, and struggled to where Captain Eliot Dufferin, commander of the *Aurora*, sat in the forward control room. Under a two-G field it felt like climbing stairs with a man on your back.

"Yes, Ensign?" Captain Dufferin was a short, tubby man with a high-pitched penetrating voice. He also had a reputation as a person with his own view of new recruits. He sat on a raised dais in the control room, and stared down his nose at Jeff as though he had discovered a caterpillar in his salad.

"It's about my cabin, sir." Jeff was already doubting the wisdom of his decision to come forward.

"I see. What is it? A pea, perhaps, under your bunk mattress that's keeping you awake?"

"No, sir. But the cabin hasn't been cleaned since we left low Earth orbit."

"Indeed?" Captain Dufferin looked very serious. "It hasn't been cleaned. Not even once?"

"No sir." Jeff knew he was being played with, and he also knew he could do nothing about it. He couldn't even turn and retreat without the captain's permission.

"I wonder how a thing like that could have happened?" Captain Dufferin stared up to the transparent ceiling and the stars beyond, as though for inspiration. Then he leaned down so his angry red face was close to Jeff's. "Ensign, do you know the number of servants that a junior officer has on a navy ship? No? Then I will tell you. It is *zero*—even if your name happens to be *Kopal.*"

"Yes sir." Jeff was learning something new about the significance of his own last name. "I'm sorry, sir."

"Sorry? For what?" Captain Dufferin turned away. "You will be sorry, but not yet. Go aft, Ensign. Back to your cabin. You will have plenty of time to clean it and polish your brass-work—because I don't want to see your face again until we have passed through the node."

Jeff, panting in the high-G field, returned amidships and went into his cabin. He wasn't used to being spoken to like that, but what could he do? The whole incident completed the proof of his lack of value, even to the lowly Border Command. Except for meals, he stayed in his cabin. He cleaned. He polished.

When he was tired of that, he lay on his bunk and tried to sleep (every position was uncomfortable), watched briefing materials on navy ships and weapons, or queried his cabin information feed. There was lots of information about the Messina Dust Cloud, its physical composition and dimensions and history. It was a region the size of the solar system, and after its discovery a hundred years ago the whole cloud had become a stamping ground for independent explorers and ex-ploiters and traders, plus ne'er-do-wells of all kinds. The present form of government—ominously, in Jeff's opinion—was contained in files marked "Authorized Personnel Only." He soon learned that that select category excluded him. Any query with the words *Cyborg Territory* in it suffered the same fate. Some people knew what was happening. Jeff was not to be one of them.

He thought he was eager for the flight to the node to finish. Then he would find out what was going on. But when the countdown to the transition at last began, he found himself not so keen.

The response of the information feed to his new questions sounded cool and blasé. *"Your concerns are groundless. The effects are all psychological. You may feel as though your body is being twisted and sheared in two, but that is all in the mind. You will emerge from the node transition in the same physical condition as you enter it."*

Which was to say, in Jeff's case you'd come out with sweating palms and a feeling that you might wet yourself. He was having trouble drawing a full breath.

He stared at the approaching node beyond the *Aurora*'s port. Half an hour ago it had been a tiny point of light. Now, although the drive had been cut back to a low value and the ship hardly seemed to be moving, the node shone as big and bright and cold as a hunter's moon—the moon that had been rising on the evening when Jeff left Earth. That moon was now so far away that he could see neither it nor Earth, crouched together near the tiny bright disk of the Sun. "How much longer to transit time?"

"Seven minutes and fifteen seconds. The transition sequence has already been initiated."

"Has there ever been any trouble with a transition?"

"Not when the node entry was correctly initiated. The complete list of fatalities shows that they have only occurred when a ship or an individual attempted to make a transition without a suitably defined target node."

That was what Uncle Drake had done. "Node hopping without a defined destination," Jeff's father had called it. As a game! So his reckless uncle was, in a curious sense, part of the cautionary tales of the Space Navy.

"Do people and ships always come out where they intend to?"

"Unless the approach velocity vector is incorrect. That has happened, and it can yield an unexpected destination. However, hundreds of thousands of node transitions are made every year, with never a problem." The information feed changed tone. "Three minutes to node entry. *Return to your bunk and remain there until transition is complete.*"

The warning was unnecessary. Jeff lay supine, restraining straps already in place. But why restraining straps, if the effects were all psychological? The twists and shears were supposed to be purely imaginary. And why fatalities, for that same reason? He could breathe no more easily now than he had under two Gs of acceleration.

"Two minutes to transition. *The ship's drive has been turned off until transition is completed.*"

That was the answer to Jeff's unasked question. They were suddenly in free fall again, and without restraints he might drift off anywhere in the cabin and be hurt when the drive turned back on. The straps were a good idea. Less good was the response of his stomach to more free fall. He thought he had got over that in low Earth orbit, but a twinge of nausea—or was it nervousness—was gripping his insides.

"One minute. *Following node entry, the Aurora will*—forty-five seconds—*be automatically controlled. At entry minus five seconds, all power will be turned off, including computer power. The Aurora is automatically programmed to*—twenty seconds—*emerge from Node 23 in Cyborg Territory, twenty-seven light-years from Sol.*"

Jeff wished he were a computer himself. It sounded so calm and certain. He, as usual, was terrified. His insides were in stressed-out turmoil. He clung to the thought of what he had been told. They were in the right place, and at the right speed. They had a well-defined destination. Nothing could go wrong.

Except that there was a first time for everything.

"Ten seconds. *Prepare for node entry.* Seven—six—"

The lights went out. The computer was silent. Jeff waited, in frozen horror. If power never returned. . . .

He told himself that things were fine. They were inside the node, and he could see the predicted rainbow blur of color. He felt perfectly normal. If this was all there was to it, then he had been a fool—

Except that suddenly things were not fine. *He* was not fine. Not at all. He felt his stomach, already uneasy, beginning to rotate in one direction while the inside of his head went in another. He closed his eyes, then opened them again. It made no difference. He could still see the rainbow internal glow of the node, even with his eyes squeezed shut. That glow was beginning to turn, a hundred ways at once. He was riding a giant multicolored whirligig, that every few seconds chose to vanish and reassemble itself and turn all the parts of him in different directions.

He decided that he had no choice. He was going to throw up. That's all he seemed to have done for the whole of the past two weeks; throw up onto—and into—officers' boots; throw up in bags on the way to Earth orbit; and now it was happening again, throwing up in a situation where his stomach didn't even feel *connected* to his mouth.

How could that happen? His throat was here, his stomach way over there.

It was a relief of sorts when a final spin took him off in a direction where there were no directions. Jeff felt himself twisted out of space; and in the ultimate blackness of nowhere, he felt the bliss of nothing at all.

It seemed as though he had been unconscious for hours, but it must have been no more than a few seconds. The information feed was saying, *"Transition plus one second. Node transition is successful and complete."*

"Where are we?" Jeff spoke more to prove that he was alive than for the answer.

"Where we should be. The object directly ahead of the Aurora *is the Messina Dust Cloud. To human eyes, it has a reputation as one of the most beautiful of known celestial objects."*

Jeff was staring on the forward screen at a scene unlike anything he had ever seen. The Messina Dust Cloud appeared as a great blue and purple haze, shot through with streaks and swirls of brighter colors—greens and yellows and glowing crimsons. Those rainbow lines and curves defined currents and whirlpools, which like a connect-the-dots picture provided an outline for a set of broader patterns. Jeff recognized those as the sluggish space rivers of dust and gas described by the information feed. Within them lay invisible pockets of stable transuranic elements, carried around some unseen cloud center.

And somewhere in that hazy nimbus—not too close, Jeff hoped—lay the cloud reefs. In those regions of intense electromagnetic and gravitational fields, something very strange happened to space-time. That's where you might find the big prizes, the shwartzgeld and the Cauthen starfires. People explored the reefs for them at their peril—though it was difficult to imagine anything so gorgeous as being dangerous.

"In spite of its beauty," the information feed said, as though it possessed a direct pipeline from Jeff's brain, *"the Messina Dust Cloud is the home of great and undefined perils. Reefs and space sounders have been responsible for the loss of many ships—"*

"I know all that, and I've seen the data on space sounders. I don't want to hear it again."

"—in circumstances which cannot be explained. They—"

It was a relief to hear Captain Dufferin's nervous, high-pitched voice, cutting into the emotionless information feed.

"We are clear of the node. All ship systems are in working order. Crew to the main deck."

The *Aurora* was once more under drive, but now it was set to a low cruising level. The trip from Jeff's aft quarters forward, so difficult under a two-G acceleration, became an upward drift.

He had been on the main deck only once before, when he first boarded the *Aurora*. At the time it seemed small and cluttered. Now nine people fitted into it easily. Almost the whole ship's complement must be present. Jeff, wondering who was flying the *Aurora*, realized that he had never seen a couple of these people before—not even once, not even at meals. Where had they been hiding? He went to squeeze into the only available seat, next to one of the strangers. She was a huge black woman with short frizzy hair, who showed her teeth at him. He hoped it was a smile.

Captain Dufferin stood on an elevated platform at the far end of the long cabin, rocking backward and forward on his heels. His eyes surveyed the whole group, pausing for a split second at Jeff before running on past him.

"I think we are all here—at last." The captain's eyes flickered once more to Jeff and away again, so quickly it was difficult to be sure. "As some of you may know, our journey out to the E-K Belt was conducted with sealed orders." The captain spoke like a machine, inviting neither question nor interruptions as he continued: "Sealed orders are used when the mission is of particular importance. The electronic scrambler that guarded our mission files was unlocked only ten minutes prior to node transition. After this meeting it will be available to any crew member who wishes to examine it. However, I have listened to it already. I now propose to present to you a brief summary of its content."

The black woman next to Jeff wriggled on her chair—her bottom overflowed the seat—and emitted a sound that could have been either a groan or a deep breath.

Dufferin stared down his nose at her, but went on, "Node 23 provides access to the Messina Dust Cloud and associated regions. These include the planets Solferino and Cauldron, of the star Grisel, and also the planet of Merryman's Woe."

"Know that. Don' nee' no lecsher. Giv's sumthin new."

The black woman spoke so softly and in such a peculiar accent that Jeff could only just hear and understand her. At the same time he was afraid that she might be audible to the captain. He moved a little away from her on his chair and tried to look as though he were nowhere near—not easy, when she seemed to fill the whole space around her.

"In its earliest days of development, the Messina Dust Cloud had no real government." Captain Dufferin continued as though reading a lecture. "It was sparsely populated, and the explorers and traders operated more on a basis of mutual need than of written laws. For most of the time, they worked independently and even competitively, exchanging only essential materials and information. Part of each year was spent back at Sol, selling goods and reequipping the ships. That phase ended when production capability appeared in the Cloud, together with local markets. It was no longer necessary to make the annual and expensive trips through the node. The Cloud inhabitants began to move toward a more structured society with its own laws. They established a governing body for the Cloud, to operate under guidance from Sol. At the same time, a dangerous and perhaps fatal trend began."

Captain Dufferin's briefing had a quality that Jeff had noticed in his uncle Fairborn. Every word and every syllable was delivered with no expression and with exactly equal emphasis. That, together with Dufferin's steady rocking backward and forward on his heels, produced a hypnotic effect; after a while you stopped listening—no matter how hard you tried, or how interesting or important the material.

Jeff found his eyes roaming around the assembled group. Out of a total of nine people, he recognized seven, including himself and Captain Dufferin. The two strangers were the fat woman next to him and a slight, wizened man with red hair, a big nose, and the look of an angry rooster. The pair had something in common.

What was it?

It took a few moments, then Jeff had it. The big woman and the little man over on the right looked *sloppy*, with smudges of dark at wrist and elbow. They slouched in their seats and were dressed in a casual and haphazard way that no one would ever confuse with the smart style of a navy officer.

So who were they, and what were they doing on board a Space Navy ship? Had Captain Dufferin been lying when he said there were no servants on the *Aurora*?

Jeff turned back to the captain and realized that Dufferin had been speaking all this time. Tuning in again, Jeff realized that he had nearly missed something important.

"Completely different attitude toward machines," Captain Dufferin was saying. "Development in the Messina Dust Cloud was permitted to proceed for close to a century without laws or limits. Twenty years ago, it seems that claims were made to the government of Earth, by Messina Cloud representatives, that machines had been constructed in the Cloud with an intelligence equivalent to or greater than that of humans. Naturally, our government pointed out the statutes that limit machine development and intelligence. We emphasized the natural and inevitable human antipathy toward intelligent machines."

This time the growl from beside Jeff could not be missed. Fortunately, Dufferin was too infatuated with the sound of his own voice to be willing to stop. He merely glared in their direction and went on: "After that, it seems, there was a long period of quiet. Nothing more was said to Sol government about intelligent machines, and combinations of humans and machines were never discussed. It was with great horror that Sol government learned, less than one year ago, of highly perverse activities taking place within the Messina Dust Cloud. Contrary to all the laws of God and Man—"

"God 'n' *Man!*" The woman muttered the words loudly, right, it seemed, in Jeff's ear. He wished he could turn invisible. "You hear him? Wha' 'bou' God 'n' *Wimmin?*"

"Contrary to all the laws of God and *Man*, as I say." Captain Dufferin looked daggers—not at the woman, but at Jeff. "Contrary to those laws, researchers in the Messina Cloud have been building cyborgs, hellish mergers of humans and machines. Such actions must be stopped, and they will be stopped. We will stop them. We have received instructions from our government as to how to proceed."

We? Jeff reviewed the head count. Assuming one person was now flying the *Aurora*, that gave a grand total of ten. It was hard to guess the number of Cloudlanders, humans and cyborgs scattered through the vast region ahead of them, but there could be millions. And the *Aurora* was a small ship, armed with the Space Navy equivalent of a squirt gun.

We will stop them. Those instructions on how to proceed must be really something. Jeff leaned back, prepared to be amazed.

"After this meeting," the captain went on, "I will broadcast a message prepared jointly by headquarters staff of both Bor-Com and CenCom. It is an order to the governing body of the Messina Dust Cloud to surrender peacefully to the *Aurora* and accompany us back to Solspace. It warns them that a refusal to do so may involve dire consequences for the entire population of the Dust Cloud."

Captain Dufferin paused. "Any questions?"

There was a long pause. Jeff couldn't believe it. Apparently that was it, the whole plan. The *Aurora* would order the government of the Messina Dust Cloud to give in, then sit and wait. As for questions, Jeff had a hundred; but he didn't want to be the one to ask.

Finally a hand was raised over on the right. It was the bantam redhead.

"Captain, are other BorCom ships on the way here? I mean, like, reinforcements."

Dufferin shook his head. "We do not judge that to be necessary. It is well known that the inhabitants of this region do not favor the use of weapons, and never have."

"I know that, sir, but I mean—"

"If there are no other questions?" Captain Dufferin surveyed the group. "Very well. You are dismissed. You may return to your duties."

He marched rapidly out of the room. Most of the group left after him, talking among themselves. In half a minute Jeff found himself with just the two strangers. He expected they might introduce themselves, but instead the woman stared at the man disapprovingly and shook her head. "Questions, questions. Russo, you orter know better. Jinners don' do that."

"I know." The shriveled little man scowled. "But I had to ask. I may not be big, and I may not see good, and I may not hear good, but when it comes to a smeller"—he reached up and tapped the side of his beaky nose with two fingers—"I got the best. 'Specially for trouble. An' when old Squeaky says we jus' send a message, an' tell the Cloudlanders to lie down an' roll over, why then—" He paused and pointed a finger at Jeff as though he had just noticed him. "He with you?"

"No," the woman said. "You right." She turned to Jeff. "What you doon here?"

Jeff didn't know. He was just sitting. Since no one had assigned him duties, he had no reason to be anywhere. But it was obvious that the other man had known that he was there—so why the fake surprise at Jeff's presence?

"I'm not doing anything here."

"Then you ought to get the hell an' gone," said the man. But the woman raised a broad, black hand. "Hol' it, Russo." Then, to Jeff, "You the Kopal, right?"

The Kopal? "I'm Jeff Kopal, yes."

"And you even looks summat human." She surveyed the long cabin. "We'll see. You wanna listen, all right. Not here, though. Come on with us."

She slid her ample behind off the chair and started to head aft.

"Hooglich!" the man said. "He might be one of Squeaky's."

"Then we'll fin' out, won' we?" She kept going. "An' the sooner we know, the better."

Russo trailed along after her. Jeff, not at all sure he was doing the right thing, followed. He knew he was being manipulated, but he didn't have any idea why. He went through a round, sliding hatch and found himself in a part of the ship where he had never been before. The cabins were more filled with equipment than the rest of the *Aurora*, and yet neater.

The woman stopped and flopped into a huge chair just wide enough for her broad behind. She indicated that Jeff should sit down.

"I'm Hooglich," she said. "That there's Rustbucket Smucker—Russo, for choice. How you call?"

He couldn't decide if she was asking his name, or what he preferred to be called. "I'm Jefferson Kopal, Jeff for short."

"An' I'm Mercy Hooglich. Hooglich for short an' for long. So, Jeff Kopal. You new to navy, new to here. What you think 'bout what Squeaky say?"

"Squeaky?"

"Captain Dufferin," Russo said. "Squeaky for short, but he don't know it."

Jeff wasn't sure what the others were up to. The only thing he could think of was to be absolutely honest. "I'm not a spy for the captain, if that's what you were worried about. But how do I know that one of you two isn't?"

Hooglich chuckled and slapped the tight-stretched cloth of her pants so that a wave of fat undulated along her thigh. "Hear the man, Brother Russo. Us spies? But we not. We jinners, an' jinners make bad spies—all navy tell you that."

Jinners? Jeff thought he knew all the ranks in the Space Navy, but this was new to him. He was finally forced to shake his head.

"I'm sorry. I don't know what a jinner is."

"You don't?" Russo's red eyebrows rose until they seemed ready to meet his hairline. "Why, we're the most important people on this ship, that's all—on any ship."

"But Captain Dufferin—" Jeff remembered the advice his father had once given him, talking about the Space Navy: "If you're not sure what it is, salute it." But he couldn't see himself saluting Hooglich or Russo.

"Forget ol' Squeaky for a minute." Russo rocked backward and forward on his heels in a fair imitation of the oscillating captain. "He don't know sweet fanny about anythin'. An' he's no worse than the rest of 'em, with their ribbons and stars and white hats. Take as many admirals and commanders and captains and mates as you like, you still can't run a ship. Engines and servos and sensors and life support, they're what makes a ship work. An' *we* run *them. Jinners run ships!*"

He spoke the final words like a rallying cry, and Jeff realized what had seemed familiar about some of the people listening to Captain Dufferin. He had seen smudges like that often enough—on himself, after a session on the old aircars.

"You're engineers! Jinners are engineers. You service the drive and the attitude control system and air system and navigation system and you operate the communications system and autochefs and computers."

The words came out of him in one great burst and he had to pause at last for breath. He realized that he had been sitting down when Russo was speaking, but somehow he was now on his feet.

The other two stared at him, then at each other. Finally they turned to give Jeff a longer second inspection.

"Well, how 'bout that," Hooglich said slowly. "Proves yer never can tell. But you was right, Russo. I think mebbe we cotched us a live one."

She grunted as she raised her bulk from the chair.

"Brother Kopal, how'd yer like me to give yer a look-see roun the real bizness end of the *Aurora*?"

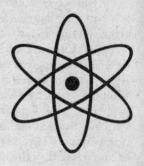

CHAPTER SIX

LET me ask you, Brother Kopal." They had reached another part of the ship that Jeff had never seen, a long descending corridor running right around the circumference of the inner hull as it spiraled aft. Russo had not come with them, and the helical tunnel was not much wider than Mercy Hooglich. As she led the way she spoke to Jeff over her shoulder. "Back on Earth, you got servants, right? Cook, cleaner, valet, butler, an' all."

"Yes." Was she criticizing him? He had no say in who worked at Kopal Manor, the servants were just *there*. Anyway, he didn't feel that they really worked for *him*. He was always uncomfortable when he had to ask anyone to do anything.

"So where they live, Brother Kopal?"

"In the house, like the rest of us."

"An' which part of house?"

"Downstairs. In the basement levels."

"So. It same here. Same in all navy. Jinners—us—us live down on lower levels, near the engines."

"But why? You seem to run the whole ship."

"Why you think?" She turned her head. "Wouldn't wan' people, would yer, like me an' ol' Russo—dirty people from Pool—rubbin' 'gainst them cap'ns 'n' admirals."

She was confirming what Jeff already suspected. She was from the Pool, Earth's great mass of unemployed and unemployables. Her speech was unlike that of the few Pool people he had met, but it was even less like anyone's in the Kopal and Lazenby circle of acquaintance. How had someone from the uneducated Pool made it into the prestigious Space Navy?

That was something to ponder over as they moved into a new section of the ship, where the broad midsection curved from its maximum width and began to narrow toward the rear. Jeff had examined the *Aurora*'s profile when he approached to board. It had the form of a swollen fish, enormously bloated in the middle to a near sphere. On the top, secured to the hull, was the little pinnace that could serve either as a space runabout or an emergency lifeboat. At the bow, where Captain Dufferin had his control room, the ship narrowed to a thin spike twenty meters long. The transparent bubble of an observation nacelle sat out at the very end, accessible only through the narrowest of crawlways. Jeff or Russo might wriggle out along it, Hooglich never. Aft—where they were heading—lay the engine room, and beyond that the fluted tail fins of the Diabelli fusion drive.

Jeff knew a good deal about the Omnivore engines of the drive. But he had never actually seen them. He had the shakes at the prospect—not the unpleasant tremor that accompanied family events, but something curiously pleasurable.

"And here we are, Brother Kopal." They had reached a little control panel beside a circular plate in the floor. Hooglich tapped in a four-digit sequence. "Now we hafta wait. Take a few seconds to cycle."

The plate began steadily turning around its center.

"How did you know my name was Kopal?" Jeff asked. "I mean, you knew it before anybody said it."

She laughed, a full-throated guffaw that set her whole body jiggling. "Through the 'vine—the grapevine, that is. The navy's the worst place in the universe to keep a secret. You find gossip tagged onto the end of almost every official communication. Before you came here there was talk for days. A Kopal and a Lazenby were joining the navy less than a week apart. The Lazenby goes to Central Command, no surprise there—but the Kopal ships out on a BorCom dumpship like the *Aurora*, with a captain who's known to resent all Kopals because he's not one. That makes no sense. No one seems to know what's going on—and that includes me."

She stared at him expectantly. Jeff stared right back at her. He knew exactly why he was on the *Aurora* rather than in Central Command, but he didn't want to talk about it. Instead, he said, "What happened? Your speech is different. I can understand you easily now, and I couldn't before."

She gave him a grin, with more and whiter teeth than a human head should hold. "Well, I guess you jus' be gettin' smarter. Or mebbe you think it 'cause we way aft, none of yer hi-ups officer comes this way. Wouldn't do, eh, 'f us dumb folk from the Pool start talkin' the top-chat line, like ol' Cap'n Duf'rin. Bes' talk like this-aways, see, makes navy peoples feel good."

"Now you're faking it again. But you were willing to talk normally to me just now. How do you know I won't go and tell the captain that you can talk perfectly standard navy talk when you choose?"

"Maybe you'll do that. Be my guest, tell him anything you like. Do you think that would be a good idea, though?"

It took less than a second to decide. "No, it wouldn't."

"Quite right. For one thing, Captain Dufferin probably

wouldn't believe you. And if somehow you did manage to persuade him—it wouldn't be easy, he has a head like Stedman plate—he'd hate you for bringing him bad news. It's the old story: Shoot the messenger."

"If you're willing to talk to me, why did you make such a big deal at the beginning of my being a Kopal?"

"Because you are one. Because it *is* a big deal. Anything involving a Kopal makes waves through the whole Space Navy. That's simple fact. Lazenbys are important, too, but Kopals are *it*. That's not the only data point, though. You see, I put a lot of faith in my instincts. I also trust Russo's big sniffer. After we took a good first look at you and saw you staring at the control panel, Russo gave me a wink and whispered 'Jinner!' I agree. You're a Kopal, no doubt about that; but you're a jinner, too, if ever I saw one. That's one strange combination. Did you ever take machines apart?"

Jeff nodded. He began to describe his work to restore the old aircar in the barn—"Manuals are for sissies," Hooglich said at one point—but he couldn't take his eyes off the circular plate. It was turning, slowly, slowly. At last it stopped and began to rise clear of the floor without any visible support. His voice faded.

Mercy Hooglich moved forward. "Come on. I can see we'll get no sense out of you 'til after this." She led the way down a turning staircase beneath the plate, remarking as she went, "There's an elevator, pretty useful if you're climbing up forward and the drive's on high setting. But we're only at one-sixth G, and you'll see more this way."

Jeff followed her and found himself in a tall cylindrical chamber about ten meters high. Ladders ran around the walls, and a walkway—vertical, now that the drive was on—ran along the middle of the room. Set in a hexagonal pattern between the walkway and external wall were half a dozen innocent-looking blue cylinders, each one about four meters long and no more than a meter across.

"Is it all right if I—" Jeff paused, his hand reached out halfway to one.

Hooglich nodded. "Go right ahead. Touch if you want. But you won't feel anything."

Jeff placed his fingertips on the side of one of the pale blue tubes. The surface was cool to the touch, and he felt—or imagined—a slight vibration there. It was hard to believe, but under his hand sat the burning heart of a Diabelli Omnivore. The drive was on, and the fusion reactions must be taking place within a few inches of his fingers.

"Hydrogen fusion at the moment," Hooglich said. The fat woman was observing Jeff closely. Most people in the Diabelli chamber were blue-funk nervous, even if they tried to hide it. They knew they were within feet of temperatures as hot as the inside of a star. This visitor appeared enthralled. "Hydrogen is easy to find, most places you go. But if we don't have hydrogen we can live off the land. The Omnivores use anything lighter than iron as fusion fuel." She patted the bulbous cylinder affectionately. "Nothing heavier than iron, though. You see, Brother—"

"I know. Iron is where the binding energy per nucleon reaches a maximum. If you fuse anything heavier than iron, it *takes* energy instead of giving it."

"Hmm." She stood staring at him, her head cocked to one side. "Where'd you pick that up? Not in navy training, that's for sure."

"I've had free access to query links as long as I remember."

"Maybe you have. But most people don't access science stuff, even when it's available. Anyway, the Omnivores can operate in five different modes, depending on what's available." She tapped a point near the top end of the cylinder. "Fusion takes place right here, inside this section. Sometime when the drive is off, if you like I'll pull an Omnivore head and let you see what it's like inside. Interested?"

"Sure!"

"I thought you'd say that. And here, see"—she was descending farther, to a ring of complicated displays and switches—"we have the indicators and controls. The drive can be turned on and off here, by individual Omnivore units if we want to."

"But I thought the control room for the drive was up front, on the bridge with Captain Dufferin. In fact, I saw it there."

"I'm sure you did. But commands given there all come here prior to execution. They can be overridden from here, too. Of course, that would only be done in an emergency."

"What sort of emergency?"

"That's a good question." She pursed her lips. "I don't know—until it happens. Let's put it this way: Do you feel comfortable knowing that Squeaky Dufferin is making the decisions for all of us? He has the worst reputation in the whole fleet, you know—and that includes officers in CenCom, Sol-Com, *and* BorCom. He can't make up his mind, can't fly a ship, and can't keep control of himself. Why they put him in charge of a tricky assignment like this, I'll never know."

"If he's so bad, why do you ship with him?"

"You think people like me and Russo have much choice? We're not like you, a Kopal, with the whole universe open. We take what we can get, and feel lucky to have it. Squeaky's the worst, but there's others nearly as bad."

"But how did you get out of the Pool? I mean, Pool people, they're—"

Jeff stopped. He had been going to say what all his family stated as self-evident truth, that Pool people were ignorant and lazy and uneducated.

"Pool people what?" Hooglich scowled. "Stupid?"

"Well. . . ."

"If you were going to say that, you'd mostly be right. The Pool's no different from anyplace else—full of dummies. But the people who run the Space Navy understand what a population bell curve is. Do *you*, Brother Kopal?"

She said it like a challenge. Jeff knew the answer, but he wasn't sure he could state it clearly. "It means that in a big population, you'll have lots and lots of people who are about average. Say, of average height. But if the population follows a bell curve, you'll always get a few people who are really tall or really short."

"Good enough. And a normal distribution—that's the fancy name for a bell curve—also applies to smarts. Did you know that most navy jinners come from the Pool? But you should see the tests we had to take. We struggled every step, eighteen hours a day; the tests got harder and harder and harder. You, you're a Kopal. You waltzed through, roses all the way, an' everyone applauding."

If only she knew! It was a relief when she went on, "But enough of Pool and people talk. What do you think of the drive?"

More than enough people talk. She had no idea by how narrow a margin he had scraped into the navy, or how his cousins, uncles, and aunts felt about him.

He forced his mind away from that dead-end subject. What did he think of the drive, and the whole power and control system of the *Aurora*?

"It's—it's—" He couldn't find a suitable word. Colossal? Sensational? Awe-inspiring?

"It's great," he finished weakly.

"When you first see it, you think that." There was a gloomier note in Mercy Hooglich's voice. "But then you look at the whole fleet, and you realize that there's been little change in the design of the Omnivores for over half a century. Oh, they're more compact and a bit more powerful. And now we have the catalyzed drive, too—you know what that is?"

Jeff didn't, but he was willing to try a guess. "Something to make the fusion reaction take place at a lower temperature? Like the catalysts you get in chemical reactions."

"You'll make a real jinner yet. When I first came into the navy, used to be that heavy element reactions wouldn't start in until the Omnivore internal temperature hit a billion degrees. Billion and a half, for fusing oxygen to silicon and iron. Now, nothing in there goes above ten million."

Jeff tried to visualize ten million degrees. He failed.

"Catalyzed fusion is nice to have," she went on. "But it hasn't made a *fundamental* change to space travel, the way the nodes changed it. Free-fall and high-G travel is just as uncomfortable now as it was when people first went to space. What we need is—" She stopped dead, and her face lost all its expression. "Oh my sainted Santa. The Anadem field, and the Messina Dust Cloud. I wonder. Could it be that?"

"What?"

"Nothing worth talking about." But Hooglich had been transformed from a focused and enthusiastic explainer of the *Aurora*'s engines and control systems to a woman whose mind was clearly far away.

"Nothin' for talking about," she repeated. "Not yet, at leas'. Come on. I gotta fin' Russo 'n' talk. Mebbe he know."

It was as though her speech, ahead of her body, was already moving toward *Aurora*'s forward section. As they approached amidships, she turned her attention for a moment back to Jeff.

"Never did tell me one thing, did you? An' I ask it right out, I 'member. So again: How come you on the *Aurora*?"

This time there was no escaping. Jeff started to tell the whole sorry story, about the Kopal and Lazenby families, and how Myron and Myra fitted the model for bravery and competence, while he didn't. He was getting to the final disastrous riding event when she interrupted.

"Uncle Giles—that be Giles Lazenby?"

"That's right. He's my uncle, my father's cousin."

"Not your uncle, then. Second cousin."

"I know. But I've always called him uncle."

"You close to him?"

Jeff hesitated. He saw a good deal of his uncle, but emotionally he felt as far away as you could get. He never had any idea what Uncle Giles was thinking.

Hooglich read his face and cut in before he could answer. "Let me tell you somethin' 'bout Uncle Giles." Her Pool

speech style disappeared again as she went on, "Everybody in
the Space Navy knows of Giles Lazenby. He was never an admiral, and he's not a Kopal—though maybe he'd like to be—but
he pulls terrific weight. When he was in the service, he was the
head of security forces. That's a mighty powerful position.
Word has it he kept—and still keeps—the dirt on everybody in
the navy. They're afraid of him. What he wants, he gets. Is
there any reason why he might want you in BorCom?"

"I can't think of one. Maybe to get me out of the way, so
his own son, Myron, can shine?"

Mercy Hooglich shook her frazzle-mop head. "That bird
won't fly. If he wants his Myron to look good, and you always
do *worse* than Myron, Giles Lazenby would make sure you two
stayed together so people could make comparisons."

"Then I don't know. Maybe Uncle Giles had nothing to
do with my assignment here." But Jeff felt convinced that that
was not true. He had been pretty much out of it on the night of
the riding meet, but he did remember one thing: Uncle Giles
in the conference room, saying, "We are proposing, and they
will approve, assignment to Border Command." It seemed an
odd way to put it. Surely, the navy proposed, not civilians—not
even influential retired officers.

"Let it set." Hooglich waved one brawny arm, dismissing
the subject and Jeff in one sweep. "We fin' out sometime. You
git on forrard. I gotta gabble Russo."

He spiraled on higher in the ship, up the long narrow corridor that would take him to his own cabin. Since he had not
been offered a single assignment, or a suggestion of one, after
his arrival on the *Aurora*, he had no thought that his absence
might be missed. It was a shock to enter his cabin and see a message blinking urgently on his communications panel: *Report at
once to the bridge.*

He still had no thought of trouble as he headed forward,
to where Captain Dufferin was pacing his raised dais in the
middle of the control room. The captain halted as Jeff entered,

and advanced to the edge of the platform so that he was high enough to peer down on his visitor.

"Ensign Kopal. What have you been doing?"

"Looking around the ship, sir. I thought I ought to know as much about it as possible, and there were parts I hadn't seen. Engineer Hooglich took me aft and showed me the engine room and drive."

"She invited you to see them?"

Jeff sensed some kind of trap, though not perhaps for him. "No, sir. I asked her to show me."

"I see." Captain Dufferin went back to pacing the raised dais, his hands clasped behind his back. "You realize, do you, that I could charge you with a failure to discharge your duties?"

His duties? He didn't know he had any duties. That was clearly the wrong thing to say. "I'm sorry, sir. I thought that I was off duty after the general meeting ended."

"An officer on my ship, Ensign, is never off duty. Even a junior officer such as yourself. Also"—the captain swung to face Jeff—"it is not appropriate that an officer socialize with the engineers. They are of a different social class. I am astonished that I need to remind you, above all, of that fact. You are, are you not, a *Kopal*?"

Dufferin spat out the last word.

"Yes, sir."

"Then behave accordingly."

"Yes, sir." Jeff stood at attention. The captain seemed to have lost interest. He wandered over to stare at the controls, and then up through the hemispherical bubble above the bridge.

At last Jeff cleared his throat. Dufferin swung around. "Yes, what is it?"

"I didn't know if I had been dismissed, sir."

"You have not." Dufferin gestured upward. "Since you have this burning desire to explore parts of the *Aurora* unknown to you, I will allow you to indulge that curiosity to the full. Proceed at once to the observation nacelle and familiarize yourself with its functions."

"Yes, sir. Should I then return here?"

"No." Dufferin again turned his back on Jeff. "We will soon be approaching the region of the Lizard Reef. You will remain in the observation nacelle and cool your heels, at least until such time as the reef has been passed."

"Yes, sir. Should I make observations?"

"That is entirely up to you. We will be at our point of closest approach to the reef in approximately seven hours. Do you have questions?"

Yes. Why are you doing this to me? "No sir."

"Then proceed. I will inform you as to when you may return. Until then, I do not want to see you or hear from you under any circumstances."

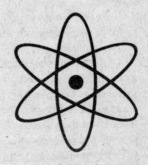

CHAPTER SEVEN

THE spike leading to the observation chamber was even narrower than it looked from the outside. Jeff, squirming up the ladder of a narrow chimney barely two feet wide, thought of the stories he had read as a child. Growing up in a Kopal household, many of those tales had been of old Earth navy days; of voyages to unknown lands, of cannibals and mutinies and floggings and keelhaulings, of pirates and treasure troves and hanging in chains.

Those times were long gone; but what he was doing now must surely be little different in spirit from the old crewman punished for some trifling offense. This was the equivalent of being sent to the crow's nest or crosstrees at the top of a mast, to hang and hover there as long as the captain chose to leave him.

At least there would be no gale-force winds to tear at him, no days of pitiless sun glare or of snow and hail to freeze his body.

The little observation room, when he finally inched his way out to it, was not designed for comfort. He gulped and shivered as he poked his head through the entry hatch. Maybe wind and driving rain would not be so bad. Seen from inside, the wall of the nacelle that he was entering was perfectly transparent. He seemed to be facing open space, with nothing between him and the great luminous shroud of the Messina Dust Cloud. Below him as he scrambled through the hatch lay the rounded front of the *Aurora*, the expanding eldritch glow of its drive barely visible behind the curved bulk of the hull.

He had to stand up and grope with his fingers to find the bubble of the nacelle's wall. He learned that he was in a spherical chamber only five feet high, so he could never fully stand up. When he closed the hatch through which he had entered, a fold-out chair on top of it allowed him to sit down. The chair could be rotated, to give a view in any direction. He could also pull up a rudimentary control panel, with access to the ship's knowledge bank and communications system. And that was all. There was nothing to eat, nothing to drink. If he needed to use a bathroom, he was out of luck.

Jeff sat down and turned the chair so that he was staring straight up, in the *Aurora*'s direction of travel. Nothing was supposed to happen for the next few hours, and he could certainly use some time to think. He was accustomed to the idea that a member of the Kopal family was regarded as someone special, from whom a superior level of performance was expected. That, to someone incapable of outstanding performance, was bad enough. It was even worse to learn that many people were going to hate him, not for anything he had done, but simply because he was a member of those privileged Kopals.

Why had he been sent out to the Messina Dust Cloud,

working for Border Command? It had seemed straightforward enough when it first happened, a technique to make sure that he was far from home where his mediocre performance and lack of courage could not embarrass the rest of the family.

Mercy Hooglich had put her fat finger on an obvious problem with that explanation. He had to agree with her; Uncle Giles would do anything he could to show Myron's superiority to Jeff. That should have meant assignment to Central Command for both of them. So there had to be some other explanation of why he was here—and also, according to Hooglich, a reason why the *Aurora*, lightly armed and with a minimum crew, had been set the impossible task of persuading the people of the Cyborg Territory to surrender. Were the two things related? He couldn't see how. And what did Hooglich mean, when she spoke of the Anadem field? Although he had spent endless hours browsing the science banks—"Utter wa-a-aste of time," Aunt Willow had sniffed—he had never come across it.

He keyed a query into the science knowledge bank and listened to the quiet reply. *"No direct entry. Cross-reference to speculation bank?"*

"Yes."

"Level?"

Jeff wasn't quite sure what that meant. "Elementary?"

"Cross-reference performed. From the speculation bank, elementary level: the existence of the Anadem field has never been confirmed. The possibility of such a field was proposed in a series of theoretical papers by S. Macafee. According to Macafee's calculations, the Anadem field would permit a modification of space-time, of such a nature that local inertial nullification would be achieved in the vicinity."

So much for the elementary level.

"Does that mean that if you were on a ship using an Anadem field, you would not feel any acceleration?"

"If you were in the correct location, that would be true. The Anadem field, if one existed, would be a displacement field. Some parts of the ship, close to the field, would feel the effects of acceleration

much diminished. Other parts, however, would experience an augmented acceleration."

Jeff could sort of visualize what was being said. It was as though you had the power to move the acceleration forces, so that instead of feeling them where people were located, they would be effective only in places where machines and equipment were found.

"Why is this only considered speculation? Do other people question the results?"

"Sol system experts claim that the analysis by S. Macafee is obscure, and some of the base assumptions are questionable. However, others claim that devices employing the Anadem field already are in use."

That answer was oddly stated. *Sol system experts.* Why not just "experts"?

"Who and where is Macafee?"

"No information is available on the background and training of S. Macafee. A possible location is currently listed as the Confluence Center."

"I never heard of that. Where is it?"

"The Confluence Center is located within the Messina Dust Cloud. Coordinates are as follows. . . ."

Jeff ignored the long strings of digits that came over the communication link. He had at least a partial answer to the sudden change in Mercy Hooglich. The navy grapevine must associate the rumored Anadem field with the Messina Dust Cloud. That meant Cyborg Territory, the target of the current mission. In Hooglich's mind the *Aurora*'s mission, and even Jeff's own presence, were linked in some way with the Anadem field.

How?

Jeff stared at the lilac and purple nimbus of the cloud. Somewhere, somewhere out there within the unknown depths, lay a place known as the Confluence Center. Somewhere within that Confluence Center sat S. Macafee—man or woman, or even cyborg. Nothing had been said about that.

And somehow, in a way that Jeff could not begin to imagine, Mercy Hooglich thought that their mission, Macafee, and the Anadem field might be linked.

Jeff realized that he was no longer staring vaguely at the expanse of the cloud. His eye was drawn, again and again, to a single pinwheel of darkness.

"Directly ahead. Is that the Lizard Reef?"

"The Lizard Reef is not directly ahead. Our trajectory will actually take us clear of it. However, the object that you refer to is the Lizard Reef."

"Why does it look that way? It's like a whirlpool."

"In the middle of every reef lies a ring vortex. That is a dense ring of dust and gas, rotating in on itself. The vortex stability is maintained by an electromagnetic field. What is observed is not the field itself, but the cloud of dust around it. The middle of the vortex forms a hole in the middle of the ring."

Jeff could see it, now that he knew what to look for. A hole of utter darkness lay like the pupil of an eye at the exact center of the swirl.

"If a ship passes through the exact center, there will be a big change in speed but no ill effects. The danger of a reef comes in an inaccurate passage through the eye. A ship that goes through even slightly off-center is torn apart."

The pinwheel seemed remote, decorative, and harmless against its background of the great dust currents of the Messina Cloud. It would be easy, in ignorance, to stray too close. Jeff checked the *Aurora*'s course vector from the ship's database and confirmed that they would pass comfortably clear of the heading listed for the Lizard Reef.

He glanced up again, reassured—and saw not one but two swirls of darkness in the sky ahead. The second one had appeared in the minute or so while he had been checking the ship's course vector. And the new one seemed to be moving.

Could a reef do that? Or was it some illusion, an effect of the *Aurora*'s own motion?

He looked more closely at the second dark patch. It no

longer matched the Lizard Reef in appearance. Now it was surrounded by a silver glitter, tiny sparkles that dotted the near vacuum of the Messina Dust Cloud with a million flecks of light. As he watched, those dots of light dwindled and faded, to leave behind emptiness of a curious clarity.

An octagonal shape appeared where the sparks had been. Around its perimeter sat eight ragged blue-white tendrils, pointing outward and thinning gradually to invisibility. Next to the tendrils the pattern of background stars was compressed and distorted, as though the object was imposing its own eightfold symmetry on space itself. As he watched, the shape increased its size. It was moving to lie directly ahead of the *Aurora*.

Jeff caught his breath. He switched the communications link to connect him with the bridge of the *Aurora*.

"Captain Dufferin." He hardly recognized his own voice, it was so hoarse and nervous. "This is Ensign Kopal."

"Kopal! Didn't I give you direct orders not to—"

"Captain, we are about to suffer a space sounder encounter." Jeff's voice cracked on the last word, and he had to swallow before he could go on. "It's almost directly ahead of us. And it's getting closer—fast."

Myron would have done it exactly right: Observe with a clear eye and a calm head, while at the same time comparing what he saw with what he had learned about space sounders.

Jeff knew all that, but it made no difference. He was not Myron. Nervousness mixed with enormous excitement was turning his head into a gigantic stew pot where facts and fancies clashed in a bubbling maelstrom of ideas. It didn't help that he could hear Captain Dufferin shouting orders over the communication channel, his voice so high in pitch that Squeaky was the only possible nickname. The captain must have picked up the image of the sounder on his observation screens, and obviously he didn't like what he saw.

That was all right. Neither did Jeff. Space sounders were supposed to be found only in the neighborhood of reefs, but the Lizard Reef was far ahead and here was a sounder, out in open space and closing in on the *Aurora*. The sounders were known to have some strange attraction for the gemstones known as Cauthen starfires, but unless a ship had a starfire on board the sounders were supposed to be harmless. The *Aurora* had no starfire on board—but there was no doubt that the sounder's attention was on the ship.

The distance between the two was closing steadily. From his position Jeff had a view of the sounder's long, tapering body, kilometers of near-perfect blackness occulting the pale glow of the Messina Dust Cloud. The octagonal shape at the front had become a great maw, surrounded by its eight blue-white tendrils. According to navy files, that maw could stretch wide enough to engulf a full battle cruiser—a ship fifty times the size of the *Aurora*. There were stories of vessels swallowed whole, their crews carried off to nowhere so fast that the final desperate messages were redshifted to a small fraction of their original signal frequencies. They were traveling at some large fraction of light speed—and still alive, not crushed by the monstrous and near-instantaneous acceleration. No Sol scientist had any explanation as to how that could happen.

The sounder filled a quarter of the sky ahead when the captain's next scream reached the observation bubble. It sounded to Jeff as though he was calling, "Emergency stations! Emergency stations!" but his voice was overlaid with a scream of interference, a deafening *shreep-shreep-shreep* that set teeth on edge. It was the call of the sounder itself, filling space with high-energy radio signals. Against that background, Jeff could hardly hear Dufferin's frantic instructions.

The emergency stations were amidships, in the main body of the ship where the pinnace was located. It was tiny compared with the main ship, but if the *Aurora* ever had to be abandoned the pinnace had the power and supplies to carry the crew to safety.

He stood up to stow the folding seat away, so that he would be able to lift the hatch and start back along the narrow shaft that led to the main hull. His hand was on the seat back when the *Aurora*'s drive went without warning from low to high power. Instead of the light acceleration of easy cruising, the ship surged forward.

Even if he had been ready, Jeff would have had trouble remaining on his feet. He fell forward over the folding chair. It collapsed under his weight, sending him crashing to the floor of the bubble. He landed hard on his arms and chest, barely able to protect his face with his hands. Lying unable to move, he both felt and saw the long column that supported the observation bubble flex and whip under the sudden force of the drive. The floor of the nacelle resonated beneath his chest with the deep, groaning note of a gigantic organ pipe.

He rolled over, braced himself on his hands, and struggled to his knees. He had to get back to the main hull. If anywhere at all was safe, that would be it. Even if the sounder swallowed up the *Aurora*, the crew might still escape in the pinnace.

New shouts and screams were coming over the communication channel, Dufferin's high-pitched cries mingled now with some deeper bellow. It sounded as though a furious argument were going on below. The *shreep-shreep-shreep* of sounder interference became louder. Jeff looked out, away from the ship. The *Aurora*'s evasive action, far from losing the sounder, had brought it closer. The black maw seemed only meters away, spanning the sky.

He paused for a moment, imagining he saw a spark of iridescence deep within the mouth's dark cavity. Could that be a Cauthen starfire, the fabulous gem that had sparked the original exploration and development of the Messina Dust Cloud? If so, he might be the first living person who had ever seen one, *inside* a sounder.

His sanity returned. *There'd be time to think about historic firsts only if you remained a living person. Get back to the main hull!*

He pushed aside the shattered chair and struggled to lift

the hatch. The little plate seemed to weigh a ton. Before he could move it, another sharp pulse of force came from the *Aurora*'s drive. The spike holding the observation nacelle curved through thirty degrees, sending Jeff rolling around the curved floor of the bubble. Moments later, the drive cut back to such a gentle thrust that he was almost floating.

As he rose to his feet Jeff had his second attack of sanity. The sounds coming through the communications link suggested total chaos in the control room. Dufferin must have been trying anything he could think of, blindly, to escape the sounder. And as long as the *Aurora* veered and darted erratically, in random directions and with variable thrust, Jeff would never be able to make his way through the narrow shaft to the main hull. He would be all right on the ladder now, with the drive throttled back almost to nothing. But how long would that last? Another pulse of two or three Gs, like the one they had just experienced, and his grip would tear free. He would accelerate helplessly down the twenty-meter drop. At three Gs, a fall of one tenth of that distance could be deadly.

He was stuck in the observation nacelle. His only possible escape route was too dangerous to use. That realization forced a decision: If he could do nothing, he would do nothing. It calmed Jeff completely. He rolled onto his back, cushioned the back of his head on his hands, and stared up at the blind face of the sounder. It had so grown in size that he felt he could reach out through the transparent wall of the bubble and touch one of the floating blue-white tentacles.

That was an illusion, he knew, an effect created by the sounder's immense size and the lack of anything to provide a scale of distance. The sounder was still probably a hundred meters away. The maw was opening wider, as though preparing to ingest the ship. It was impossible to believe that the object he was looking at was not a sentient creature, well aware of the presence of the *Aurora*.

Both ship and space sounder had turned during their past few seconds of violent maneuvers. The observation bubble now pointed not toward the glowing face of the Messina Dust Cloud, but to an expanse of open starry sky. Jeff could see an octagonal pattern of distortion imposed on that background. Far too many stars were visible, as though space near the sounder had been drawn in and compressed by its presence.

He tried to estimate the rate at which the maw was increasing in apparent size. Unless something changed, the *Aurora*—or at least its observation bubble, which was the part that most concerned him—would be within that dark mouth in less than thirty seconds.

The knowledge that you were about to die was supposed to calm you. It didn't work that way at all. Jeff, gazing down the maw, felt an all-over terror. He didn't want to die. His pulse was pounding faster and faster, his guts were knotted with the fear of imminent pain and death.

The blow, when it came, felt as though his heart was smashing out of his chest. A terrible, overwhelming force crushed him, molding his body to the rounded contours of the little chamber. In navy centrifuge tests he had endured as much as seven Gs. This was nine G, ten G, what? More, far more, than anything he had ever experienced. Part of the broken chair was digging deep into his shoulder, but he could not change his position by a millimeter.

His eyes would not move in his head. He saw only a shrinking and darkening circle, straight in front of him. The maw was near the center, and he stared at it. It was coming closer—fast—but at the same time it was sliding to one side. The observation nacelle filled with the writhing glow of one of the blue-white tentacles, then suddenly that ribbon of light was also moving past. Jeff saw the broad side of the sounder, like a wall of darkness speeding by. There came a crackle of discharge, as sheets of pink lightning enveloped the *Aurora* and pulsed within the interior of the bubble. The electronic *shreep-shreep-shreep* of the sounder rose to a new maximum.

The *Aurora* leapt forward as though goaded by the energy pumped into it. Jeff had not believed that the acceleration could possibly increase again. But it did. The new force that pushed him to the unforgiving floor went beyond intolerable. He no longer cared what happened to him. He just wanted it to stop.

It didn't stop, and it didn't stop, and it didn't stop.

And then at last, as the world darkened and he slid into unconsciousness, it did.

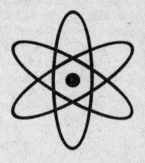

CHAPTER EIGHT

THE world was black as Jeff lost consciousness. When he awoke it had turned completely white. Other than that there seemed little difference.

He had not been able to move then; he could not move now, not even a finger. His chest was rigid, so constrained that he could barely breathe. As the scene before his eyes came into focus, the uniform field of white took on a pattern of ruled lines. He realized that he was staring at a flat ceiling made up of big square tiles. As he watched, a flicker of red and green came and went.

Nothing like that existed in the observation nacelle. There was nothing remotely like it anywhere aboard the *Aurora*.

Where was he? He felt as though he had been unconscious for days.

He tried to lift his head. The effort produced a stab of pain in his neck, but it was worth it to be able to move again. He craned forward to look at his body. From his neck down his trunk, arms, and legs, he was totally encased in a rigid white cast. His head was the only thing he could move, and he could lift that only a couple of inches and hold it up for only a few seconds. Soon, even though he was in a low-G field, he was forced to lie back and stare again at the ceiling.

He heard a clicking sound from his left. He wanted to turn in that direction, but the effort produced a worse pain.

"Is someone there?"

Even his throat hurt. The voice that came out sounded nothing like his own.

He was answered by another and louder clicking, then a deep purr like a great cat. He could smell something, an odd odor like oil and cinnamon. Pain or not, he had to see what was beside him. He gritted his teeth and slowly forced his head to turn to the left.

The first thing that came into view were two long, spidery arms. They were made of metal or some dark plastic, and they had three separate joints. A warning voice in Jeff's head said, "Cyborg Territory." He grunted and turned his head farther in spite of the pain. He was afraid that the arms would end at a deformed human torso and some metallic monstrosity of a head. What he saw was not much more reassuring. Both slender arms—and six more like them—attached to a rounded gold tube shaped like a giant wine bottle. A tangled snakes' nest of wires grew out where the cap should have been. The body leaned toward a tall metal cabinet, whose surface was covered with tiny glowing hemispheres that formed an always-changing pattern of red and green lights.

The mop head of wires turned slowly in his direction.

"You are awake," a jerky voice said. "As the monitors

indicate, exactly on schedule. That is excellent. Do you know who you are?"

That wasn't the question most on Jeff's mind.

"I'm Jeff Kopal—Jefferson Kopal. Who are you?"

"I am Tilde. Wait here."

The wine bottle rotated rapidly to a horizontal position and scuttled away on all eight limbs like a great spider. Jeff wondered, Was *that* a cyborg; part human with a machine's limbs and casing? He had no idea of the forms taken by the inhabitants of Cyborg Territory. As for "wait here," what option did he have?

He could not stay with his head twisted to one side, it was too painful. He turned slowly back to his original position.

Where was he, and how had he come here? And what had happened to the *Aurora*? He felt sure that their final surge of acceleration was far beyond the ship's rated maximum.

He could hear a new sound to his left, an unnerving kind of scraping noise. He had to find out what it was. He turned again, slowly and painfully, and felt enormous relief. A fat black face, all worry and scars, was just a couple of feet away from his.

"Hooglich!"

"Tha's me." She turned, and he realized that the scraping was caused by a heavy chair that she was dragging along behind her. She plumped her massive behind onto the seat and settled down next to him. "How you doing?"

Pain all over, and as uncomfortable as you could get. Even a wimpy coward couldn't say something like that.

"I'm all right. What happened?"

She grunted. "Oh, mebbe ten million things." She dropped her Pool style of speech. "All right, Brother Kopal. Where would you like me to start?"

"Tell me everything."

"That might be difficult. I don't know everything. But I guess you realize that we got away from the sounder—otherwise we wouldn't be here."

"Where's here?"

"On board a Messina Cloud ship. Am I going to talk, or are you going to keep interrupting?"

"I'll be quiet."

"Right. From the beginning, then. The first that me and Russo knew we were in trouble was when Captain Dufferin threw the *Aurora* onto high G. We realized then there was some sort of problem, but being Squeaky he of course didn't bother to say what. We kind of figured it out, though, when the image of the sounder appeared on the forward screen. By the way," she made a face that Jeff would not like to have met on a dark night, "you may as well hear this from me as from anybody. According to the captain, you are entirely to blame for what happened. You were supposed to be in the observation nacelle to keep an eye out for sounders, and you didn't notify him of danger until too late."

"He didn't send me for that!" Excitement made Jeff's voice crack to an embarrassing imitation of Captain Dufferin's. "I noticed the sounder, but he didn't tell me to keep a lookout. He sent me there to *punish* me—for talking to you."

"I believe it." She did not point out that Jeff had interrupted again. "That's our captain, every time. He's never to blame for anything. I didn't even know that you were out at observation point 'til it was all over. Russo and I assumed that you were with the rest of the officers, at emergency stations and cushioned for high-G maneuvers. Otherwise, we'd never have done what we did." She gestured to Jeff's body cast. "And you'd not have needed that. Of course, if we hadn't acted we might not have escaped from the sounder. If it's any consolation, I'm in deep as you—'taking action contrary to officer's command,' the record says."

"What did you do?"

"Russo and I were down aft. We couldn't see what was happening on the bridge, but it was obvious from the way the *Aurora* was being thrown around—all fits and starts—that

Dufferin didn't have any idea what he was doing. And we could see the sounder, closing in on the ship. So . . . I took over. The commands for the drive arrive aft before execution. I overrode them. I put the *Aurora* onto ultrahigh emergency thrust, something the manuals warn you never to try—I'm in big trouble for that, too; but the people who write manuals don't have sounders chewing at their rear end. The log shows we touched twelve and a half Gs before we got clear, seven more than the engine danger level. Ruined the Omnivores, of course. I'm charged with that, too, wanton destruction of navy property. I came close to ruining you as well, Brother; but I don't think that worried old Squeaky at all."

"You saved the ship, yet you'll get blamed for damaging the engines?" Jeff forgot about his body cast and made a painful and unsuccessful effort to sit up. "That's not fair."

"Like life. What you going to do about it?"

"I'll make sure Captain Dufferin reports accurately."

"How you'll do that?"

"I will. I can. I'm—" Jeff was about to do something he had sworn never to do. He would never say, "I'm a Kopal," and expect on the strength of that to receive special treatment.

What stopped him was not revulsion at the idea of using the family name. It was the knowledge of where he was: marooned in the Messina Dust Cloud, far from every court of appeal. Until their return to Sol-side, Captain Dufferin was the ultimate authority.

"I'm going to file my own report," he finished weakly. "When we get back."

"Which might be quite a while from now, since we're not heading for the node. In fact, we're going in the opposite direction. Want to hear the rest of it?"

Jeff couldn't nod. It hurt too much. He just closed and opened his eyes.

She seemed to take that as agreement and went on, "We blew the *Aurora* clear of the sounder. Something strange about that, a sounder showing up so far from a reef, and I've no explanation yet. Russo claims to have ideas. Anyway, the sounder vanished after we were clear, the way they do. It just faded into nothingness and left us wondering if it was ever there. But *we* were certainly there, a gazillion kilometers from anywhere in a ship with no engines. Most of the officers wanted to send out a distress signal. Captain Dufferin refused. He said a navy ship should not accept assistance from any group trying to secede from Sol. No one asked him the obvious question: What were we supposed to do, sit around in space until we starved or ran out of air? Russo and I weren't in a position to say anything. Squeaky had already accused us of usurping his authority and being partly responsible for the fix the ship was in because we ruined the engines. Russo went forward and eased you back to where you could be looked after. There wasn't much anyone could do, beyond feeding you intravenously and hooking you up to life support. You were in poor shape, but you needed better medical care than the *Aurora* could provide. A couple of the officers said as much and suggested a Mayday for medical help. They were chewed out by Dufferin for their pains. He said to keep you sedated and out of it until something changed.

"You got slowly worse. We floated where we were for close to a week, with nothing to look at except reefs and dust rivers. And still nothing changed."

Hooglich paused and gloomily shook her rat's nest of tangled hair. It sounded to Jeff as though she were telling a late-night horror story, one that finished, "So we all died."

"But something must have changed," he said. Although he had thought on first waking that he had been unconscious for a long time, he was finding it hard to believe that six days or more had vanished from his life.

"Yeah." Hooglich laughed, for the first time since she had appeared at Jeff's side. "It changed. Me and Russo, we figured we couldn't be in much more trouble, no matter what we did. So we sent the Mayday. Squeaky went crazy when he found out what we'd done. Said we'd be locked in the brig. Trouble is, the *Aurora* doesn't have a brig; it's way too small for one. After six or seven hours, he stopped frothing at the mouth—because a Cloudship rolled up alongside. I thought, thank God, we're saved. With all the excitement aboard, I'd pretty much forgotten about the ultimatum the *Aurora* had sent to the Cloud government. But Dufferin hadn't. He said the same thing again, when the Cloudship contacted us to offer help. It had used our original signal as a beacon, and it was curious to find out what the 'else' might be in our 'surrender or else'. What sort of ship had the firepower to make a threat like that to a whole colony?

"Not us, that's for sure. We were floating without a drive. We had all the destructive power of a toy in a bathtub. The *Aurora*'s weapons weren't much to start with, and the ship's drive provided all their energy. No Omnivores, no weapons.

"If you think Captain Dufferin was grateful to be rescued, or at least embarrassed by the threats we had made, you don't know the man. The Cloudship jinners came over and gave us temporary power. We agreed that the *Aurora*'s Omnivores would be out of commission without a full dock overhaul. We went aboard their ship and met their commander. And Dufferin repeated his order one more time: the Messina Dust Cloud government must surrender."

"They refused?" More and more, Jeff wondered what combination of circumstances had brought him to a ship commanded by Captain Eliot Dufferin.

"Not exactly *refused.*" Hooglich had moved over to study the bank of monitors by Jeff's bedside. "The head of the Cloudship was Captain Trask. The answer wasn't a yes, and it wasn't a no. It was more like a suggestion that the two of them could talk the whole matter over on the way to the Cloud center, where the *Aurora* would be repaired and refurbished. I'd say more like Squeaky was *humored*, the way you would some harmless half-wit. Except we all know, he can be anything but harmless."

A worry had crept into Jeff's thoughts while Hooglich was talking. At the mention of the Cloudship's captain, it moved to center stage.

"Is Trask a cyborg—like Tilde?" He turned his head, to see if the eight-legged oddity had returned. It hadn't.

Hooglich's face twisted into a scowl. "Didn't you agree not to interrupt? I'm trying to tell you something important."

"This is important."

"You horrified by cyborgs?" When Jeff said nothing, she went on. "I sure hope not, given everything. Anyway, I'll answer your question. Captain Trask is Captain Docie Trask, and if she's not all human she keeps it well hid. As for Tilde, that's a Logan—a smart machine. If Earth wasn't so hung up on keeping intelligent machines off the planet and out of the solar system, you'd have seen Logans long ago. Now can I go on?"

Jeff managed a minute nod, but he was thinking of the first thing she had said. "You horrified by cyborgs?" Was he? Probably. He was frightened by plenty of other things. "I sure hope not, given everything." What did Hooglich mean by that comment? It suggested that although Captain Docie Trask and Tilde the Logan didn't happen to be cyborgs, other beings on this ship, or wherever he was being taken, would be.

"The other thing I want to talk about, Brother Kopal, is *you*." Hooglich chose the perfect word to bring Jeff's attention back. "I said you were in bad shape when Russo brought you down from the observation bubble, but I didn't tell you how bad. I'll tell you now. You were a mess. You had a broken shoulder blade with a piece of chair still stuck into it. You had lost a liter or more of blood. You had four crushed vertebrae, burst veins in both eyes, a fracture and hemorrhage at the back of the skull, two dislocated hips, hematomas all over your arms and legs from blood pooling on the undersides, and five broken ribs. I think that's all."

Jeff heard the catalog of injuries with a mixture of horror and disbelief. Certainly, he didn't feel good. But with all those things wrong, shouldn't he feel far worse?

"Am I on painkillers now?"

"Not according to the monitors. Do you want to be?"

"No." Jeff risked a slight side-to-side movement of his

head. It wasn't his imagination; the pain was less, each time that he moved. That was impossible—unless he had lain unconscious for months and been slowly healing for all that time without knowing it. "How long has it been since the sounder?"

"Nine days."

And five or six days of that had been waiting, before the Messina Cloud ship came onto the scene. He had been receiving proper medical treatment for only half a week. It was all impossible. He ought to feel like death, far worse than he did.

"How long before the cast comes off?"

"Not my department." Hooglich stood up. "Also, you are scheduled for more beauty sleep in just a few minutes."

"I don't want to go to sleep. I want to talk to Captain Dufferin. If he puts in my record that I'm to blame for the loss of the ship, and that gets back to Sol and my family—"

"I'm sorry, Brother Kopal." Hooglich sat down again. "Sorry three different ways. First, Squeaky already put it into the official record. You, me, and Russo are all labeled as bad guys. Second, there's no way we can stop it getting back Solside."

"Yes, there is. Nothing can get back to Sol unless it goes through the node, and you said we're heading in the opposite direction."

"True, and true again. *We* are heading for Confluence Center, the place on the other side of the Cloud where the dust rivers meet. But Squeaky isn't. I said I was sorry three ways, and I mean it. The third way is that two days ago, Squeaky and the rest of the *Aurora* officers made a break for it. When everything was quiet they went back to the ship, blew the pinnace clear, and hightailed it for the node."

"We have to stop them." Jeff tried to raise his head, but he couldn't do it. The monitor by the side of his bed was hissing, and dark waves were moving in to obscure the ceiling. His tongue seemed too large for his mouth as he mumbled, "We can't, we can't let them. . . ."

"Sorry, Brother Kopal." Hooglich was a million miles away, her voice dwindled to an echoing thread of sound. "It's too late. You see, Captain Dufferin is going . . . going to. . . ."

Jeff did not learn what their superior officer was going to do. Because he himself was gone.

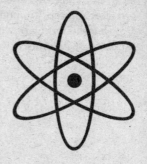

CHAPTER NINE

WHEN Jeff awoke he was sure that this time he had been unconscious for a much longer period. First, he was in a different room, a square-sided blue-walled chamber with a door on one side and an outside port in the wall opposite. Second, he was lying on a normal bed, with no sign of medical equipment. Third, his whole body cast had been removed. He looked down at himself and found that he was dressed in shirt and pants of a soft dove gray, with comfortable loafers on his feet.

Finally, and most important, he did not hurt. Anywhere. He turned his head. Not a twinge. He could sit up easily, swing his feet to the floor, stand up, and head across to the port. Nothing felt sore or damaged or delicate. In fact, he felt better than he had ever been. There was only one source of discomfort—a hunger that started to gnaw inside him as he approached the port.

He was tempted to turn and go at once to find something to eat, but the sight of the sky outside held him. Although he was still in the Messina Dust Cloud, this was a different part of it. Here, the great dust rivers coiled and curled and twisted, in braided strands of gold and pink and deep purple. This was where the streams of ionized dust, moving in response to the Cloud's gravitational and electromagnetic fields, must meet and intermingle.

Not everything visible was a natural feature. To the left and to the right he could see long linear constructs like cylindrical spokes, glowing lilac and magenta in reflected light from the Cloud. The thirty-meter-thick spokes began at the main body of the structure, close to where he stood, and stretched away kilometer after kilometer to infinity.

This could not be a ship. It was too big. It could only be Confluence Center.

And if he were here—memories of his last awakening were returning—then Eliot Dufferin was already Sol-side, reporting on Jeff's failure. It was unlikely to surprise any of his family. Except for his mother and Uncle Lory, no one would really be upset.

As he examined the sky again, seeking some pattern that might tell him the direction of the node, he became aware of another mystery. He had weight, not far from the weight he had on Earth. Confluence Center was big, but not big enough to produce a gravitational field. Unless the Center was rotating fast enough for centrifugal force to give the sensation of weight, he should be floating. Yet his view of the Cloud was static, with no sign that he was turning in relation to it.

He could see no sign of the node that the *Aurora* had used

to reach the Messina Dust Cloud. The change from his last Cloud position made everything unfamiliar. The node could be beyond any one of the glowing patches—or behind him, on the other side of the sky.

That would have to wait. His hunger had passed beyond reasonable to ravenous. He turned to head for the open door and heard an odd scuffling beyond it.

As he walked forward, he heard a hissed "Stop that! I only wanted to *look*. I've never really seen one."

"You can't." More scuffling. Then, "You were told to stay away. Come on. Ouch!"

"It's your own fault. Let go of me!"

Not Hooglich, and not that funny machine, either. What was it called, Tiddler? No, Tilde. He must still be a bit groggy from waking up.

Jeff walked through the open door and emerged into a blue-walled corridor that ran thirty or forty meters before curving away out of sight. Just outside the door a strange tableau met his eyes. A stocky boy of six or seven with bright black eyes and a mop of dark curly hair was trying to pull free. Holding him from behind, one hand on his shoulder and her arm around his neck, was a tall, strongly built girl about Jeff's age. She had short-cut hair the color of fresh straw, and his first impression was of a younger version of his own cousin, Myra. That changed when the struggling pair moved and he had a good view of her face. She was panting with the effort, and fair devil's eyebrows scowled above a pair of startling blue eyes.

The two caught sight of Jeff at the same moment. They stopped tussling and slowly moved apart. They stared at Jeff, the girl sheepish and the boy openly curious.

At last the boy spoke. "Huh," he said. "He doesn't look anything special. He looks *normal*."

"I told you," the girl said. "What did you expect? A freak show?"

"Well, when people say he's a Kopal *and* a cyborg, you'd think—"

"Do you mind?" Jeff stepped closer. They were talking about him as though he wasn't there.

"It's *his* fault." The girl was speaking to Jeff but she gave the boy a punch on the shoulder. "We knew you'd be waking up now, and I was told to come and get you. Before we go inward, I'm supposed to see if you need anything. But nobody asked *him* along."

"Nobody said I couldn't."

"You're a piece of space junk, Billy. I don't know why we didn't leave you there."

"Hey!"

"Shut up." Then, to Jeff, "I'm Lilah Desmon."

"I'm Jeff Kopal."

"I know. And this disgusting bit of space flotsam is Billy Jexter. Do you need anything, Jeff Kopal?"

Jeff had the dizzying feeling of a situation totally beyond his comprehension. But he could answer her question without having to think.

"I need food. *Lots* of food."

"Easily done. Come on."

Lilah led Jeff along the corridor. The boy trailed along behind, muttering, "Cyborgs do eat, then."

"Billy!" the girl said warningly. "Just ignore him, Jeff. He's a total animal."

Jeff wasn't taking much notice. As they walked, he seemed to become lighter and lighter. Also, something very strange was happening inside him. Was it all the side effects of hunger? The pangs had grown and grown until he was unable to think about much else. He didn't care what he was given to eat, he would chew happily on a dead dog. His mouth watered at the prospect. "Can we hurry?"

"Nearly there." She took them along a curved section of the corridor, and into a room leading off it. Half a dozen tables sat in the center, and one wall held half a dozen autochefs.

Lilah waved her hand. "It won't be anything much, unless you are willing to wait a few minutes. I can—"

"No. No wait."

She turned to stare at him. "Well, all right. Sit down."

The next two minutes were the longest in Jeff's life. It became worse when the smell of hot food wafted over from the autochef. Billy Jexter had seated himself opposite and was staring steadily at Jeff, who scowled back. When a bowl of soup and a loaded plate appeared in front of him, he stopped looking at anything. He ate and drank and drank and ate until there was no room inside for another morsel. At that point he stopped, leaned back, and took notice again of his surroundings and the other two people.

Billy Jexter was still staring at him, but with a new expression. "Wow. I've seen Link Musterthwaite eat, and I've seen Fat Winkleman. But I've never seen anybody eat as much and as fast as that."

Jeff recognized a compliment when he heard one, and he realized that the look was admiration. He didn't deserve either. He had never gulped down food like that before, and he didn't think he ever would again. He must have been badly starved— and there was an obvious explanation.

"How long was I unconscious?"

"Let's see now." Lilah began to count on her fingers. Jeff waited. He wouldn't be surprised by any answer, weeks or months or even a year. To heal the injuries he had suffered took a long time.

She finished her figuring and said, "Altogether, from the time you were hurt, it's been ten days."

"That can't be right!"

"Why not?"

"Well, Hooglich told me it was nine days from the sounder encounter when I first woke up. I felt terrible then, and she told me I was in awful shape. Now you are telling me that it's less than forty-eight hours later, and I feel better than I've ever felt."

She sat down opposite and regarded him with her head

to one side. "You don't know, do you? You really have no idea."

"I'm not sure he is one," Billy said. "I think they were kidding. He doesn't look like one."

"One *what*?" Jeff had taken as much gibberish as he could stand.

"A cyborg," Lilah said quietly. "But there's no doubt about it. You are."

A cyborg? Jeff stared down at his hands, as though they might suddenly turn to metal claws. "What are you talking about? I'm not a cyborg."

"You are," she repeated. "If I hadn't known before I saw you eat, I'd know it now."

"You're crazy. This is Cyborg Territory, but I'm not one."

"Sit down." Jeff had started to stand up—amazingly, he was starting to feel hungry again. He ignored her and kept going. "Look," she said as he headed across to the autochef. "I think we're talking past each other. What do you mean when you say 'cyborg'?"

"A combination of human and machine." Jeff wasn't quite sure what that meant. His own mental picture was of a poorly defined image of flesh and metallic parts, combined in some vague yet definitely unpleasant way. "Perhaps a man's body with artificial arms and legs. Artificial eyes, too, maybe."

Billy snorted in disbelief, and Lilah asked, "Why would anybody make a thing like that?"

"I don't know." Jeff spoke through a mouthful of bread. "To fight as a soldier? You ought to be the one to answer that. I'm from Earth, this is Cyborg Territory."

"It is not. Look at Billy, and look at me. Do you think we're part machine?"

He turned and stared at both of them, seeking anything he might have missed on the first inspection. Either of them would not have been out of place on Earth. "No," he said at last. "I don't. But you say I am. I don't see the difference between us."

"There's a *huge* difference." She came to stand by him. "You ate a ton of food a few minutes ago. Now you're eating again."

"So what? I'm hungry."

"I can see that. Don't you know why? The big difference between us is that Billy and I weren't in a major accident ten days ago, and just about killed."

"So?"

"So you needed medical treatment—urgently. Our people didn't wait to ask. We just did it."

"I appreciate whatever you did."

"I hope you will when you *know* what we did. We didn't want you to lie helpless and miserable for weeks and weeks as your body recovered naturally. Our engineer doctors examined your injuries, then added the machines to you."

"Machines?" Jeff took another look at his hands and arms. "I don't see any machines."

"Of course not. They were injected, just a few milliliters of them. Tiny machines, too small to see, the size of a cell or smaller. Smart machines, too, able to recognize and repair bodily damage. And self-replicating machines, that would multiply as needed using your own body's supplies of raw materials. That's why you're starving—you have to keep them supplied and you're swarming with them. Like it or not, Jeff Kopal, at the moment you are a man-machine combination—a cyborg, if you prefer to use the word that Sol-siders seem to like."

"What's going to happen to me?" Jeff had a vision of himself as the machines inside took over, turning him into some kind of clanking mechanical monster. "Am I going to . . . change?"

"Sure." She seemed to be confirming his nightmare, but before he could react she continued, "You're already changing—back to the way you were before you were hurt. If you're feeling well, it means that the nannies—nanomachines—have rebuilt you inside and are close to finishing their job. They made you eat because they needed raw materials, and they'll make you sleep if they want your nervous system closed down for adjustments. They'll stop functioning when they are all done, in another day or two; then the nannies will be naturally excreted from your body."

"I know what *naturally excreted* means," Billy said happily. "It means you'll shit machines. It sounds painful."

"Billy Jexter!"

"Well, it does."

"You don't have to say things like that." Lilah spoke as though her argument with Billy was an old one. She turned to Jeff. "You can see why nobody wants him around."

Jeff had little interest in talking about Billy Jexter's habits. Something else was on his mind. "Is that the only kind of cyborg you have—little machines that you use in medicine?"

"No. There are other kinds of nannies that we use to build things. That stuff's boring, and I don't know much about it. Why does it matter?"

"Back on Earth, the Messina Dust Cloud is called Cyborg Territory."

"That's only 'cause Earth is afraid of machines. You don't have them there, do you? You have slaves instead."

"We have machines, of course we do." But Jeff knew it was a half-truth. Smart machines, like Logan, were prohibited.

"What about human slaves, then? People whose job is just to serve other people. Are you going to tell me you don't have them?"

"Well. . . ." The servants in Kopal Manor didn't *have* to work there, they could leave anytime. But no one did, because the alternative was the Pool. Hooglich had made it clear how unpleasant that option was. People would hang on to their jobs no matter what. Maybe there was slavery on Earth, even if it wasn't called that.

"See," Lilah said. She had correctly read Jeff's hesitation.

"Which would you rather have: intelligent machines to help you, or human slaves?"

The answer was obvious, but a sudden memory prevented Jeff from speaking. He recalled his mother, fighting for breath with her ruined lungs. The nannies could have cured her in days, rebuilding everything damaged in the accident. The difficult operation for lung replacement would have been avoided.

Lilah seemed to have a natural ability to read his emotional state. This time she stood up and quickly said, "Well, never mind that. We'll have time to talk about anything we feel like . . . later. But now we have to get moving. I was sent to bring you to central axis, and she'll be wondering where we've got to."

"Who will?"

"Mo— Connie Cheever." Lilah had an odd smile on her face, and Billy hooted with laughter. At Jeff's blank look, she added, "She's—er, the general administrator of Confluence Center. The nearest thing in the Cloud to an overall boss of operations."

"Why does she want to see me?"

"You'll have to ask her. But it makes sense. I mean, you are a Kopal, you must know what the Sol navy is up to. And as for you"—she turned to Billy Jexter, who had stood up with the other two—"you are specifically *not* included in this invitation. So bug off."

Billy scowled and stuck his tongue out at her. "I don't care if I go with you or not. I bet he doesn't know anything worth hearing."

He ducked under Lilah's swipe and skipped out of the door. Lilah moved after him. "I'll get you, Billy Jexter," she shouted along the corridor.

Jeff, watching the two of them, decided that Billy didn't deserve punishment. He had the situation exactly right. Jeff knew nothing worth hearing, and he wanted to be informed as much as anyone.

What *was* the Sol navy doing? Was Jeff's own presence in the Messina Dust Cloud tied up with that? And was Uncle Giles Lazenby, the smiling and devious master plotter, somehow behind it all?

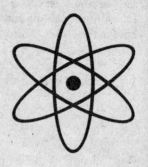

CHAPTER TEN

I'M as much to blame as anybody," Lilah said. "Billy's an orphan, his parents were lost when a rakehell went too near Dodman's Reef. He was only four when it happened. Since then he's been a sort of mascot for Confluence Center. He goes where he likes, does what he likes. We're all used to him popping up anywhere."

"Doesn't he have school?" Jeff was listening, but half his attention was elsewhere.

"Of course he does. That's only for part of the day, as long as the Logans can keep him there. He has plenty of time left for mischief—and he uses it. I bet he knows the interior of Confluence Center better than anyone. He has ways through the tunnels that even the Logans can't tell you. I'm glad I'm not in charge of him."

"Mm." Jeff was counting his footsteps as he walked. He estimated that they had traveled close to a kilometer. "How big is Confluence Center?"

"Do you mean across, or along the axis?"

"Either one. *Is* there an axis? I mean a spin axis."

"There used to be. The Center grows all the time, it's been building for a century. From one side to the other—not counting the external tunnels—it's a couple of kilometers. And the thickness, along the spin axis, is about half a kilometer."

Jeff had been trying to judge his effective weight as they walked, and from that the field in which they moved. It had changed from near Earth gravity at the beginning to a point where they were close to floating along. Now it was slowly increasing again. If Confluence Center were rotating, that would make sense. They had started at the outside, where the centrifugal force caused by the rotation was a maximum. Then they had approached the spin axis for a while as they walked, so the centrifugal force that created the effect of gravity became less; and now they were heading out again toward the perimeter. But Lilah's words seemed to destroy that idea.

"You say there *used to be* a spin axis," he said. "What happened to it, and what's there now?"

She paused and her blond eyebrows lifted. "You're interested in weird stuff, aren't you? Are you a jinner, like the other two?"

"Hooglich and Russo? They say I am, but I don't think so."

"Well, you sure sound like one. Nobody sensible cares about weight and spin and that sort of rubbish. The way I've heard it, Confluence Center was spinning until about ten years ago. Then they stopped it. I remember the way it was before, and it's better like this."

"But if it stopped spinning, everything ought to be close to free fall. Confluence Center is in open space; there's no gravity around here."

"There certainly is." Lilah slid a comb from her pocket, released it, and caught it again as it fell slowly toward the floor. "What do you think that is, if it's not gravity?"

"I mean, there *ought* to be no gravity. There's not enough mass for gravity."

"Complain about it to Administrator Cheever, then."

"It's not an *administrative* issue."

"Then talk to Simon Macafee—if you can find him. I never met him, but they say he likes that sort of stuff."

"Macafee." Jeff halted in his tracks. "I saw that name when I looked up the Anadem field in the query system. Is Simon Macafee the one who invented it?"

"They say that, but I don't really know. I don't care, either. He's supposed to be a real loony, and that's all I can tell you about him. Why are you worried about nonsense like that?"

Jeff gave up. Lilah was pointedly not interested in anything to do with science—even science that affected her and the whole of Confluence Center. He wondered if she was interested in anything.

She was walking along the long spiral of the corridor, and as he caught up with her, she asked, "What did you mean, when you said that you didn't know what the Sol navy was trying to do?"

"I don't know their strategy. I'm an ensign. The navy doesn't tell its plans to junior officers."

"Not even to you? You're a Kopal. Everyone says that Kopals run Sol's navy, even if they don't travel much beyond the Sol system. How did you come to be here?"

How, indeed? Jeff said, "I don't know. I guess I fell off a horse."

If he had intended a conversation stopper, it was a failure. Lilah stopped, grabbed him by the arm, and swung him to face her. Her blue eyes blazed. "You've ridden a *horse?*"

"Ridden one, groomed one, fell off one—lots of times. I was taught to ride before I could read."

"Oh, my God. That's so wonderful."

Jeff's opinion of Lilah Desmon went down two notches. He was thinking, What sort of idiot doesn't care why there is a gravitational field at Confluence Center, but is fascinated because I can ride a horse? He said, "I even own a horse. It's a mare called Domino."

"You're so *lucky.* I've *dreamed* about owning a horse since I was three years old."

"Are there horses out here?" Maybe his idea that they were found only on Earth was wrong.

Lilah shook her head. "Not a single one. I only wish there were." She grabbed his arm and started to tow him back along the corridor. "I have to show you my rooms. I've got pictures of horses all over my walls, and a million questions about them."

"I thought Administrator Cheever was waiting for us." It was better to say that than to tell Lilah Desmon that horse pictures were one of the world's most boring items, up there with horseflies and horse sweat and horse manure, and Aunt Delia Lazenby's unspeakable horsey tea parties.

Lilah stopped pulling at him. "Ooh. She is. I forgot. You have to go to your meeting. Will you come and see my rooms? And talk with me about horses?"

"Sure."

"Promise? Later today?"

"Sure." *Much* later, if Jeff had anything to do with it. He followed Lilah, and in another couple of minutes they were entering a huge hemispherical room with a smooth, hard floor. The curved wall had been made into one giant display that showed the misty glories of the Messina Cloud. Sitting in the middle of the room at a round table, dwarfed to insignificance by the scale of the chamber, were three people: Russo, Hooglich, and a second woman.

Jeff was no close observer of features and appearances, but even he could see the resemblance between Lilah Desmon and the stranger. The woman was an older version of Lilah, with darker, shorter hair and with lines in her forehead and at the corners of her eyes and mouth.

Lilah led him forward, and he halted and came to full attention.

"Took your time, didn't you?" the woman said. She was talking to Lilah.

"Billy Jexter was with us. We had to get rid of him."

"Ah," the woman said, as though a reference to Billy explained everything. She glanced up at Jeff, studying his rigid stance. "Hello. I'm Connie Cheever. How are you feeling?"

"Very well, thank you." Jeff doubted that she wanted to hear how nervous he was.

"Good. If you feel tired or hungry, don't try to fight it. Eat, or drink, or lie down, as soon as the feeling comes over you. Otherwise, the nannies will make you do it. They are good, but they're not too smart. They don't tell you when they're finished. Are you hungry or sleepy now?"

"Not at all."

"Then sit down. You don't have to stand like a statue if you don't want to."

She was amazingly casual, not at all like the highest authority in Confluence Center.

Jeff held his rigid position. "Am I a prisoner of war?"

"What war?" Connie Cheever waved a hand. "Come on, sit down before you burst. There is no war so far as I know, although a few hours ago I received a message from a Sol-side ship. The *Dreadnought* has passed through the node into the Cloud, and it wants to meet with us here."

"I know that ship," Hooglich said. "Destroyer class, not much firepower in spite of its name. Strange. The *Dreadnought* is a Central Command vessel, not Border Command. I wonder what *that* means."

Jeff's leg muscles were tightening. He decided he might as well give up standing to attention. As he sat down he asked, "Did the message from the ship mention me?"

"I'm afraid it did." Connie Cheever glanced around the table. "All of you, you and Hooglich and Russo. You are all officially described as deserters from the Space Navy."

"That's absolute nonsense." Russo's beak of a nose glowed pink with fury. "If I could get my hands on Captain Eliot Bloody Dufferin, old Squeaky would—"

"Be patient, and maybe you will. He might be on board the *Dreadnought*. I gave them directions for Confluence Center, and they'll be here in about a week." Connie Cheever turned to Lilah, who had shown no signs of leaving. "You're not part of this meeting, but if you want to stay, you can. On one condition. When you speak the first word, you leave."

From what Jeff had seen of Lilah, that wouldn't take very long. But she said, "I promise, Mother. Not a word."

That disposed of one question. He had wondered why someone her age would be sent to bring him to a meeting with the administrator. She sat down at the table by his side, while her mother went on, "The three of us have already talked about the *Aurora* and what the Sol navy thought it could possibly achieve here. I'd like to hear your impressions, Jeff Kopal. Before you were told by Captain Dufferin, had you ever heard anything about the Cloud seceding from Sol?"

Jeff had to think. He felt as though he had known about that for a long time—but how long? Finally, he had the answer.

"It was before I left Earth—before I even joined the Space Navy. A month and more ago. I asked the query link at Kopal Manor about the places where Border Command operated, and it came back to say that Node 23—the node that serves the Messina Dust Cloud—was one of the trouble spots. It said the node threatened to secede from Sol control."

"Interesting." Connie Cheever glanced at Hooglich and Russo. "But untrue, of course."

"I told you," Russo said. "There's something else going on here—something that has nothing to do with any secession. Only I don't know what."

"That's why we're talking. And now we've disposed of one possibility." Connie Cheever turned to Jeff. "I'm not trying to be mysterious. The Cloud has never threatened to secede from Sol, even though we have our own government and no need for support from them. We've been economically self-sufficient for fifty years, and there's nothing new on that front. We did tell the Sol-side authorities that we won't pay node use charges anymore, because we maintain this node and we make less use of it than they do. But we told them that *recently*, in just the past couple of weeks. Your query link gave you information earlier. So unless somebody on Earth can see the future, this doesn't explain the talk about us seceding."

Lilah had been following everything closely. "It's as though someone *wants* to start a war and is looking for a reason," she said.

Jeff glanced over at Connie Cheever and waited for a reaction. The administrator merely nodded. "That's a very intriguing and useful suggestion. We'll have to consider it, because Sol is certainly acting that way. Thank you, dear." And, as Lilah began to smile in satisfaction, "But now, of course, you have to leave."

"Muv! You can't do that. I was *helping*."

"You were indeed. But rules are rules. Not a word, I said at the start; and you agreed. So off you go."

Lilah frowned, but at last she stood up from the table, glowered around, and walked head-down to the door of the chamber. Connie Cheever waited patiently until she was almost outside, then called after her, "Thanks again, dear. See you at dinnertime."

Jeff revised his ideas about the atmosphere in Confluence Center. Easygoing it might be, but *rules are rules*. He would not speak until he was asked to.

"The question is," Connie said thoughtfully, "What is there here that's *worth* starting a war over?"

"The stable transuranics?" Hooglich suggested. "Or the Cauthen starfires?"

Connie shook her head. "You need the Logans and the nannies to collect transuranics on a commercial basis. Sol government won't use either, so it's cheaper for them to buy from us. As for starfires, they lead to so much trouble from the space sounders, no one in her right mind tries to collect them any-more. It's a mystery why Sol might want to stir up war. We have a hundred thousand people here in the whole Cloud, they have ten billion on Earth alone. They could ship every one of us there and not even notice a difference. We do have ten million smart machines. But they don't want any part of those."

"I tell you." Russo stood up and stamped his boot on the floor. "It's right underneath here. This is what they want."

"The Anadem field?" Hooglich asked.

Russo nodded vigorously. "Isn't this something the Cloud has refused to sell—refused to admit you have, almost?"

"We have refused to sell," Connie said. "But that wasn't my decision to make. It's Simon Macafee's invention, and he has made his position clear. He'll give it for use free in the Cloud, but he won't let it be sold or given to Sol. I can't see how they'd use it if they had it. Are there free-space colonies in the Sol system?"

"Some. Mining mostly." Hooglich scratched at her head. Her hair, to Jeff's eyes, had not been combed since the last time he saw her. "No, it's the Space Navy that would be most interested in the Anadem field. If you had a neutralizing field for acceleration, you could make fast transits at ten G or more, and your crew would never feel it. Russo's right, that might be a reason to start a war—so you could come here and grab the Anadem field, and no one able to stop you. Once Earth had the secret, what could the Cloud do about it? There's an old saying:"—she switched to her Pool accent—" 'Big sticks, good arguers.' But there's still a problem. The people on Earth don't start wars easily. You'd have to give them a reason—a better reason than a new invention, or the loss of a small ship like the *Aurora*."

The others were nodding. Obviously, they knew something that Jeff didn't. In the past few days, the Anadem field had apparently gone from navy rumor to hard reality. But he knew something that maybe would be news to them. The Space Navy didn't build its own ships, not one of them. They were constructed under contract. And by far the biggest and most

successful contractor, ever since the time of Great-grandfather
Rollo Kopal, was Kopal Transportation.

Jeff opened his mouth and found himself reluctant to
speak. It had been drilled into him since he was a toddler: He
was a Kopal, and he wasn't supposed to tell outsiders anything
about the company operations or business.

"Maybe we can talk to Macafee," said Hooglich at last.
"See if he'll change his mind."

"Maybe we can," Connie agreed. "And maybe we can't.
The first job will be to find him."

"Isn't he here, at Confluence Center?"

"I don't know. I can't even guarantee that he's alive. We
never track people who don't want to be tracked, and he's been
a solitary for years and years, a kind of wandering hermit. No
one knows where he came from, nobody knows where he goes.
One time he vanished for a couple of years, and all he said when
he came back was that he had been out among the reefs, studying them and everything to do with them. He's shy with people,
but every now and then he pops up with some new gadget and
gives it to us. We got the Anadem field that way. If he wanted
to, he could have made a fortune. But he doesn't care. He wants
privacy, and we give him that in return for what he gives us."

"Privacy," Russo said. "Isn't this more important than privacy? Suppose the main CenCom fleet comes through the
node. It has enough weapons to turn the whole of Confluence
Center to plasma."

"If the main fleet comes through, I'll certainly worry about
that. Maybe we'll just surrender and get it over with. Meanwhile, I need to think." Connie Cheever pulled a black oblong
toward her from the middle of the table, pressed the side, and
spoke into it. "Lilah, I said I'd see you at dinner, but are you free
now? If you are, I'd like you to take Ensign Kopal, feed him if
he needs it, and show him around the Center while the Logans
make accommodations. If you're not here in five minutes, I'll
get someone else to do it."

Lilah appeared suspiciously fast, only a few seconds after

Connie Cheever's call. Jeff decided that she must have been lurking outside the door. Maybe she was trying to listen, and maybe she had succeeded. Security seemed far less tight than at Kopal Manor, where closed doors were the rule for all important conversations.

In any case, Lilah's arrival was too rapid for Jeff. He wanted time with Hooglich and Russo. While Lilah was still at the door he turned to Hooglich as she was levering her bulk out of her seat. "The Anadem field," he said rapidly. "People keep talking about it, but I don't know how it works."

"Join the club. Me and Russo talked earlier. We know what it does, but we don't understand how it works, either."

"But what is it?"

"I can tell you that." Hooglich sat down again. Connie Cheever and Russo had left, but Lilah was waiting impatiently at Jeff's side. He ignored her and a strange moment of dizziness, and kept his attention on the big woman.

"Take two solid rings of matter," Hooglich said. "Make them the same size, and place them one above the other with the same center, like this." She drew what she had described.

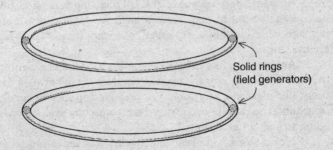

Solid rings
(field generators)

"Got it?"

"Sure." Jeff struggled to concentrate. "What are they made of?"

"The Anadem field here works with solid carbon rings,

because there's plenty of that in the Cloud; but apparently you can use pretty much anything.

"The region between the rings can contain any kind of material, but let's suppose that it's vacuum. In practice it makes no difference what it is, because the Anadem field doesn't care. Here's what a cross section of the rings looks like, if you make the cut through their centers." She drew another simple picture underneath the first.

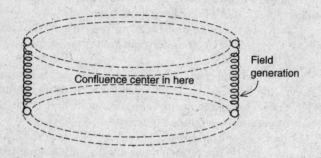

"All right?"

"All right." Jeff was aware of Lilah fidgeting at his side, but he couldn't attend to that. He was having trouble concentrating, and what Hooglich was saying was important. "How big are the rings?"

"Any size you like to make them. For Confluence Center, they are big enough for the main structure to sit in between the rings, like meat in a sandwich. For a Cloudship they normally fit around the middle part, where crew quarters are. Are you going to keep interrupting?"

"Not a word." He realized that he was repeating what Lilah had said to her mother, and she was scowling at him.

"The Anadem field is produced by a resonance *between the rings.*" Hooglich added a set of spiral lines to her drawing. "It's a vector field, and it produces a body force. That means a force like gravity or acceleration, one that acts on every piece of material. But it's not gravity. The force is strong right between the rings, and falls away fast as you get farther from them—much faster than the gravity inverse square law. It looks like this, where the arrows show the direction of the force and their length shows the force strength." She took another sheet, repeated the cross-sectional drawing of the rings, and added to them a lot of arrows. They were long and straight in the cylindrical region directly between the rings, and shorter in the middle. Outside the ring region they rapidly dwindled away to nothing.

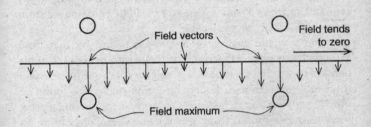

"With the Anadem field switched on at Confluence Center, in the region between the rings you have a force pulling you to the floor, the way we do now. It feels like gravity, but as I said, it isn't."

"So one ring is down below us, and the other one is up above our heads?"

"That's right."

"Why did Russo stamp his foot on the floor?"

"What do you expect him to do, stamp his foot on the ceiling?" Hooglich waved her arm. "Go on, out of here. You're at the silly stage."

Jeff stood his ground. She was right. He was approaching

the limits of patience for Mercy Hooglich, and some other limit for himself. But there was a mystery to be explained. "Just one more question."

Hooglich wrinkled her nose. "I don't know about that."

He took it as agreement and said, "You and Russo seem to think that the Anadem field would be a great thing for the Space Navy, because a ship could make trips at higher accelerations. I don't see how. Wouldn't the field just make you feel *heavier?*"

"I said you'd reached the silly stage, and that proves it." She took the last sheet she had drawn on and handed it to Jeff. "Go figure for yourself. I'm out of here."

She left him staring at the page with Lilah tugging at his arm and saying, "Thank Heaven, I thought you'd never stop. I've been waiting for you *forever.*"

Jeff saw the answer in five seconds, but by that time Hooglich was gone. He stuffed the page into the pocket of his pants. He wanted to follow her and explain that he wasn't a total fool, even though his last question made him look like one. He couldn't do it, because suddenly he was feeling a great weakness. He wanted to lie down somewhere, anywhere, on the floor, on the table if he had to. It wasn't hunger, it was something else.

Lilah didn't seem to notice. She took his arm, and he had no strength to resist. "This way," she said, as she pulled him along. And then, "Well, what do *you* want?"

Jeff found that his eyes had somehow closed. He opened them and saw that she was not talking to him. Billy Jexter had popped up from nowhere.

"You said I couldn't come to your meeting," Billy said, "but it's over now."

"How do you know?"

"I was listening. I heard everything."

"You little sneak." Lilah didn't ask how. Jeff wondered if people in the Cloud knew what a private conversation was. His eyes closed again, beyond his control.

"This is another meeting that doesn't need you," Lilah was saying. "We're going to my rooms. So you can just go away again."

"What's wrong with him?" Billy said.

Jeff tried to open his eyes. He couldn't do it. He heard somebody saying in an excited voice, "He's falling over," and "Look out!" and "Catch him!" He wondered who they were talking about.

And then it didn't matter anymore.

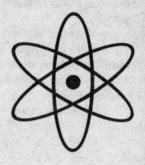

CHAPTER ELEVEN

THE nanomachines were efficient, but they were not intelligent as a human is intelligent. Their function—their only function—was to preserve the life of the body into which they had been injected, and they did that single-mindedly. If they must modify a human radically in order to succeed, they would do it.

Jeff had been a difficult case. Without massive changes, he would die. The nannies did not hesitate. Lungs and heart were replaced by powerful pumps of resilient plastic. Eyes were eaten away by strong acid solvents, and crystalline sensors, more sensitive and adaptable than human retinas and lenses, grown in their place. The entire digestive system was disposed of, and a small nuclear power pack installed in the belly as energy source. Taloned metal claws, a superior alternative to human hands, formed the end of the tough inorganic sinews and cables of modified arms. Finally, a glittering and metallic exoskeleton replaced tender skin. Now the host could survive anywhere, even in a hard vacuum. His new home would be outside, naked under the silent stars.

Jeff became conscious slowly, knowing what had been done to him. He lifted his arm and opened his eyes, expecting to see a taloned paw outlined against the glow of the Messina Dust Cloud.

What he saw was his own familiar right hand, trembling with tension. He was wearing a long-sleeved shirt of pale brown that ended at the wrist. A perfectly normal wrist. Above him, no more than two feet away, the blind face of a display screen peered down. He gasped, dropped his arm to his side, and closed his eyes again. The nightmare was just that, the product of his own imagination. The fear of Cyborg Territory had been planted deep.

He lay for a few minutes, eyes closed. It seemed to have become a way of life: the slide into unconsciousness in one place, the awakening somewhere completely different with no certainty of his own condition.

He felt fine; rested and not sick or hungry or thirsty. He no longer trusted those feelings. Maybe he was not a cyborg in external shape, but he lacked the final say in control of his own body. The micromachines decided what he would do, when he would eat, whether he would sleep or wake.

He heard the creak of a chair to his left. He opened his eyes and looked that way. He thought he might see Tilde, or Hooglich, or maybe even Lilah or Connie Cheever. Instead he was staring into the bright eyes of Billy Jexter, only a foot away. The dark head nodded. "Hi. I've been watching you. Hooglich said to call her the second you looked like you were going to wake up. So I did."

"What happened to me?"

"Dunno. But Galen says you ignored the warning signals. You tried to override the nannies. That *never* works, and you passed out."

"I don't know Galen. Do I?" Jeff at the moment was not sure of much.

"Dunno. Galen's a Logandoc. Galen delivered me when I was born, Lilah says. But I don't remember that."

Mention of Hooglich had Jeff feeling for his pocket. Neither the page she had drawn on nor the pocket itself was there. Someone had changed his clothes. He started to sit up, then had second thoughts. He didn't want to collapse again. "Is it all right for me to get up?"

"Dunno. But Galen says the nannies are done with you. You won't fall over, if that's what you're worried about."

Jeff eased himself off the bed. "How long was I unconscious?"

For a change, Billy had an answer. "Since last night. It's morning now. Want to know a secret?"

"Where are my old clothes?"

"Dunno. Maybe Lilah took 'em. She's been in and out of here ten times while I've been watching you. She wants to talk to you." Billy came closer. "I have a secret. I know something you don't know."

The look on Billy's face said that he was bursting to tell, if someone would just ask. Jeff deliberately didn't. He wasn't interested in the secrets of a six-year-old. He had his own problems. He was a failure—again—and this time he had been labeled a deserter. He couldn't even send a message to his mother, explaining what had happened and defending his name.

Again he thought of her burn-scarred face and months-long struggle to breathe, and of the awesome power of the nannies. Nanomachines could have cured her in days. Did the people of the Messina Dust Cloud have it right, and Earth's government have it all wrong?

Yes, in his opinion, but it was a dangerous thought. Was it even the thought of a traitor?

"Am I a prisoner here?"

"Huh?"

Billy obviously wasn't the person to ask. The idea of prisons and prisoners didn't seem to have reached the Messina Dust Cloud.

Jeff moved away from the bed and prowled around the room. It was sizeable, maybe four meters square, windowless and simply furnished with bed, desk, terminal, easy chair, and a small autochef. He saw a small heap of things sitting on the desk. It was the contents of his pockets: a locket with a picture of his parents, a couple of pens, an old compass which had no possible value in space, a small brass weight shaped like a sea horse, his personal computer, and the sheet of paper, several times folded, that Hooglich had given him. They were the only signs of anything personal in the room. The walls were a plain buff in color, leading to a sterile overall effect, as though no one had ever lived here. The empty cabinets and cases along one wall seemed to confirm that.

There were two doors, in opposite walls. The first could be locked from the inside. The second led to a small bathroom. Jeff peered in and felt a sudden and overwhelming urge to use what he saw.

Billy was sitting cross-legged on the bed when Jeff came out. He had a self-satisfied expression on his face. "Said you would, didn't I? Did it hurt?"

Jeff took his cue from Lilah. "No. But what I'm going to do to you will."

Billy was off the bed and at the outer door before Jeff could add, "Whose room is this, anyway?"

"Why, it's nobody's." Billy understood from the question that the threat had been withdrawn, and he stepped back to the middle of the room. "What I mean is, it's yours. The Logans put it together for you. They'll put your stuff in later and decorate it any way you want. Don't you like it?"

"It's perfectly fine." Jeff had no "stuff," more than what he stood up in or what sat on the desk. The rest of the things he had brought with him to space had been left on the *Aurora*. But he had another idea to struggle with. From the sound of it, the interior of Confluence Center changed all the time. Connie Cheever had mentioned that the loner Simon Macafee could be holed up in a place specially made for him by the Logans. It wouldn't be difficult to fabricate new living areas anytime you wanted to, when a hundred smart machines served every human. And there was plenty of interior space. How much?

He could have gone over to his computer, but it wasn't worth it. Jeff stood and did the calculation in his head. If the main body of the Center was a cylindrical disk two kilometers across and half a kilometer thick, then, even without the external corridors, that provided a volume of a billion and a half cubic meters. Be generous and allow a space of a thousand cubic meters for each apartment and its support facilities. You had enough room for a million and half people. Connie Cheever had said there were only a hundred thousand in the whole Messina Cloud. Confluence Center was nowhere near capacity.

"Billy, I think you lied." It was the deep voice of Hooglich, interrupting his thoughts. "You told me he was awake. Looks like he's dreaming to me."

Jeff turned to her. "I was just calculating something."

"Ah. That's all right then. Calculations are sacred." She was as big and bulky as ever, but she had changed into a uniform of pale blue that fitted better than anything she had worn on the *Aurora*. Her clothes were also a lot cleaner. "How are you feeling, Brother Kopal?"

"Better. I asked a really stupid question last night." Jeff had to get this out of the way, before any other subject came up. He went across to the desk, unfolded the piece of paper, and marked a set of lines on it with one of the pens.

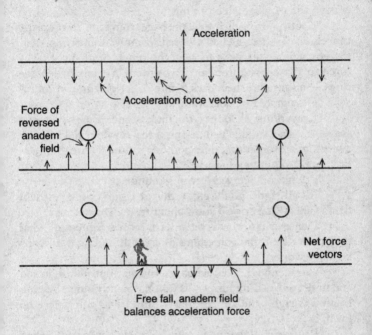

Acceleration

Acceleration force vectors

Force of reversed anadem field

Net force vectors

Free fall, anadem field balances acceleration force

"You were three parts zombie," Hooglich said. "I knew you'd figure it out, either before you passed out or right after you woke up."

He held the page toward her. "I realized as soon as you left. Acceleration is a body force, the same as the Anadem field. So if you want to accelerate hard *this* way"—he moved his finger upward to follow the lines he had drawn on the sheet—"and not feel it, you set up an Anadem field that works the opposite way round from the one here on Confluence Center. The field produces a force on anything within the double rings in the same direction as the acceleration. If you make the field strength right, the forces from the Anadem field and the acceleration will cancel each other out."

"Locally." Hooglich took the page from him. "If it exactly cancels *here*"—she touched it—"halfway toward the rings' center, you would still feel a force at the center. And you'd feel a force in the other direction if you were right between the rings." She gave the sheet back to him. "All right. You've got it."

"Of course. It's really simple."

"Everything is, once you understand. But when you *don't*. . . . And we don't understand the Anadem field. Don't confuse *what* something does and *how* it does it. Are you feeling up for something harder?"

"I think so." Jeff was learning caution.

"It's all right. You'll enjoy this, it involves the Anadem field again. What do you know about *reverse engineering*?"

"I've seen the words, but I have only a vague idea what they mean. Isn't that something to do with finding out how a machine works?"

"Close enough." Hooglich led the way out. Jeff followed and noticed that Billy Jexter was trailing silently along behind. Lilah was right; the kid seemed to wander as and where he liked.

"Reverse engineering is used," Hooglich went on, "when you want to duplicate some gadget a company makes, and the company won't tell you. Sometimes the device is sealed, so you can't dismantle it without destroying it." She was taking them on a path where their weight rose and fell, but overall there was a steady increase. It meant they were winding their way toward the outer perimeter of Confluence Center, where the Anadem field was strongest. She seemed to know exactly where she was going. Jeff noticed that Billy had vanished. The conversation was beyond him, and he must have grown bored.

"So what you do," Hooglich said, "is you buy a few of their machines. You put them through their paces, with every input you can think of, and you measure the performance and output for every set of circumstances. Maybe you try to probe the interior with ultrasonics, or X rays, or neutrinos—though that's always dangerous; the probes might destroy the machine. When you've learned all you can, you build a machine of your own. Ideally, it will be the same inside as the ones you bought. If it's not, but it's good enough so it mimics their performance exactly, no one will ever know the difference."

They had emerged through a little door into a great narrow corridor, ten meters wide and scores high. It ran smoothly away on either side until its own curve hid it from view. Waiting for them, lounging easily against the far wall with a smug look on his face, was Billy Jexter.

"Slideway shortcut," he said. "I guessed where you'd be going, when you talked about the Anadem field. I could have told you a good way."

"But you didn't," Hooglich said. "Why not? You're a pain in the butt, Billy."

"Well, you never asked." He glanced from side to side, and his voice dropped. "I know a secret."

"I know a hundred." Hooglich turned to Jeff. "You'll never find a better use for reverse engineering than this one. No one knows where Macafee is, but we have the Anadem field right here, to play with any way we like."

"Did Connie Cheever say it was all right?"

"More than that. She suggested it. The Cloud jinners are all working on it, too."

"Why? Why not wait until Simon Macafee shows up, and just ask him?"

"A call went out, but there may not be time to wait until he chooses to show up." They were ascending a spiral staircase made of an open lattice of metal. "What Russo warned, of a whole CenCom fleet coming through the node, actually seems to be happening. A coded message came in from one of the harvesters close to Node 23. At least forty fleet ships are already through from Sol. There may be more on the way. The administrator is asking if we can increase the Anadem field strength, add drives to Confluence Center, and be ready to boost away from danger if we are attacked."

"That doesn't sound like reverse engineering."

"It's on the way to it. You might say we don't really have to know how the field works, just how to change its settings. But we don't know what else might happen when we make the field stronger. The more we understand of the basics, the better. That's what we'll be working on."

They had climbed the spiral staircase all the way to the top, where a small boxlike room with one door and no windows perched just under the metal ceiling. Hooglich was almost too big to get inside. She somehow squeezed through. Billy had wandered away again. His attention span seemed to be short. Jeff ducked his head and followed Hooglich.

He had been expecting some kind of control center for the Anadem field. What he found was a room bare of equipment. Russo was sitting like some strange idol, cross-legged and with folded arms, against the far wall. Hooglich went across, grunted at the effort, and lowered herself next to him. She gestured to Jeff to sit down.

He remained standing. "I thought you were going to work on modifying the Anadem field."

"We are. You are. We'll join the Cloud jinners in just a few minutes. But first. . . ." She turned. "Russo, how does it look?"

He raised his head and tilted it back, as though the great nose was sniffing the air. He nodded. "They don't have the slightest idea of security. But so far as I can tell, this is a place that can't be overlooked or overheard from anywhere."

"Not even by Billy Jexter?"

"I won't guarantee against that little imp. But I hope we're snug."

"We'll have to risk it and talk." Hooglich turned to Jeff. "You must be wondering what this is about. Me and Russo, we think we're all in bad trouble."

"We are." Russo sniffed. "My smeller tells me. It's never wrong."

"You mean, because of the report that Captain Dufferin made?"

"That, and a lot more than that. Russo's been thinking, and he believes he's finally figured it out." Hooglich turned. "Go on, Rustbucket. This is your show."

"I'd like to be wrong. But"—Russo tapped the side of his nose—"I don't think so. Remember when we were back on the *Aurora*, and nothing seemed to make sense? We had a teeny little ship with just about no weapons, run by a captain known through the whole fleet as all mouth and trousers. And we were sent to tell everyone in the Messina Dust Cloud to surrender to us—or else. That was the first piece of strangeness. But there was another one, and it seemed to have nothing to do with the first. That was *you.*" Russo pointed a gnarled finger at Jeff. "A Kopal, the first ever to be sent to BorCom. What were you doing shipping with us?"

"I told you. Back on Earth, I made a real mess—"

"Yeah, yeah. I heard all that. We know Giles Lazenby was involved, too. But if you follow fleet talk, when it comes to Brother Giles the simple explanation is *never* the right one. And as the Hoog said to you and to me, if Giles wanted to make his own kid look good, he'd have put you, Jeff—no offense—next to Myron, where people could compare and contrast the two of you.

"Then there was what we were told on the *Aurora* about secession, which Connie Cheever says is nonsense. The Cloud never thought for a minute of seceding from Sol. That's where I was stuck, until your little sweetheart, Lilah—"

"She's not my sweetheart! She's—she's—" Jeff groped for words strong enough. "She's a *horse fanatic.*"

"Is that right? I never saw a horse, not live at least. Ate it a few times, back in the Pool. Not bad, when you've been living on cornmeal." Russo blinked. "Where was I? That Lilah,

she came up with a good one. The business with the *Aurora*
looked as though somebody wanted to start a war and needed
a reason, she said. Now, the Anadem field, there was a real good
reason—'specially if you happen to be Kopal Transportation."

"I didn't—"

Russo waved his hand. "It's all right, Jeff, I'm not accusing
you. You'll see why in a minute. Let's go on. Now I'm moving
from fact to theory. Somebody might *want* to start a war with the
Cloud territory, but they couldn't just up and make it happen.
Not even if a piddling little nothing of a ship like the *Aurora* was
captured or lost. Actually, I think we were sent through the
node, under Squeaky's command, *intended* to be captured or de-
feated. The sounder just made things happen a lot faster. But for
starting a war, you need something special. Can you think of
anything that *would* make everybody back in the fleet, and all
over Earth, willing to send the fleet through the node network
and teach the Cloud a lesson—and, along the way, and just by
accident, get our hands on the Anadem field? Well, suppose that
those terrible cyborg monsters in the Messina Dust Cloud captured a *Kopal*—an innocent young recruit, ensign in the Space
Navy, and a member of the proudest and most famous family in
Earth's military and commercial history." Russo pointed at Jeff.
"You. Now there's a real reason to go to war. Either to get you
back, or to revenge your death." He folded his arms. "That's
what I think. And I ask, do you see anything wrong with it?"

The whole idea made Jeff's head spin, but he could still
think. "There is something wrong with it. Your idea could only
work as long as we're out here. The moment we got back and
told people in the fleet and on Earth the full story—"

Jeff paused, and Russo nodded.

"You just got it," Hooglich said softly. "I told you he
would, Russo. For the scheme to work, we wouldn't be going
back to tell our stories. Not now, not ever. There's only one way
to make sure of that. In the next stage of the operation, three
people have to die: Russo, and me, and—most important of
all—Jeff Kopal."

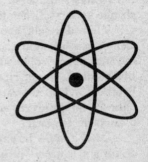

CHAPTER TWELVE

JINNERS seemed to be jinners, anywhere in the universe. They were not strong on ceremony. Jeff was introduced to a bunch of Cloud engineers by name, and ten seconds later he was one of the group, to be noticed only if he spoke. Hooglich and Russo asked for working details on the Anadem field generators. Different features were pointed out, and the technical arguments began at once.

Jeff didn't mind that he was excluded. He had plenty to see, and lots to think about.

He was standing with the others on the catwalk that circled the perimeter of Confluence Center. Two hundred and fifty meters above him hung the stupendous upper ring of the field generator. The lower ring lay an equal distance below. Both rings shimmered with a peculiar clear glow, like the change in the sky when Jeff first saw the space sounder.

He had weight, about the same as on Earth. Confluence Center possessed too small a mass to produce noticeable gravity, and the environment should have been close to free fall. But he didn't forget Hooglich's warning: "Watch your step, Brother. Fall off the catwalk, and you'll head straight down until you hit the lower field-generating ring. It's not gravity, but it can be just as fatal."

After a while the jinners all ascended in an open-sided elevator and squeezed into a control room perched fifty meters below the upper ring. Anyone who had ideas on field modification gave them—loudly. There was agreement on how to adjust the field setting, but no agreement on how big a change could safely be made, or what might happen afterwards.

Jeff listened for a while, but it mostly seemed to be confessions of ignorance. He wandered back outside, took the elevator down, and started to pace along the spidery strand of the narrow catwalk. After an hour of watching and thinking, he had formed an opinion of his own. He was reluctant to offer it, because all the other people had more experience; but if Simon Macafee were anything like the genius he was supposed to be, surely he wouldn't have built a potential for disaster into the Anadem field generators. They ought to be a fail-safe design. Also, Jeff had learned something from his own efforts back on Earth: Size shouldn't be confused with complexity. He could take an aircar apart and put it back together with no trouble. The same attempt with his expensive wristwatch had been a fiasco. He had thrown away the random mess of bits and pieces he was left with, and told everyone he had lost the watch.

The gigantic scale of the rings above and below did not mean that the Anadem field itself had to be complicated. It might have a simple governing equation, as simple as the Newtonian law of gravity. But without some basic understanding of *principles*, any effort at reverse engineering was doomed to fail.

Hooglich and the other jinners would probably never agree with that. Maybe Jeff wasn't a jinner after all. He loved to take things apart, but more than knowing *how* they worked, he had to understand *why* they worked. The reason he could rebuild the old aircar was because the physical principles that allowed it to rise and move through the air were clear in his head.

He kept walking. He was lost in his own thoughts, and the control room was far behind. He wasn't worried. The rings extended around the whole circumference of Confluence Center; eventually he must return to his starting point.

He had begun at a point on the perimeter that faced out into a dark region of space. Now he was far enough along the great exterior circle of Confluence Center to glimpse the misty light of the Messina Dust Cloud through the ports. He paused. Somewhere out there, picking a path through those braided rivers of dust and glowing gas, a ship from Central Command was on its way. Behind it, waiting near the node, sat scores or hundreds of other navy vessels.

Did he believe Hooglich and Russo, that the three of them were marked for death? From what he had seen, the other two didn't much want to return to Sol and the Space Navy. They were perfectly at home among the Cloud jinners, where there was no threat of a return to the Pool.

He was in a different position. He *had* to go back. He was the only thing that stood between Kopal Transportation and a company takeover by his uncles and aunts.

He thought of Uncle Giles. How far would his uncle go, to advance his own interests and those of his children? Certainly, he would arrange for Jeff to be sent to a far-off assignment in Border Command, while Myron and Myra served in prestigious Central Command. But would he plan murder? Did the long arm of his influence extend all the way here, to the Messina Dust Cloud?

Jeff wanted to say no, definitely not, of course not. But he couldn't do that: Something in Uncle Giles's perpetual smile said that anything was possible. Jeff felt a shiver up his spine. When the *Dreadnought* arrived, he would be very careful.

He started walking again. After a while he felt his weight increase, pressing his feet harder on the catwalk. Soon it returned to what felt like the old value. The jinners were having fun, tentatively exercising the controls to vary the strength of the Anadem field. It would take a high acceleration to fly Confluence Center away from fleet attack. Jeff had heard that some of the Space Navy ships were capable of short acceleration bursts of ten Gs or more, without ruining their drives.

Jeff picked up his pace. He couldn't imagine that the jinners would intentionally boost the Anadem field to multiple G values, but accidents happened. The lattice of the open catwalk was probably stronger than it looked, but he felt alone and very exposed.

He stared ahead, wondering if he was past the halfway point. If not, he ought to turn around. He saw a distant black dot on the catwalk. Exposed, yes; alone, no. Someone was coming the other way.

It might be Hooglich or Russo, telling him to get back to work. But the colors were wrong. Instead of Hooglich's dark mop or the red of Russo's hair, he saw a gleam of blond hair topping an outfit of startling white.

Lilah. He had promised last night that he would go and see her horse-infested rooms, but he had passed out before she could drag him away. If she had gone to the trouble to track him down on the outer rim of Confluence Center, she was a worse nutcase than he'd realized. He had known horse fanatics—all girls—back on Earth, and apparently twenty-seven light years wasn't enough to get away from them.

He waited until she was close, then said brightly, "Hi. Were you looking for me?"

"You? No." She looked splendid in an all-white jumpsuit, but her tone was icy. "I didn't even know you were out here. Why are you?"

"I'm helping the jinners to adjust the Anadem field."

It was true enough in general, even if it was a bit of an overstatement of his own role. If he had expected approval, he didn't get it. Lilah gave him another black look. "*You're* the ones messing about with the gravity, are you? I wish you'd quit it. I came out here to find Billy Jexter, and you're not making it any easier. Have you seen him?"

"He was with us a couple of hours ago. When I started talking to Hooglich and Russo, he wandered off. I thought you tried to avoid him."

"I do. But he has been going round all morning making a big deal out of some secret he says he's found in Confluence Center. When he saw me I was grounded, for—well, never mind for what—so he knew he couldn't show me whatever it was. But I promised Billy that he could show me later. He said he'd be out on Level Twenty-nine, Ninth Sector, Fifth Octant. So when I got free, I came to look for him. You see, I keep *my* promises."

If that was Lilah's idea of a subtle hint, Jeff was not impressed. He stifled his natural reaction, and said, "If you like I can show you where he was, last time I saw him."

"That would be a start."

"We need to go to the Anadem field control room. Which way is quicker, to keep going as I was, or turn around and head the way you were going?"

"I haven't the slightest idea." She was staring away from Jeff, toward the rim ports. "I don't know anything about the Anadem field."

Know, or care, said her tone. Jeff was still in Lilah's doghouse. He wanted to shoot back, "And I don't care anything about the stupid horse pictures you have plastered all over your walls." But he could not afford to get into a fight with her. The only other people he really knew at Confluence Center were Hooglich and Russo, and they were almost as much strangers as he was. He needed information about the ship coming from Sol, especially anything relevant to him. Billy Jexter couldn't be a source for that kind of information; but Lilah was Connie

Cheever's daughter, and she could probably find out anything—if she was willing to try.

Instead of arguing, Jeff turned and started back the way he had come. He felt a bit sneaky, as though he had already taken advantage of Lilah's family connection. He eased his conscience by saying over his shoulder, "After you are done with Billy, why don't we go to your room."

That ought to have produced a favorable response. It led instead to a long silence, and then, at last, an uncomfortable and uncertain reply. "All right. I guess we can do that if you want to."

Jeff kept walking. He had been thinking, half an hour ago, that he was perhaps not a real jinner. He was too interested in the abstract principles that lay behind the machinery. But whether he turned out a jinner or whether he didn't, one thing was sure: You knew where you were with jinners. You didn't find yourself listening to what they said, then spend the next ten minutes wondering what they *meant*.

The gravity made another sudden up-and-down dip as they circled the Center perimeter, giving Jeff's stomach an uneasy lurch. He stopped and grabbed at the catwalk rail. The jinners were still playing games with the Anadem field. Lilah, forced to walk behind him on the narrow catwalk, had the grace not to complain, though he did hear a snort of annoyance.

The elevator leading up to the control room finally became visible from the curve of the catwalk. Jeff could see a few of the jinners, lounging around the control-room door. They were obviously still in session. He pointed to the place where he had left the interior with Hooglich and Russo. "Billy was through there when I last saw him, in a chamber full of cloudy green tanks with big blue duct pipes along the walls."

"Air generation and circulation plant. It's one of his favorite haunts; he says you can get anywhere in Confluence Center by following the ducts. We could have reached it in a quarter of the time if we'd come through the interior. Why didn't you tell me that in the first place?" Lilah pushed past him and headed for a branch off the catwalk.

Because I didn't know it, you dummy. Jeff hurried after her. His annoyance with Lilah was growing. He hadn't been at Confluence Center more than a couple of days, part of that time unconscious, but she seemed to expect him to know his way around. He'd like to take her to Earth, and see how *she* got on *there*.

Confluence Center, like a Space Navy ship, had a double hull. The region between the two hulls was normally air-filled, so there was access to the Anadem field rings and the controls without needing suits. The same space could be emptied of air, when vacuum operations were required. Lilah was now leading Jeff through a lock into the true interior of Confluence Center, where a breathable atmosphere was maintained at all times.

"Close the door behind you," she said. "Quick."

Jeff didn't need to be told. They were moving into a warm, steamy room where the walls dripped moisture and wisps of white fog curled around the edge of the lock. The lights were bright, and great tanks of cloudy green algae filled the interior. There was a stink in the air, ripe, rotting, and juicy.

"I don't know how Billy can stand it." Lilah had her hands in front of her nose and mouth and was hurrying toward a door at the far end. "He always goes this way."

Because no one wants to follow him, Jeff thought. He followed Lilah's lead, put his hands over his nose, and tried not to breathe until he was through the other door.

"Billy! Billy Jexter!" Lilah called.

Jeff peered around him. This was someone's living quarters—or had been. The new chamber was poorly lit, and his eyes had not yet adjusted from the previous brightness. Even so, there seemed to be a dinginess and an air of neglect in the room's walls and furnishings.

"Does Billy live here?"

"Nobody does." Lilah was staring around her in irritation. "Damn. I felt sure we'd find him here. This part of the Center isn't used at the moment, but Billy likes it because he can do what he likes."

She pointed at the once-white surrounds. On them someone had drawn and painted crude pictures of spaceships and dinosaurs and planets and people. One whole wall was a hideous human face, with a smaller face, equally distorted, forming the nose. Small red handprints walked up the opposite wall and continued all the way across the ceiling.

"Won't he get into trouble for this?" Jeff was feeling envious. It was exactly what he had wanted to do with his own rooms when he was six or seven years old, and never been allowed to.

"Why should he? If someone wants to use it again, the Logans will have it like new in a couple of days." Lilah was walking around the neglected chamber, running her hand along a chair back and inspecting the dust it brought away. "That wretched child. Well, he's had his chance. I've done my bit. Let's go. There's nothing here."

Jeff was not so sure. He felt that he had seen something, he was not sure what, and the sight sent a tremor running from his spine to his legs. He put a hand on Lilah's arm. "The face," he said softly. He gestured to one painted wall. "Look at the little face inside the big face, the one that forms the nose."

She swung around, turning him with her. "Billy Jexter!" she shouted at once. "You rotten little weasel. Come out of there."

The face on the wall seemed to split into two, moving aside to reveal Billy's grinning features. Jeff realized what had caused his odd discomfort. Those had been Billy's dark eyes, peering out at them through the empty sockets of the wall painting.

"Gotcha!" Billy said. "Wait a minute." His face disappeared, and after a few seconds the person himself came running into the room.

"You're lucky." Lilah didn't hide her irritation. "Lucky that Jeff saw you. Me, I'd have been out of here. And I wouldn't have come back."

"Nah." Billy was coated with dust, as dirty as anything in the room. "You wouldn't have got away. I've been trailing you two for ages. I saw you before you even came off the catwalk."

"You're pushing your luck, Billy." Lilah made a move to sit on one of the battered chairs. She changed her mind when she saw how filthy it was. Her all-white outfit wouldn't survive the first encounter. "I came here because I promised you that I would. Now you have five minutes to tell me. After that, I don't care what your wonderful secret is. I'm heading back to Level Two."

"I bet you don't. I'm not going to tell you, I'm going to show you. Do you have your locator on you? Otherwise, we can use mine."

Lilah unfastened a pocket of her jumpsuit and pulled out a grey oblong as long and as wide as a finger.

"What does it show?" Billy asked.

Lilah bent over and peered at the side of the oblong. "Exactly what you'd expect it to show. We are in the Ninth Sector, still in the Fifth Octant, but we've moved in a little and are now on Level Twenty-eight. To be completely precise, this is Habitation Chamber 106,788."

She was answering questions that Jeff had been wondering about but never got around to asking. Confluence Center contained thousands of kilometers of tunnels and corridors and shafts and ducts, serving hundreds of thousands of interior chambers. How did you specify a particular place?

The answer to that didn't seem too difficult: You divided the interior into regions—levels and sectors and octants—and used them as coordinates. You also gave each chamber a number. But there was a more difficult question: How did you know where you were?

The handheld locator, small enough to fit easily into a pocket, was the answer. It gave the coordinates of your current location. Presumably it worked anywhere in Confluence Center, and it was a fair guess that it could also serve as a route planner, providing an efficient path to anywhere you wanted to go.

"Don't put your locator away," Billy said. "Follow me, and keep an eye on it."

He went back through the same door he had come in. Lilah followed. Jeff, assuming he was included in the invitation and more curious than he wanted to admit, went after them.

They were in another chamber, not much different from the one that they had left. Billy headed for a small opening in the far wall, no more than three feet high. He crawled through, at the same time as Lilah said, "Habitation Chamber 106,787. No change in level, sector, or octant. Are we supposed to follow you in there?"

"Sure." Billy's voice came back, sounding hollow. "Once you are inside, keep your voices down."

Lilah pushed her head through the opening and pulled back. "It's *filthy* in there!"

"It is a bit. Not so loud!"

She bent lower, muttered, "One day I'm going to kill that kid," and eased her way in through the opening. Jeff went after her, crawling on his hands and knees. At first he thought there was no light at all. He moved forward, until his face came into contact with something that had to be Lilah's well-padded rear.

He heard a hiss from in front of him. "Do you mind! Slow down! I can't see a thing. Billy!"

"Shh! I'm here, right in front of you. Wait a minute, and you'll get used to it."

"This had better be good, Billy."

"It will be."

Jeff's eyes were finally adjusting. He realized that it was not nearly as dark as it seemed. Light bled in every few yards through rectangular grilles. The tunnel that they were crawling along must be part of the giant ventilation system that carried breathable air to every part of Confluence Center.

"Can you see your locator?" Billy whispered. His face was a pale oval, a couple of yards beyond Lilah.

"Yes."

"What does it say?"

"We're back to Level Twenty-nine, Ninth Sector, Fifth Octant. We're not in a habitation chamber—as if we didn't know. We're in Air Duct 93,469. Billy, this is ridiculous. I'm not crawling any farther. I've had it."

"Just a few meters more. Then you'll see."

Lilah did not answer, but Jeff saw the white pants moving away again in front of him. He could feel the dust and grit on his hands. She was right. This had better be good, or Billy was one dead brat.

The "few meters" turned out to be highly optimistic. Jeff crawled on forever, silently following the faint white beacon of Lilah's rear end. The duct was curving down. It was another stage in the descent of Jefferson Kopal, reduced from a uniformed officer in the proud Space Navy to a deserter following a girl's wriggling buttocks down a grubby tunnel. Was it possible to sink any lower? For some reason, his personal disgrace upset him more than Hooglich's warning that they might all be killed. He would risk death anytime for a chance to explain to his mother that what had been said about him was not true. Maybe there were things worse than death. Maybe people would die rather than be disgraced.

Lilah halted and put an end to his gloomy train of thought.

"Right," Billy whispered. He had stopped, too, and turned to face the others. "Now look at your locator."

There was a long silence. Jeff could not see what Lilah was doing. Then her voice came, low-pitched and puzzled. "This is impossible. There must be something wrong with it. It doesn't show anything at all."

"I know." Billy was triumphant. "But there's nothing wrong with it. I tried yesterday with three different locators. They all said the same thing."

"What does it mean?"

"It means that we are in a part of Confluence Center that the locator system doesn't know about."

"There's no such place. The locator knows everywhere, even new facilities that the Logans have only just finished. Are you saying there has been a malfunction?"

"I don't know what a *malfunction* is."

"It means that something isn't working."

"Then I'm not saying that. Come on."

"Where? I thought we'd finished."

"You think I'd call *that* a big secret? That there was a bug in the locator system?" Billy's face was invisible to Jeff, but he could hear the scorn in the voice. "I don't think there's been a *malfunction*. I think the locator doesn't work because it's been fixed not to work."

"Who would possibly do that?"

Billy did not answer. He said, "Come on," turned, and again began to crawl away along the tunnel.

The others followed. Jeff noticed that they were now moving slightly uphill, which meant they were heading toward the upper ring of the Anadem field. He wondered how Hooglich and the others were doing. It had been a while since he had noticed any variations in local gravity.

The tunnel was also growing in width and height. Soon Lilah paused, stood up, and walked upright. Jeff followed suit, but he had to keep his head bent. Billy, much shorter, had given up crawling ten meters back and was far ahead. He was standing on tiptoe with his face pressed to the tunnel wall. As Jeff and Lilah approached, he turned to place his finger to his lips and gestured to the wall.

The ventilator grille was big, about three feet wide and a foot deep. The three of them could stand side by side and peer through.

Jeff moved to a position between Billy and Lilah. He found himself eight to ten feet above the floor of a huge room, looking out upon it from a vantage point high on one wall. The room was packed with equipment, meters and pumps and monitors and generators. On the floor, right in front of Jeff, one thick plate of metal was poised above another, while a delicate device like a balance for measuring small weights stood between them. Nothing seemed to be supporting the upper plate. On the left was an isolated silver cylinder. It seemed to have no function and no part of it moved, but the air around it was filled with faint sparkles of light. Over to Jeff's right stood a machine of black metal with a double ring above and below, like a doll's-house version of the Anadem field generator encircling Confluence Center.

At first Jeff thought that the room was empty. Then a figure crouched by a featureless black cube in one corner rose upright and came wandering slowly back toward the middle of the room. It was a man, tall and slightly built, with narrow sloping shoulders and a head that craned forward like a bird's from a thin neck. He had long, wild hair, pushed casually back off a high, narrow forehead, and a full sandy beard so bushy that most of his face could not be seen. He advanced to a single chair in the middle of the mess of equipment, sat down, and stared into nothingness.

Billy nudged Jeff. He jerked his head to indicate that they should retreat. Jeff touched Lilah on the arm, passing the message on, and all three moved a few yards to stand on the other side of the tunnel.

"I told you," Billy whispered. "I told you I had a real big secret. Look at your locator, Lilah."

"I did." She held it out toward the others. "This place doesn't exist. That *man* doesn't exist. This whole thing is impossible. Come on, Billy."

"Where are you going?"

She turned. There was black grime and grease in her hair, and dust all the way along the front of her white suit. At some point she must have touched her cheek, because there were smudges of dirt there also.

"Going?" She ran the back of her hand across her nose,

adding another dark streak of filth. For the first time, Jeff saw another side of Lilah, one more like the daughter of the chief administrator of the Messina Dust Cloud. She seemed utterly unaware of her appearance. "Why, we're going to talk to that man," she said firmly. "It's our duty. We have to find out what he's doing, and why he's been messing around with the Con-fluence Center locator system. And he'd better have some good answers."

She turned to Billy Jexter. "Come on, Billy. You say you know the interior better than anyone. Prove it. Show us a way into that room."

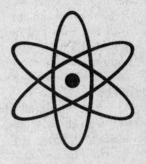

CHAPTER THIRTEEN

BILLY had never been into the actual chamber. As he explained, the man had always been there when he looked through the grille. Billy wasn't sure he ever left. It took a couple of tries, but Billy regarded Lilah's words as a challenge, and finally they were standing at a **huge** pair of doors wide enough to drive a bus through.

"Nonstandard specification," Lilah said. She was eyeing the doors. "You'd have to give the Logans special instructions for them to make something this size. Are you sure, Billy?"

"I'm not sure he's still there. But I'm sure this is the room, the one we were looking into."

"That's all I need. Give me a hand." Lilah grabbed one

door handle and gestured to Jeff to take the other. Working in unison, they pulled the doors wide. Lilah went through at once, with the other two close behind.

The man had not left. In fact, he didn't seem to have moved at all. He was still sitting in the chair and staring at nothing.

As the doors opened he turned his head. "Hello," he said mildly.

And that was all. He ignored them, rubbing at his bearded chin with the fingers of his left hand and from time to time pursing full lips.

Billy looked ready for instant retreat. Jeff wasn't sure what he would have done, but he didn't have to find out. Lilah walked forward to stand right in front of the stranger. She put her hands on her hips.

"Did you fix the locators' databases so this room doesn't show on them?"

"I did." The words were spoken quietly, in a soft, precise voice.

Lilah had been ready for denial, and the open admission surprised her. She regarded the seated man, then said in a voice no louder than his, "Why would you do a thing like that?"

"For privacy, of course. Why else?" The man slowly rotated his head for a good look at Lilah, Jeff, and Billy. Jeff saw eyes of pale gray that even when they stared right at you seemed to be seeing through and beyond you.

"I used to think that privacy was easiest to find far away from people," the man went on. "But it didn't work. No matter where I went, someone seemed able to track me down and ask me questions. So I adopted a different principle, one I read of long ago. If you want to hide a leaf, the best place to do it is in a forest. So the best place to hide a person should be in a crowd. If I stayed right here in Confluence Center, among so many swarming tens of thousands, then surely I would pass unnoticed. Unfortunately. . . ." The man smiled for the first time, and Jeff thought it was a gentle, friendly smile. "Unfortunately, your presence proves that idea is also false. I am now in need of a different principle."

The way he put it made Jeff feel they ought to apologize for intruding. But the man went on, "Never mind. I would have been forced to put in a personal appearance, anyway, within the next twenty-four hours."

"Why?" Lilah asked. "I mean, if we hadn't found you. . . ."

"I tend to lose myself in my work, enough to ignore most external distractions. However, it is hard not to notice when the body-force field changes around you and affects half a dozen delicate experiments. Someone is experimenting with the Confluence Center's Anadem field. I see no way that they can do any damage, but I would rather seek direct confirmation of that." Jeff didn't remember moving, but he found himself standing in front of the man.

"You are," he said. "Aren't you? Simon Macafee. I mean, are you—"

"I am indeed," the man said. "I am Simon Macafee. And now you three have the advantage of me, because although you were perspicacious enough to track me to my lair, I have no idea at all of any of your names."

"I'm Billy Jexter," Billy said promptly. Now that he had met the mysterious stranger, all his fears had gone away. "I'm the one who found you."

"I will not go so far as to thank you for that."

"And I'm Lilah Desmon."

"Whose father, as I recall, is in charge of Cloud boundary exploration, and whose mother is the general administrator." Macafee turned to Jeff questioningly. Once again Jeff was aware of a look that went all the way through him.

"I'm Jeff." He paused. Did his last name matter? He was likely to be disowned and disinherited anyway, as soon as the false report of his destruction and desertion of the *Aurora* reached Earth. But it was still his name. "I'm Jefferson Kopal."

"Kopal?" The gray eyes took on a new light. "A famous name indeed, in Sol's military and commercial circles. Might you be a member of that family?"

For a hermit and a recluse, Simon Macafee seemed to know an awful lot. Jeff nodded. *If you went all the way to the edge of the universe, would that be far enough to escape the shadow of your name?*

"A descendant, possibly, of the redoubtable Rollo Kopal?" There was a twist to Macafee's lips that suggested he did not altogether approve of Rollo's reputation.

"My great-grandfather." Jeff lifted his chin. His mother had told him, You are responsible for your own actions—but not the actions of your ancestors. "My father was Nelson Kopal."

Was. He regretted the word as soon as it was out of his mouth. He had implied what he should have kept secret, that his father was no longer alive.

If he hoped that the comment would glide by unnoticed, he was disappointed. Simon Macafee said at once, "Was? You mean your father is dead?"

"Yes. He died in a space accident." And let's hope there's no way *that* statement can ever find its way back to Earth.

"I am sorry to hear it." Macafee was not just mouthing the words, he actually did sound sorry. "But what are you doing here, so far from Earth and Sol? The Cloud is remote territory for any descendant of Rollo Kopal."

Simon Macafee had an uncanny ability to ask questions that Jeff did not want to answer. But there was no choice. Jeff gave a short and edited version of the events leading up to his joining the Space Navy, mentioned his assignment to Border Command, and spoke of the injuries that had caused him to be brought here following the *Aurora*'s close encounter with a space sounder after passing through Node 23 into the Messina Dust Cloud. The last point took Macafee's thoughts off in some other direction. He sat silent for a few moments, then said, "A space sounder, you say, over by the Lizard Reef?"

"Fairly close. But not as near the reef as other people claimed it ought to be. It was out in open space."

"Now that is most interesting." Macafee stroked absent-mindedly at his beard. "Were you frightened by the experience?"

"I was terrified." Jeff's gaze was fixed on Simon Macafee, but from the corner of his eye he thought he saw Lilah frown at the admission of fear. She was probably like Myron, scared of nothing.

"I am sorry to hear that," Macafee said. "I suspect, Jefferson Kopal, that I may have done something with my experiments much worse than anything you did in disturbing my privacy. I think I owe you."

"What are you talking about?" Lilah asked.

"I will not tell you now. But if you three come here tomorrow, I may be able to show you something to reduce your fear of space sounders." Then Macafee added, as though he were having second thoughts, "Show you, that is, if you are permitted to leave Confluence Center. Are you?"

"I am," Lilah said at once.

"I can go anywhere I like," added Billy.

From the expression on his face, that was an absolute lie. As for Jeff, he had no idea where he could go and where he couldn't go. No one had told him anything. But Macafee was done with that subject. He was moving on.

"As I have often said, successive anomalies are more likely to be causally linked than to be independent events." He saw from the looks on Lilah and Billy's faces that they had no idea what he was talking about. "What I mean is, if two peculiar things happen, one after another, the second one often follows as a result of the first. For instance, a Kopal"—he nodded at Jeff—"comes to the Cloud, is hurt, and arrives at Confluence Center. Soon after that, the strength of the Center's Anadem field is varied, for the first time ever. Are these events independent, or does one derive from the other?"

"They are linked." Lilah jumped in before Jeff could answer. She explained that the loss of the *Aurora* was being blamed on Jeff by that ship's captain. "Though of course he had nothing to do with it; Muv says it's just a pretext for aggression. Sol government is making threatening noises, and now they have this other ship, the *Dreadnought*, on the way, and maybe a fleet to follow. So, just to be on the safe side, mother wants the Center to be moveable at high acceleration. For that, we need to be able to change the field if we have to."

Jeff stared at Lilah. She didn't actually blush, but she had enough conscience to avoid his eye. All her claim to have no idea at all about the Anadem field, or why it was being worked on, had been pure nonsense. It had been done to annoy him. She probably knew more about the field than he did.

"I'll take care of changing the field strength." Simon Macafee spoke absently, and his gray eyes remained fixed on Jeff. "If I may offer you a word of advice, Jefferson Kopal, you should be extremely careful when the ship from Sol arrives here. Perhaps things are not what they seem. I must think now. There are many factors to be considered."

Macafee was saying much the same thing as Hooglich and Russo. Jeff waited for him to explain or elaborate, but he did not. He leaned back in the chair, and it was as though a light was extinguished behind the gray eyes. Once again he was staring at nothing.

After a few seconds Lilah coughed. "Er, Mr. Macafee. About tomorrow."

The head with its shaggy mane of hair turned.

"You still here?" Simon Macafee waved a long-fingered hand. "Away, avaunt. As I said, you may come back tomorrow. *Provided* that all of you"—he speared Billy in particular with a skeptical look—"by that time have adult permission to make a trip with me. If not, there is no point in returning." He pointed to the right. "You will find that direction leads you most easily to the central levels."

The dismissal was so inarguable, not even Billy tried to say another word. The three moved in thoughtful silence, until after five minutes of wandering through chamber after deserted chamber, Lilah said, "My locator is working again! This is Level Nineteen, Eighth Sector, Fifth Octant. We're back in known territory."

"I know *that*," Billy said. "I know the way from here." The silence had been unusually long for him, and now the words came tumbling out. "He didn't say we ought not to tell people about him being back here in Confluence Center, did he? I mean, he said he'd be coming himself, so he could work on the field, and then everyone will know where he was hiding. And if I don't tell anyone we met him, how can I get somebody to write and say it's all right for me to go with him? I really want to go. I will be going, won't I?"

"Depends," Lilah said. "I think he intended us to tell people he'll be fixing the field himself. He doesn't really like the jinners messing with the controls, even if he's sure it's safe for them to do it. I don't like it, either. I'm going to pass word along to Muv. As for *you*." She turned on Billy, who was hovering close to her side. "I'll see if I can get permission for all of us to go with Macafee—provided that you stay out of my way, and you don't bug Jeff or me *at all* for the rest of today."

"Deal!" Billy bounced with excitement. "Do you know the way home?"

"The locator will tell me."

"Then I'm out of here. See you tomorrow." They were standing in the connecting section between two tunnels. Billy ran forward five steps and turned the corner. Jeff, following, saw two long, straight corridors—and no sign of Billy.

"Where is he?"

Lilah came to his side. "Don't ask. It's a Billy Jexter specialty, instant disappearance. He's just showing off for your benefit. Come on. I need a change of clothes."

Jeff didn't blame her. It was hard to believe that an hour or two ago her suit had been so gleaming white and spotless. Now she was as smeared and streaked and striped as the grubbiest jinner in the Cloud. Jeff was just as dirty, but a change of clothing was the least of his worries. Why couldn't Lilah have banished *him* from her presence until tomorrow, instead of Billy Jexter? He had dozens of things to think about; he could use a few hours to himself to put his problems in order.

There was the *Dreadnought*, still far off but with an approaching, ominous presence that he could almost feel. Simon Macafee's perplexing warning, to be careful when the ship from Central Command arrived, only made the situation more disturbing. Hooglich and Russo, from the look of them, were quite happy to be listed as deserters, and they might choose to stay in the Cloud permanently. But Jeff's position was not so simple. He was a Kopal, with the Kopal name to protect—even if he hadn't chosen to be born one, and even if he didn't like most of what the family stood for. What would he do, if he was ordered to return to Sol aboard the *Dreadnought*? He didn't have a choice. He was still a navy ensign—unless he had been drummed out already, without the chance to make a statement in his own defense.

Then there was Macafee, the mysterious Cloud wanderer whom Jeff somehow trusted for no reason he could put a finger on. Maybe it was because Macafee seemed to be interested, like Jeff, in knowing the *why* of things, more than in money or fame or position. To be free to spend years wandering the reefs, just to learn what was there—that was better than being an admiral. Even the peculiar statement, "I may be able to show you something to reduce your fear of space sounders," was tolerable when Simon Macafee said it. Jeff tried to imagine those same words spoken by Uncle Giles Lazenby. The thought made him shiver. And yet, although Simon Macafee and Giles Lazenby seemed as different as any two human beings could be, there was a peculiar resemblance that Jeff could not begin to explain.

That was what he ought to be doing: sitting alone, thinking through everything that had happened since the day of his acceptance into the Space Navy, trying to form a rational picture from it all. Instead he was going to spend the next few hours listening to a sermon in praise of horses.

Why had he been stupid enough to suggest today as a good time for his postponed visit to see her rooms? Only because he felt guilty about using Lilah's family connections, and so far he had not used them at all; his promise, judging from the frozen look on her face, had earned him not a scrap of credit with her.

It was too late to back out now. They had been moving steadily inward, toward the middle of Confluence Center, and Jeff was starting to recognize his surroundings. Lilah led them through a big cafeteria-recreation area, down three floors in a little service elevator, and through a wide transparent pipe that ran across a no-man's-land filled with unfamiliar and riotous vegetation.

Ten more steps, along a corridor marked with identifying purple and orange stripes, and Lilah halted in front of a sliding door.

"Here we are," she said lifelessly. "After you."

Jeff went in. It was as bad as he had feared. The living room was four meters by four meters, with a high ceiling. One of the walls, opposite the entrance, had two more doors in it and was relatively plain. The other three provided a hymnal of horse worship. A life-size 3-D projection showed a white stallion, rearing up and pawing the air with his forelegs. The walls offered a changing sequence of holograms, realistic depth images of show horses grazing, galloping, foaling, nuzzling, or trotting. Small horse statues, plastic and stone and glass and even wood, stood on every available surface.

Jeff waited for the gush of words that in his experience horse fanciers offered to anyone who would listen. Instead, Lilah avoided looking at him, gestured to one of the inner doors, and said, "If you'd like to take a shower, go ahead. It's in there."

"I have no change of clothes."

That finally earned him a look, a very odd one. "I guess you're not used to Cloud service. Just put your old clothes in the disposal, next to the shower. The Logans will have a new set for you before you're out and dry." As he moved toward the door, she added, still in the same dead voice, "I'll fix food while you shower. Is there anything particular that you would like?"

"Whatever you dial." The mention of food made Jeff hungry. "I'm easy to please. You order it, I'll eat it." He hurried through the door before she could change her mind. If she preferred to put the horse talk on hold, that was fine with him.

He found himself in Lilah's bedroom, dominated again by the horse motif. A bathroom, surprisingly large, lay beyond it. He took his time with the shower, using water as hot as he could stand and hoping it would sluice his worries away along with the dirt. It didn't quite work, but he felt a lot better when he emerged lobster pink, dried himself slowly, and put on the new clothes provided by the dispenser. He returned to the living room prepared to suffer. Lilah had earned the right to talk. All he had to do was sit and listen and nod agreement in the right places.

There was no sign of her. He followed the smell of hot food, went through the other door, and found himself in a little kitchen. Lilah was there, bringing half a dozen filled dishes out of a compact autochef and setting them on the table.

"Good timing," she said. "Everything is ready. Help yourself, and I'll take my shower."

"But what about you eating?"

"Don't worry about me. I can get something later." Still she did not meet his eye. As she hurried out, turned into the bedroom, and closed its door firmly, Jeff finally realized what should have been obvious ten minutes ago. Lilah didn't want to talk to him. From the way she was behaving, she didn't want him here at all.

He sat down at the little table, helped himself to generous amounts of food, and began to eat steadily. Lilah had chosen the dishes carefully, and everything was well prepared. He hardly noticed the taste. He had to add Lilah's behavior to his list of mysteries and concerns. Presumably it was something he had done, something new since his last unkept promise. But without a hint from her, he would never guess what. Something he had said? He struggled to remember their conversations. It seemed to him they had not said much to each other at all; most of the talk had been with Billy or with Simon Macafee.

Lilah returned as he was examining what was left in the dishes. His absentminded eating hadn't left very much for her.

"Listen," she said, before he could apologize. She slid into the seat opposite. She was pink and well scrubbed, wearing a long green robe with her golden hair bound up in a pale blue towel. "This is probably going to make you really angry. But I can't do it."

Jeff stared at her. Her face was earnest, and she presumably thought she was telling him something. He had no idea what.

"You can't?" he said.

"No. It isn't your fault, and it's not my fault. It's just the difference between the way things are on Earth and here in the Cloud. You can't stay."

She stood up. Jeff followed her lead and did the same. "You want me to leave?"

It was her turn for confusion. "Well, I didn't mean right this minute. Not if you don't want to. I just assumed you *would* want to, as soon as I told you." She turned pinker yet. "You don't have to leave at once. I'm just telling you that you can't stay with me all night. Like on Earth."

"All night," Jeff repeated blankly. "Like on Earth." He collapsed back onto his chair. It was suddenly obvious what had been going on.

"I didn't mean to give you a bad time." Lilah was still standing, rigid and awkward. "I didn't even realize what you meant, until you said you'd come to my rooms after we were all done with Billy. And I'm not saying that everything we do in the Cloud is right, and the way things are done on Earth is wrong. Any place with ten billion people has to be obsessed with mating and breeding. You and your cousin have probably been with a hundred different girls. But for me—and here. . . ."

The strange thing was, when she put it that way Lilah could well be right. Ever since they were teenagers, Jeff had watched Myron at dinners and parties and dances and meets. His cousin had an easy way with girls. He never seemed awkward or embarrassed or less than totally sure of himself. While Jeff fumbled and blundered and wondered what to say next, Myron moved. Before the event finished he would be exchanging numbers or notes—or wandering off with someone, well before the end.

Jeff stood up again. *If you want to know the truth, I have never spent a night with any girl, here, or on Earth, or anywhere else. That's not a boast, it's a confession. I'm probably no more moral than you think any Earth person is moral.* That's what he wanted to say. What came out was, "You don't have to worry that I'll make a pass at you, or try to talk you into sleeping with me or letting me stay the night. Because I'm going."

It made a fine exit line. Jeff spoiled it a bit by turning at the door and adding, "Oh, and yeah, thanks for the dinner."

Lilah said not a word. She clutched her robe, up near the neck, with one hand, and stared at him with astonished blue eyes.

Once outside her rooms, Jeff didn't know where he was—physically or emotionally. But after what had just happened he couldn't face going back in and asking Lilah for directions. He wandered aimlessly from corridor to corridor, until at last he found a place that he recognized. As he was heading from there toward his own rooms, he passed Hooglich going the other way.

She grinned at him. "Hey, Brother Kopal. Didn't take *you* long this morning to get fed up with work. You look tired. What you been doin', tail-chasing?"

Jeff shook his head and kept going. He was sure of one thing: he might look tired, but he couldn't possibly look as worn out and weary as he felt.

When he dropped into bed, he puzzled over something else that Hooglich had said. *This morning.* Was it really this

morning, when he and Hooglich and Russo and Billy left the
heart of Confluence Center to seek the rings of the Anadem
field?

It was, he decided as he drifted off.

Cloudland days must be at least a hundred hours long.

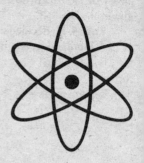

CHAPTER FOURTEEN

JEFF awoke late, lethargic and confused. For a while he stared up at the ceiling, not sure where he was. Maybe it was the effect of the monster meal he had eaten in Lilah's rooms, but his sleep had been uneasy and filled with dreams.

Dreams of Earth. It was hard to belief that he was not there, in the house where he had lived all his life. And strange dreams, too. For the first time in months, Jeff's mind had been occupied by thoughts of his father. They were sitting in the sunlit breakfast room at the end of the east wing of Kopal Manor, and Jeff was explaining that he didn't want a career as a navy officer or a business tycoon. He would rather be a scientist or a jinner. Nelson Kopal listened carefully. Instead of objecting, and repeating the inflexible rules laid down by Rollo Kopal, he seemed sympathetic as he had never been before.

Except that Nelson Kopal was dead. Jeff had known that, even in his dreams. The father talking to him across the breakfast table at Kopal Manor had Nelson Kopal's voice; but he had Simon Macafee's eyes and beard and slow, gentle speech. His words echoed the idea that Florence Kopal had urged on Jeff since infancy, a thought so different from the standard Kopal litany: "You are responsible for *your own* actions, Jeff. You are not responsible for the deeds of your ancestors."

Had Simon Macafee actually said that to Jeff, during their meeting yesterday? Jeff didn't think so. He had thought them, himself, when Simon asked about Rollo Kopal; that was all.

The moral was this: Do what you want with your life, and don't let other people force you into something different.

That was easy, for most people; but if you were a Kopal, with a family name to protect and a century of tradition ordering your behavior. . . .

Jeff eased out of bed and stood swaying and rubbing his eyes. He realized there was another reason for the odd dreams. While he stood unmoving, his weight increased and a few seconds later decreased. Now it felt exactly the same as Earth gravity. He suspected that he had been subconsciously aware of changes like this during the night, of the local field rising and falling. He had simply folded them into his dreams, making Kopal Manor, along with its buildings, stables, flower beds, pastures, and all, rise from the surface of Earth and soar away into space.

Hooglich and her fellow jinners were at it again, fiddling with the Anadem field. Or maybe it was Simon Macafee this time, emerging as he had promised from his long solitude. That idea propelled Jeff from his rooms and toward the main operations room of Confluence Center.

Macafee was not there. Lilah was. So, fortunately, was Connie Cheever, sitting across from her daughter at the round table, because Jeff was not sure what he would have offered Lilah as a greeting.

"He's been here, and he's out on the perimeter," Connie said, as Jeff skidded to a halt and she saw the expectant look on his face. "He'll be back. You really had fun yesterday, didn't you? Lilah told me the whole story."

Jeff nodded. Not quite the whole story, he hoped. Lilah was paler than usual, and the dark smudges under her eyes suggested that she hadn't slept much.

"We've been discussing your trip off Center with Macafee," Connie went on. "It's not as simple as you might think, because of what else is going on. Your navy ship will be here in two or three days, depending what route they take."

Jeff had been doing his best not to think about that. It was not *his* ship. Quite the contrary. When the *Dreadnought* arrived, everyone told him to be careful. But careful *how?* The situation was beyond his control—unless he could manage to be far away from Confluence Center, somewhere in limbo with Simon Macafee. A lot more might hang on Connie Cheever's decision than she realized.

"We can be back before the ship gets here," Lilah said, damning Jeff's hopes. "Simon Macafee says he can show us everything that he wants us to see in one day."

"Yes, I heard him. But if you knew Simon a bit better, you'd realize he has less sense of time than anyone in the Cloud. He's quite likely to *say* he's going somewhere for a day—and show up a month later."

"We can keep an eye on him. We'll make sure he doesn't stay away for a long time, and we can't go very far in one day. There's nothing dangerous one day's ride from here. Oh, please, Muv, *please* let us go. If we don't, Billy Jexter will be so disappointed."

"I see. Now it's all for the sake of little Bill-ee, is it? You have a heart of gold, Lilah. But you don't have to give me a sob story, because I've made up my mind."

"Oh, Mother, we would only—"

"I said, I've made up my mind. Don't make me change it. You see, I've decided to let you go." Connie Cheever was smiling, but she did not look amused. "It's not because of Billy Jexter, and it's not because I don't like to disappoint the two of you. I have a better reason. The Sol government is trying to push us around. We can't allow that. If they want to send a ship to visit us, that's fine."

Simon Macafee came drifting in as she was speaking. She gave him a nod and went on, "But for us, *Dreadnought* or no *Dreadnought*, it's going to be business as usual. We're not going to start doing something, or stop doing something, just because we're having visitors from Sol-side."

"Which is just as well." Macafee joined them at the table. "I've been with the jinners. I could increase the Anadem field, to two G or ten G or anything you like. And they tell me they could add Omnivore drives to Confluence Center. But if we do that, and try to run away, there'll be a ton of damage. The extension corridors were added after the Anadem rings were installed. They are not within the influence of the field, and at high acceleration they'll bend and crumple like straws. You'd be throwing five years of work down the drain. I agree with you, Madam Administrator, running away is no answer."

"So what is, Simon?"

"I'm thinking on that." He rubbed at his sandy beard. It grew full on the cheeks, and his eyes seemed to gleam out from a thicket of whiskers. Today his curly hair fell unrestrained over his forehead. "I have ideas, Connie. They need a bit of work, but meanwhile you shouldn't change anything."

"I won't. Unless I have to. I rely on you, Simon."

"Not even the plans for Confluence?" asked Lilah.

Her question meant nothing to Jeff, but clearly it did to Connie Cheever. She hesitated, unsure of herself for the first time.

"Not even Confluence," she said at last. "I've not been thinking much about that, but we won't cancel. Everything goes ahead as planned. In fact, I'm inclined to say we should start a day or two early, so by the time they arrive we'll be in full swing. That way, the crew of the *Dreadnought* can be invited as our guests. They can participate in Confluence as much or as little as they choose. But we'll go on as usual, exactly as if they weren't here. We can't let them control our lives."

She waved a hand at Lilah. "On your way, child; go get Billy Jexter before I change my mind. I have to think about Confluence, and get ready for it."

Jeff assumed that the dismissal applied to him, too. He followed Lilah and Simon Macafee out. "But what *is* Confluence?" he asked, as soon as they were far enough from Connie that he would not be overheard. "I thought it was a place—this place. But Connie Cheever says she has to *get ready* for it."

"A failure of human language." Simon dropped back to keep pace with Jeff, while Lilah hurried on ahead to pick up Billy. She said he'd be waiting in the next corridor with his fingers crossed. As soon as she was out of sight Jeff slowed down a bit. He liked having Simon Macafee all to himself, even if it was only for a few seconds.

"What do you mean, a failure of human language? What else is there?"

"There's *Logan* language—the way the smart machines communicate among themselves. They do it in a purely logical and symbolic form. The Logans are too polite to mention it, but they must be disgusted by the ambiguity and sloppiness of our languages. They will have several words for *Confluence*, depending on the meaning they want. We don't bother. We just use the same word and rely on the hearer to sort it out. For instance, if I'm talking about the Messina Dust Cloud, and I say 'confluence,' I expect you to understand that I mean the place where all the big dust rivers meet. That location wanders around—just as the magnetic poles wander around on the surface of the Earth."

Jeff was pleased with himself because he knew that last fact. The surprise was that Simon Macafee, with no direct ties to Earth, knew it also. It seemed he knew everything.

"But if I say 'Confluence Center,' " Simon went on, as Billy Jexter came skipping up to them with Lilah close behind, "then I mean not a place but a particular structure, the one we are in now. It usually stays near the confluence of the Cloud rivers, but it doesn't have to. It can wander wherever we choose to take it. Finally, there's the Confluence that starts a few days from now. It isn't a place. It is an event and a time, when all the inhabitants of Confluence Center—"

"Event, time, them's for noogies," Billy broke in. "You mean Confluence is a big hootenanny. Parties round the clock, and all kinds of games. I can't *wait*."

Even Connie Cheever became respectful when Simon Macafee was around. She regarded him as someone special, a genius unlike anyone else in the Cloud. Not so Billy Jexter. Jeff could tell that Billy thought Macafee was just some weird old guy.

"That is the way the Confluence is viewed today," Simon said mildly. He didn't act upset with Billy at all. "Nowadays it's a party. In the first days of Cloud exploration, things were different. Confluence had a real purpose then. The Cloud people out here were collecting stable transuranics, in little ships called harvesters, and they all competed with each other. But they also had a lot in common, more than they did with the stay-at-home people back on Earth. Harvester people who married each other made good matches.

"The trouble was, their children had no way to meet possible partners. But there was one time and place where all the harvesters congregated. That was where the dust rivers met, at the side of the Cloud away from the node, and they all used to rendezvous there to swap supplies and gossip before they started back for the second half of their season. So that's where they built Confluence Center. It was small and primitive at first. For the past century it has grown and grown to what we have today. But it all started out as a time and place where young people, or unattached older people, could meet and dance and court each other."

"I didn't know that!" Billy said. "Who are 'unattached older people'? Are you one of them?"

"You might say that."

"So you'll be at Confluence, and you're going to meet and dance with and court people?"

"I rather doubt it." Something in Macafee's voice suggested that meeting, dancing, and courting were his idea of a personal hell. But he went on, still quietly, "Those two will, though."

He could only be talking about Jeff and Lilah. Neither he nor Billy seemed to notice the moments of dead air that hung around the group until Billy pointed off to one side and said, "There's an exit dock that way, you know. Why don't we use it?"

"No." Macafee kept moving. "We'll be taking my own ship, the *Galileo*. It's smaller than the standard models, and it would be crowded for four people on a long trip. But this won't be a long trip, and I've made a few . . . modifications."

He offered no explanation of what that meant. Neither Lilah nor Billy asked questions. Jeff wanted to, and he might have if he and Simon Macafee had been alone. But he didn't want to look like an idiot again in front of the others. There was so much he just didn't *know* in the Cloud, he was forced to ask about everything. Even Billy was way ahead of him.

He studied the ship closely when they came to it. The *Galileo* didn't seem any different from a miniature Space Navy vessel. The profile matched a scaled-down version of the *Aurora*, and he searched in vain for any sign of Simon Macafee's modifications. Whatever they were, they couldn't be substantial.

They went aboard in silence and settled onto the acceleration couches. Even Billy was quiet as electromagnetic handlers eased the ship out of the dock and pushed it gently into open space. There were a few queasy moments as their weight decreased steadily from normal to nothing. Jeff realized that they were moving beyond the influence of the Anadem field, into the free fall of open space. Staring out of the side observation port, he saw the great mass of Confluence Center bulking alongside. The ship turned to face along the axis of the cylindrical disk, at the same time drifting out to a distance where it would be safe to turn on the drive.

Macafee, at the controls, glanced across at the other three. "All set?"

Lilah and Jeff nodded. "Let 'er rip," said Billy.

Macafee touched a pressure pad on the board in front of him. Jeff leaned back and waited for acceleration. He much preferred weight to free fall. There was a hum like a great, spinning top through the body of the *Galileo*, but that was all. He turned to Simon Macafee with a questioning look. Had something gone wrong?

Macafee did not speak, but he gestured at the screens high on the wall in front of them. The forward screen showed the misty glories of the Dust Cloud, a mottling of pink and gold and purple. On the rear screen, Confluence Center was shrinking rapidly. As Jeff watched, it went from a disk to a bright dot, then became an invisible member of the star field background.

"We're at twenty-five Gs," Macafee said. "Would you rather have a bit of weight? I usually prefer it; things don't wander away from you when you put them down."

He touched the pad again. A moment later Jeff was sitting comfortably instead of barely touching the seat. Now he understood what was happening. Simon Macafee had modified the *Galileo* by installing an Anadem field, then arranged a coupling between the field strength and the drive. The harder the drive accelerated the ship, the greater the strength of the field. The net force on the passengers could be zero, or whatever level felt most comfortable.

"How much acceleration can you give us?"

Macafee nodded approvingly. "You know what's happening, don't you? I thought you might. Not every part of the *Galileo* is within the influence of the field, so there are limits set by the strength of the hull materials. I've never taken it to the maximum, but I'm sure the ship can comfortably handle forty Gs. Maybe we'll try that for a while."

Jeff finally understood what Hooglich and Russo had been getting at. With an Anadem field installed, a Space Navy ship could reduce travel times enormously and not harm the crew. The injuries that Jeff had suffered on the *Aurora* had all been the result of high acceleration—and that had been at only ten Gs. With a forty-G acceleration available, nothing without an Anadem field would be able to catch you.

Forty Gs. When Lilah told her mother that Simon Macafee would have them back to Confluence Center within a day, Jeff had agreed with her that they would be making a short trip. But if you accelerated at forty Gs, even for six hours, you would be a long way from home.

How far?

Jeff tried to do the calculations in his head and came up with an answer he couldn't believe. Six hours at forty Gs would put you close to a hundred million kilometers out. Two days at forty Gs could zoom you clear across the Messina Dust Cloud. So much for Lilah's claim to Connie Cheever that they wouldn't be going far.

He took another look at the forward screen. Their speed had grown so that in just a few minutes he could see changes, the field of the Messina Cloud opening before them. They were heading straight for one of the twisting dust rivers, a place where the Cloud turned and folded on itself. Even at the dust river's most dense, the dust and gas were close to a perfect vacuum. The *Galileo* could plunge right through the heart of the river and not be damaged. But whatever might lie on the other side . . . that was hidden from view.

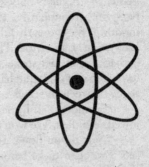

CHAPTER FIFTEEN

WHERE are we going?" It seemed a bit late to be asking, but Jeff was getting ideas. Yesterday, Simon Macafee had mentioned space sounders, and he was a man whose words always meant something. But space sounders were associated with reefs, and there were no reefs within a day's travel of Confluence Center—if you traveled at the usual accelerations.

"In about four hours we'll be approaching Miriam's Fall." Macafee didn't seem to move, but a new image sprang up on one of the displays. The glow of the Dust Cloud formed a complicated swirl of light around three darker whirlpools. "As you can see, it's an unusual situation where three reefs sit close together in a regular triangle. They have official names and numbers, Ambartsumian 13, 14, and 15. But that was too much of a mouthful for the early Cloud explorers, and they called them Larry, Curly, and Moe. The fascinating thing about these reefs is that they attract space sounders in great numbers. It's a bad day when you can't find half a dozen sounders somewhere in the space between the reefs."

"Sounders," Billy said doubtfully. "I don't think I'm allowed sounders. We won't be going near them, will we?"

"Not if you don't want to. But why don't you wait and see? I've been there before, many times—and as you can see, I'm still all right."

Macafee probably thought that he was being reassuring. Jeff didn't think so. He was inclined to agree with Billy; he wasn't allowed sounders either. He had tried them once, and that was enough for a lifetime.

"Did you tell my mother where we were going?" Lilah asked suddenly.

Macafee looked at her, then at Jeff. "All three of you are worried? If so, I'll turn around and we'll go home. I thought you'd find this exciting."

His words changed everything. Jeff didn't want to head back with his tail between his legs, having been nowhere and seen nothing. It was part of the Kopal creed: Courage is a requirement, not an elective. He also imagined Hooglich's raised eyebrows. *You chickened out, did you, when you might have learned something great? What sort of jinner would you make?*

He shook his head. Lilah, with her eye on him, said, "If you're sure it's safe. . . ."

Billy stuck his chin out and added, "I'm not afraid of any old sounders." His eyes, more convincingly, read, *Yes, I am, though.*

"It will be safe enough," Macafee said. "In fact, I'll make double sure of it. Lilah, do you know how to fly a ship like this?"

"No."

"I can," said Billy.

"Not for a few years you can't. Lilah, come here. Jeff too. I'm going to show you how to fly the *Galileo*. It's not difficult. Before we reach the Ambartsumians, you'll know enough to fly home—right across the Cloud, too, if you want."

With Billy hovering enviously over their shoulders, Jeff and Lilah learned the control panel of the *Galileo*. In the first five minutes, Jeff decided that Simon Macafee was right. It wasn't difficult. The ship almost flew itself. All you had to do was choose a destination, drive setting, and local field. And if any one of those was outside acceptable range, you would be warned. He wondered, Was it just as easy to handle something like the *Aurora*? If so, it explained how an idiot like Eliot Dufferin could be a captain. Even there, the experience of Hooglich and Russo had been available to correct mistakes.

Lilah and he took turns putting the ship through its paces. When she increased the acceleration to forty Gs, the only way to tell was by a slight increase in the background hum.

Macafee had his eye on the strain gauges. "Seems I was too conservative. We could handle another ten and be fine. But I'm not suggesting it," he added hastily—Lilah was reaching for the control pads. "Maybe on the way home."

Home. Jeff knew that Simon was talking about Confluence Center, but his own gaze turned to the side screens. Sol was there, one star among ten thousand. He had learned enough about the *Galileo* to make the display put a flashing cursor on it easily enough. But what would be the point? He would be no nearer home.

Macafee left his seat in front of the panel and walked over to a little open hatch at the side of the cramped room. "Come on, Jeff," he said.

Jeff went after him. As Macafee squeezed through he turned his head and said to Lilah, "Don't let *him* get his hands on the controls."

"Hey!" Billy complained, but Lilah smiled. After yesterday,

working the ship's controls with Jeff had at last taken away most of the tension between them.

Maybe she was forgetting what happened, Jeff thought, as he eeled his way round an awkward corner. He certainly hadn't. It was strange; before she spoke, the idea of spending the night with her hadn't occurred to him. Now he couldn't get it out of his head.

Macafee was high on the interior hull, where a tiny one-man ship only a quarter the size of the *Aurora*'s pinnace sat in a miniature dock. "Just checking one more time," he said as he opened the hatch and wriggled through. "Making sure this is ready to fly."

"It's too small." Jeff was peering in. "We'd never fit."

"We would, actually—all four if we had to." Macafee was noting switch settings. "But that's not the plan. When we get to the Ambartsumians, I hope to take a little solo ride. I assume you feel comfortable with the *Galileo*?"

"I think I could fly her anywhere."

"Well, don't get too keen." Macafee, satisfied, was emerging from the lock. "Don't leave without me."

"Where are you going?"

"Maybe nowhere. First, we have to get lucky." He didn't offer another comment until they were back in the control room of the *Galileo*, and then it was to Lilah. "We're almost at the first reef. See anything unusual?"

"Just the reef itself. Does that count?"

"Not what I had in mind. We're sounder hunting. You know the signs?"

"I think so."

"I sure do." It was burned into Jeff's brain. He jumped forward and pointed at the display. "Count them!"

Where three whirlpool smudges had blackened the veil of the Cloud, four now made big, dark holes in space. One of them was moving against the glowing curtain, growing faster than the ship's changing position could explain. At the same time as Jeff spoke, a faint but familiar *shreep-shreep-shreep* rang out from every radio-frequency communicator in the control room.

The other three turned to Macafee. This was the point where a rational captain turned the ship and ran. He stroked his beard and nodded in a satisfied way.

"Our lucky day. It's sooner than we had any right to hope." He moved to the controls, and the hum of the ship's drive went silent. "I'll be leaving now. If I'm not back in three hours, start up the drive and head for home."

"What are you going to do?" Lilah wailed after him as he entered the side hatch.

"You'll see." The hatch closed on his words. They stood silent and heard a lock cycling, then a little later the clang of spring bolts sounded through the whole vessel.

"Ship bolt separation," Lilah said. "I've heard it a hundred times. He's taking the pinnace."

"But where's he off to?" Billy had jumped to the port, while the others were watching the displays. "I see him! Oh, no. Look over here."

They crowded around the port, jostling for the best view. Looming in the center, unmistakable now and growing in size, was the once-seen, never-forgotten outline of a space sounder. At first Jeff thought it a look-alike for the one the *Aurora* had met by the Lizard Reef. A few more seconds of hard inspection, and he could see differences. This one was smaller and paler on its sides, with tendrils of a translucent luminous green rather than blue white.

The mouth, hardly more than a dark point at first sighting, was like an eight-sided cavern. Toward that pit, dwarfed by it and making no attempt at evasion, the pinnace of the *Galileo* glided onward.

"He doesn't have the drive on," Lilah groaned. "It's going to get him."

"It's all right." Jeff didn't know why Simon was doing this, but he was absolutely sure he was not watching a suicide. "If he goes inside, it's because he wants to. See, he has the manipulators out. He wouldn't do that without a reason."

Thin robot arms, designed to pick up and move objects in space, had deployed at the front of the pinnace. The little ship was moving, still with an inactive drive, right into the maw. It was visible for a few more seconds, then abruptly vanished. Space inside and around the sounder spangled with orange lights.

"Don't—he told us not to leave." Jeff was shouting at Lilah. She had left the port and was over by the control panel.

"The sounder!" she shouted back.

"It's still there," cried Billy. "It's not moving."

"Keep watching," Lilah said. "If it comes nearer, or if another one shows up—"

"We'll be out of here. Just hold it there." Jeff was crowding Billy at the port. The front of the sounder was changing, a new pattern in among the flickering lights. A blacker-than-black patch seemed to eat the space around it. "Get ready. I think something's coming out."

One more second, and he knew what it was. The pinnace was emerging, backing slowly out of the mouth.

"What's it holding?" Billy cried.

Jeff could see it too, a round object that glimmered in the grasp of the robot arm. It changed from moment to moment, and he could not quite make out what it was. The little pinnace eased clear of the sounder. It hung in space, and after a few more seconds a hatch opened. The suited figure of Simon Macafee appeared. He jetted toward the *Galileo*.

"What's he doing?" Lilah's finger was on the drive pad. She could see the screen, but the picture for her was not as sharp as the view from the port.

"He's abandoned the pinnace," Jeff said. "And the sounder is still there. It isn't moving."

"What should I do?"

"Nothing. Be ready to leave if he tells us to. He's coming back and boarding."

The sound of a lock cycling could be heard in the cabin. A few seconds later Simon Macafee came struggling through the hatch. It was an even tighter fit with the suit on, but his helmet was open and he was smiling.

"As nice and easy as you could wish. We have our insurance policy. Now we can go."

"Home?" Billy asked.

"Good heavens, no. Not after all our hard work. Make room for me." Simon nudged Lilah out of the way and made three quick stabs at the control panel. "There."

"We're going the wrong way." Jeff had his eyes still fixed on the sounder. "It's getting closer. The mouth is opening again."

He turned his head. Simon Macafee was taking no notice. Jeff stared out of the port at the approaching sounder. He was watching a dreadful slow-motion repeat of the *Aurora*'s encounter near the Lizard Reef, except that this time there was no Hooglich to produce a last-minute reprieve and escape. The mouth of the sounder did not slide away to one side and vanish. It opened, wider and wider. Inside he could see a whirlpool of night, slick and black as old oil. The *Galileo* slid smoothly into that gullet, leaving behind the friendly glow of the Messina Cloud. The great mouth closed. Outside the port Jeff saw nothing but darkness. He turned to face the others. Their faces were pale in the lights of the control room.

"What do we do now?"

"We wait for a few minutes." Simon Macafee settled himself comfortably on one of the control-room chairs. "It won't take long."

"Have we been eaten?" asked Billy. "Are we dead?"

"Not eaten, and certainly not dead. We are not going to die, either. We will be taken somewhere, very fast. I'm sorry I can't be more precise, but I haven't yet fathomed how the sounders decide where to go. Think of this as—what shall we call it?—a mystery tour."

Jeff had stronger words than that. He couldn't break down and scream, not with Billy and Lilah watching. But he wanted to.

Billy's mouth was trembling, and he seemed ready to cry. Lilah put her arm round him and glared at Simon Macafee. He regarded them both with genuine astonishment.

"We'll be all right, you know," he said. "We're perfectly safe."

"But we may never get home," Jeff said. "Sounders come and go in a way you can't predict."

"Normally that's true—unless you do something to make them predictable." Simon's expression changed from bewildered to apologetic. "Look, I'm sorry, and I ought to have explained more about what I was doing. I thought this would be an adventure for you, something you'd find exciting. This is old for me, I've done it dozens of times."

He moved to sit next to Billy. "We'll be going a long way. We are moving now, even though you don't feel anything. But the sounder will come right back to where we left the pinnace."

"How do you know?" Billy did not sound reassured.

"That's what I'm going to explain to you. Do you know what Cauthen starfires are?"

"They're a sort of jewel. Worth lots and lots."

"That's the way we think about them, particularly the people back Sol-side. There used to be a big trade in starfires, but that stopped when too many rakehells hunting them were lost. The starfires have a special meaning to the space sounders. I don't know if they make them, or if they just collect them, but the starfires are important. Some people claim that a starfire is a kind of sounder egg, something that forms part of the process of producing a new sounder. I don't agree, I think it's more complicated than that. But I do know that if you go inside a sounder and take out a starfire, the sounder may leave for a while, but it will always come back to where the starfire is."

"That's what it was holding!" Jeff exclaimed. "The thing in the robot arm of the pinnace—it was a starfire."

"Exactly. As I said, the starfire is our insurance policy. We'll take a ride in the sounder, but at the end of it we'll return to where we started."

"Where are we going?" Lilah asked.

"I have no idea. I wasn't being mysterious when I said that. Every time I've ridden a sounder it has flown me to a different place. It never takes long, though, so very soon you'll be able to see for yourselves."

"If it's that short, we can't be going anywhere very interesting." Billy was responding to Simon Macafee's confidence, and showed it by returning to his normal argumentative self.

"Wait and see, Billy Jexter. I don't know what you consider interesting, but I'm sure that *I'll* find it interesting. Anyway, we won't have to wait long before we know." Simon gestured to the port.

The awful, absolute darkness outside the *Galileo* was ending. The sounder's maw was opening again, slowly, stretching from a needle's eye to a gaping octagon. The light that entered looked fainter and whiter than the Cloud's glowing pink. It came from a striated circle in the sky that turned into a long ellipse as the sounder's mouth gaped wider.

"I can't see it properly," Billy complained. "Are we going outside?"

"We definitely are *not.*" Simon Macafee was craning forward. "If that's what I think it is, I don't want to leave the sounder and maybe find ourselves stranded out here. We would never get home."

"Out where?" But Jeff in a dizzying moment of understanding realized what they were looking at. He had seen pictures like that glowing oval in the sky, with its star clouds and spiraled arms. "That's the Galaxy! But it can't be—the Sun and the Messina Dust Cloud and everything else are all *inside* the Galaxy."

"Quite right." Macafee spoke in a faint, introspective voice. "Deep inside. I have never come so far before. We are outside the Galaxy, maybe two hundred thousand light-years out. The light you see is the combined brilliance of a hundred billion stars. I've known for a long time that the sounders have their own ways of moving through space-time, one that doesn't depend on the network nodes. I just didn't realize how far and how fast they can travel."

"Is it even *our* galaxy?" Lilah asked. "If we came so far, so fast, mightn't it be a completely different galaxy?"

She received a startled glance from Macafee. "That's a possibility I'm not sure I'm ready to deal with." He scanned the great disk of light beyond the port, as though seeking an identification label, an arrow stating SOL IS HERE. "We will certainly record an image and take it back with us. But since no one has ever seen our own galaxy from outside, I don't know what we will do with the picture. Most people will insist that anything we show them is a hoax."

"You'll have to hurry if you want an image." Jeff had noticed that the mouth of the sounder had finished its slow dilation, and was beginning an equally leisurely contraction. "It's closing."

"Two hundred thousand light-years," said Lilah. "And the journey didn't take longer than ten minutes. That means we were traveling at a speed of. . . ."

She shook her head and did not continue. Billy said, "But what's the point of coming all this way, if no one will believe us when we get back home?"

No one answered him. Simon Macafee was busy at the controls, making observations with every sensor that the *Galileo* possessed. Lilah was sitting, staring at nothing. Jeff was overwhelmed by his own thoughts. Before he left Kopal Manor, even the Asteroid Belt between Mars and Jupiter had seemed far away. Then the Messina Dust Cloud, twenty-seven light-years from Sol, had been unimaginably remote. And now. . . .

Now he was hovering high above the Galaxy, seeing it in

light that had started its way toward them two thousand centuries ago. Sol and the Cloud were no more than pinpricks of light, not even visible from this distance. In a couple of months, his horizon had changed from the cozy boundaries of the family estate, to a place where no human had ever been before.

Except that he was probably no longer there, high above the galactic plane. The mouth of the sounder had closed all the way, and outside the *Galileo* he could again see only stygian darkness.

Where were they now, he and Lilah and Billy and Simon Macafee? Were they anywhere at all, in terms that humans could understand? Or did the sounder in its wanderings take them outside the universe itself, to some other plane of existence? Even Simon Macafee admitted that there were many things about the sounders that he did not understand—and he knew far more than anyone else.

"Well, here we are," Simon said cheerfully, interrupting Jeff's thoughts. "I said you could think of this as a mystery trip, but it turned out to be more of a mystery than I expected."

The mouth of the sounder was steadily dilating. Beyond it, no more than a kilometer away, Jeff saw the pinnace hovering in space.

"We ought to say thanks for the ride," Simon went on. "Unfortunately, I don't know how to talk to a sounder, though I've recorded their radio calls hundreds of times. They are all different, and I'm sure they are messages. But I'm nowhere near deciphering them. Some day." The *Galileo* had been creeping forward, and now it was clear of the wide mouth and approaching the waiting pinnace. "Here we are. Let me pop over there and return the starfire. Then we'll head for home. I hope it was worth it for you after all. Any questions, before I go?"

"Yes." Lilah spoke for the first time since they had started the return journey. "I told Muv that you couldn't take us very far in one day, and I said there was nothing dangerous within one day's ride of the Cloud. She is going to ask where we went. What do you think I should tell her?"

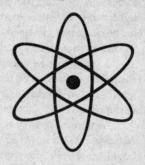

CHAPTER SIXTEEN

JEFF never did find out what Lilah told her mother about their adventure with Simon Macafee. Connie Cheever was waiting for the *Galileo* as it docked at Confluence Center, and her grim expression had her daughter flinching in advance. Lilah was expecting the worst, though she didn't know for what. As for Simon Macafee, he gave the situation one look and retreated without a word into the lock.

Connie took just enough notice of her daughter and Billy Jexter to wave them away to the Confluence Center interior. As soon as they were gone she spoke to Jeff.

"The *Dreadnought* is here. It took a faster and riskier path than I expected through the Cloud's spaceways, and we picked up its approach just half an hour ago. The ship is docking now. In a few minutes I have to go for a first meeting with their commander, but I had to talk to you first. Do you know a Space Navy ensign called Myron Lazenby?"

"He's my cousin!"

"I thought so. I've never heard you say the name, but Hooglich recognized it. He told me a number of things about you and Myron. What about Mohammad Duval, have you heard of him?"

"Never."

"Hooglich and Russo say he's bad news. A stooge for Giles Lazenby, according to them."

"Giles Lazenby is my uncle." Just saying the name gave Jeff's insides a lurch. "He's Myron's father."

"I know."

"Why are you asking about them?"

"Because Myron Lazenby and Mohammad Duval are listed on the manifest as crew of the *Dreadnought*. Mohammad Duval is the captain, Myron Lazenby is a new recruit on his first assignment. In a few minutes they will be inside Confluence Center. Confluence starts tonight—I moved up the schedule, but I never dreamed the *Dreadnought* might get here before we started. Here's my question. Do you want to be the person responsible for showing Myron around Confluence Center and taking him to Confluence? I realize that you hardly know your way around, but he is your cousin. It would be natural for you to be in charge of him, especially when the Confluence games begin. On the other hand, I can see reasons why you might not want to do it."

"I'd rather not." Jeff spoke instinctively and at once, without analyzing his feelings.

Connie Cheever stared at him. "Right. I can understand that. I'll make other arrangements. Now I have to get to my meeting with Captain Duval."

She turned and left, before Jeff had a chance to explain. But would he have explained, even if she had given him a chance? The truth was not very flattering. He couldn't see himself reciting to Connie Cheever the whole multiyear history of interactions with his cousin, Myron outperforming Jeff in every way and at every step. And Confluence, according to Billy, involved large numbers of games, just the sort of environment where Myron would shine and Jeff would sink. If he were in charge of Myron, the dreary pattern of losses would be repeated over and over.

All that, and more, had been wrapped up in his terse "I'd rather not" to Connie Cheever. She said she understood, but she didn't. Jeff was still standing, filled with feelings of his own inadequacy, when Simon Macafee emerged from the dock.

"Not pleased?" said Simon.

It took a moment to realize that Simon was referring not to Jeff's own mood, but to Connie Cheever's reaction to where they had been and what they had done.

"She's not pleased, but it had nothing to do with us and the trip inside the sounder. We didn't have a chance to say a word about that. The Space Navy ship is here. It arrived early."

"Ah." Macafee's eyes, usually remote and abstracted, came into sharp focus on Jeff. "Are they making threats?"

"No. They only just got here."

"Give them time."

"You think they came to cause trouble?" Jeff followed Macafee, who was moving away past the bare exterior docks of Confluence Center.

"Why else?" Macafee paused, and the strange eyes turned again on Jeff. "The other question is, Why? I don't mean I can't think of a reason why the Space Navy might cause trouble, I just don't know which reason to choose. Sol-side misunderstands the Cloud in so many ways."

"I know." Jeff thought back to his own fears, before he left Earth. "Did you know that on Earth they call the Cloud Cyborg Territory? Before I got here, I imagined that you were all cyborgs."

"Why would we be?"

"No one told me that. I thought the Cloud was producing some sort of superwarrior. I saw you as a kind of horrible mixture, human and machine."

"You weren't alone. I've heard that idea before. It's the way the Sol-side government likes to paint us. Come on." They had reached an unlit shaft. Macafee took two paces forward and dropped out of sight.

Jeff stood for a few seconds on the edge, peering down into darkness. It could be a fatal drop. Finally he repeated to himself, "Jefferson Kopal is a coward. He knows it, and if he doesn't do something about it soon, so will everyone else," and stepped out into space. There was a terrifying and stomach-turning interval of free fall, in which he sensed the sides of the shaft flying past him at increasing speed. Then at last he was slowing, for no reason. A few more seconds, and he was deposited in a feather-soft landing on a floor of white tiles.

"Slanting opinion a certain way by choice of words has a special name," Macafee went on, as though nothing had happened since his last remark to Jeff. "It's called propaganda. The word started out with a religious meaning, but now it's used differently. Propaganda means speeches and handouts and publicity designed to give one group a distorted idea of another. If you are going to fight somebody, or invade them, or even exterminate them, it helps a lot if your soldiers believe the other group is made up of monsters, or creatures less than human. Back Sol-side you had propaganda about the Cloud, and a big part of it was talk of cyborgs."

They had reached a chamber with a dozen exits, some of them leading to corridors, others to stairways. Macafee walked to a bench at the side of the room and sat down. He gestured to Jeff to join him.

"If Lilah and Billy are heading straight for Level One, they'll come through here. You and I took a shortcut with a little help from an Anadem field. While we're waiting, I want to walk you through a mental exercise and set your mind at rest. Let's agree that a cyborg is some mixture of a human and a machine. And let's ask how much machine, and how much human, you would want in a perfect soldier. We'll start first with pure human and pure machine, then look at mixtures. Can you list the properties or abilities that you think would be important for a soldier operating in space?"

Ten minutes ago, Jeff had been telling himself how much he hated games. He meant it, but there was one kind of game that he didn't hate at all: He loved any challenge that depended not on strength or physical coordination, but on thought alone. Apparently Simon Macafee was the same.

So. Properties and abilities useful for space warriors. The first candidate that came to mind was one that Jeff had experienced for himself, recently and painfully.

"You need an ability to withstand high accelerations."

"That's a fine start. What would you say humans can tolerate?"

"I'm not sure. Maybe ten or twelve Gs, but that's only for a short burst. Five Gs?"

"Fair enough. But you couldn't take that for long, either, a few days of it would kill you. A machine can easily be built to operate for as long as you want at a hundred Gs—a thousand Gs, too, if you ever needed it. Score one for machines. What else?"

"Perception. The ability to observe your surroundings."

"That's good. Do you know the human limits?"

"We see from violet light to red light."

"That's roughly from 0.4 to 0.7 micrometers' wavelength. Not very much, less than a factor of two in range. I can build a machine that 'sees' everything from hard X rays to long radio waves, a billion times as big a range as we have, and in at least as much detail as we see. Machines win again. What else?"

"Life support." Jeff could see where Simon Macafee was heading, but he didn't mind. This was the sort of talk he loved and almost never got—a discussion like this with Myron or anyone else at Kopal Manor was unthinkable.

Macafee nodded. "Another good one. Let's consider it in

pieces. A human can survive long-term in a pressure range from about one-third of an Earth atmosphere to a couple of atmospheres—provided we have the right gases, which in practice means oxygen plus something inert. A machine can operate in anything from hard vacuum to a thousand atmospheres or more, and it can tolerate any gas mix that doesn't dissolve it. We need food and water, too. A machine needs a power source, that's all. We have a fixed operating rate. Even when we are asleep, we use almost as much energy as when we are awake. We can't power down, or switch ourselves off for a few months. A machine can do both of those. We feel pain, and sometimes that hinders our ability to function. Try thinking clearly with a broken arm. A machine has self-preservation sensors, but damage does not interfere with its logic functions.

"We also come in standard sizes. There are adult humans who mass as little as fifteen kilos, or as much as five hundred, but I don't think either limit would be my choice for a warrior. A machine can be as small or as large as you choose, depending on needs. Think of the nannies, too small to see but still regular machines. A human is also made of fixed materials—not very strong ones. A machine can be made of anything, steel or carbon filaments or condensed matter."

Lilah and Billy had entered the room and stood listening. Simon Macafee went on talking as though he did not see them. Jeff suspected that he didn't. Macafee was enjoying himself—and so was Jeff.

"You might think you can do better by combining human and machine into a cyborg," Simon went on. "You can't. You introduce other problems. I could give you an artificial arm, able to lift tons. But the rest of your body is still flesh and bone. Try to exert all the force your arm can produce, and you'll tear yourself apart. The same problem arises if I speed up your reaction times. You'll rip your muscles if you try to move too fast. However you look at it, a cyborg makes no sense—except for the special form of cyborg where the nannies enter a human to repair it."

"You're leaving something out." Simon Macafee might be a legend in the Cloud, but Jeff was not self-conscious when he had something to say. "What about self-repair? We can do that. The Logans can't."

"True. But only because it's not the economical way to do things. Why carry a whole repair factory around with you, when you can leave it in one central place and go there only when you happen to need it? Humans are more like snails than we like to think. They carry their house around on their backs. We carry around every useless thing that four billion years of evolution has dumped onto us, hair and nails and teeth. How long since you had to use your claws and fangs to defend yourself? I know of only one area where we are superior to machines: We are still more flexible in what we can do, and more adaptable—but the Logans come closer to us every year."

"I don't think that's the only thing humans do more effectively than machines," said Jeff, and then at once wished he had kept his mouth shut.

"You don't?" Simon Macafee sniffed skeptically. "Can you name another?"

"Well, we are better"—Jeff wasn't sure how to phrase this—"we are more efficient at replication. Machines are not self-replicating."

"What's *replication?*" Billy asked. "Does that mean breathing?"

"You're thinking of *respiration*," Macafee said. "Replication means making copies."

"Huh? You mean like making copies of things with a copying machine?"

"No, Billy. I mean like *breeding*."

"Which means having children," Lilah added. She gave Jeff an unreadable sideways glance of bright blue eyes. "Rely on an Earthling to come up with *that* as his prize example."

"And it's not true," Macafee said. "First of all, many animals reproduce far more easily than humans. Second, the nannies replicate themselves until their job is done. And if you're thinking of speed of replication, a nanny or a bacterium can produce a working copy of itself in twenty minutes. Last time I studied the subject, a human took at least nine months to make. And when you're all done, a baby can't look after itself for many years." He stood up. "I'll be interested in another example if you can think of one. But I'll be amazed if you can find any case where a cyborg human/machine combination is better than a machine, in a combat situation. It's just Sol propaganda."

Macafee nodded at the others, signaling that the discussion was over. He wandered off toward one of the exits.

Billy said to Lilah, "What did you mean when you said, rely on an *Earthling* to come up with that as his example? What do people from Earth do that's different from us?"

"We-e-ell. . . ."

Jeff went after Simon Macafee. He didn't mind Billy putting Lilah on the spot, but he wasn't sure he'd like her answer.

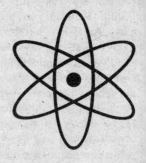

CHAPTER SEVENTEEN

APPARENTLY Confluence was a big deal, more than Jeff had realized. By tradition, it was held in the oldest part of Confluence Center, the original free-space wheel built by the first explorers and merchants of the Messina Dust Cloud for their annual rendezvous, halfway through the harvest season for stable transuranics. That whole portion of the Center was dedicated once a year to the Confluence celebration. The Logans, working around the clock, restored everything to its primitive original condition. The Anadem field in that part of the structure was turned off, and a centrifugal rotation field used in its place. The effective gravity even on the outer rim was a bit low by Earth standards, maybe a quarter of a G, but it was enough to be comfortable.

Jeff stood on the floor of the cylinder, staring around him. The original Confluence Center might be described as small by its present inhabitants, but he thought it was enormous. The length of the cylinder was at least fifty meters. The polished floor curved smoothly away from him to right and left, continuing in a great circular arc until it met seventy meters above his head. There were airlocks at the center of both flat cylinder ends, unused now but once the docking sites from which the crews of the Cloud harvesters, dressed in their finest uniforms, had entered Confluence Center. The whole interior was lit by light fixtures that ran the length of the cylinder's central axis. Looking up and beyond them, Jeff could see the heads of other people halfway around the great room. They seemed to be standing on the ceiling.

Jeff was flanked by an array of ancient autochefs, of a design unused in a century. The Logans had pulled the design from the central data banks of Confluence Center and faithfully reproduced it. Jeff wondered if any human still remembered how to program the old machines. He wouldn't know where to begin.

It was early in the first evening of Confluence. Jeff had been here for twenty minutes, apparently studying the autochefs. In fact, he was doing two things: remaining inconspicuous, and at the same time keeping his eyes open for Myron. He wasn't sure what he would say to his cousin when he met him— or what Myron would say in return—but he knew that somehow, somewhere, during Confluence the two of them were bound to meet. He wanted to follow his mother's advice to tackle an unpleasant task as soon as possible, and get it over with.

Easier said than done. Jeff caught sight of a tall blond-haired figure in a uniform of gleaming white, halfway around the curve of the cylinder. It was Myron, picture-perfect as always, standing at the edge of the dance floor. By his side, just as blond and in an off-the-shoulder dress of electric blue and a sequined white scarf, was Lilah.

They were not dancing. The music would begin in an hour or two. Then the dancers—Jeff certainly not among their number—would show off their paces.

Jeff was surprised to see the pair, at the same time as he told himself he ought not to be. Myron had the knack; he had always had it ever since he and Jeff became teenagers. He picked up girls as easily as breathing. Why wouldn't it work as well here as on Earth, and why should Lilah be different from anyone else?

Jeff wanted to get his meeting with Myron out of the way, but Lilah's presence complicated things. She would see how clumsy and inept he became whenever Myron was around. As he watched, his cousin took Lilah by the elbow with an easy familiarity and led her farther away around the cylinder.

Should he follow them? Myron wouldn't want him to. Maybe Lilah wouldn't, either. But he had to meet Myron sooner or later. He couldn't make up his mind. It was a relief to feel a tug on his sleeve and turn to find Billy Jexter at his side.

"You're not interested in *that*, are you?" Billy said. He had abandoned his usual uniform for a short-sleeved shirt and matching red shorts. He was barefoot.

"In what?" Billy's scornful gesture to the left could have been at Myron, Lilah, or the two of them together.

"In *dancing*. That's what they do over there, you know."

"I'm a terrible dancer." That was true enough, even if there were other reasons why Jeff did not want to go toward the dance floor.

"I thought you would be." Billy turned the other way. "Want to go to the Outer Loop, then, where the good stuff is?"

"I'm not sure we have the same ideas on good stuff. What's on the Outer Loop?"

"The *games*," Billy said scornfully. "Don't you know any-thing? Come on, they'll be starting any minute."

He was already moving to the right, along the upward curve of the cylinder. Games, or a meeting with Myron while Lilah looked on? The lesser of two evils. Jeff followed Billy, twenty meters along the polished floor and then down a tight spiral staircase to a lower level. What he found at the bottom of the stairs was nothing like his idea of a games area.

The games he knew came in two varieties. There were the athletic kind, contests depending on physical dexterity and coordination and strength, like archery, polo, tennis, running, football, cycling, skating, and swimming. He hadn't expected to find those in the space-limited environment of Confluence Center. Just as well, since he had no great talent for any of them.

Then there were the board games of chance and skill, backgammon and bridge and chess and poker and go. Jeff was pretty good at those, and he found them pleasant enough for a few hours of entertainment. The trouble was, he didn't care enough about the result. He had never developed the obsession and passion of a real chess or backgammon enthusiast. For him, no game competed with the delight of understanding some-thing in the real world, anything from light to lightning to lightning bugs.

What he saw on the floor of the Outer Loop didn't fit ei-ther of the game types that he knew. The annular region be-tween curved floor and curved ceiling was filled with a maze of ropes and ladders and chutes and wide tubes. A couple of dozen people were climbing around the tangle, ranging in age from children younger than Billy to adults you might think too old for games. Leaning against the wall, a dozen paces from the staircase that Jeff had descended, Simon Macafee stood gazing thoughtfully at all the activity.

"You're a bit early," he said, as they went toward him. "They're still setting up."

"Setting up for what?" Jeff couldn't make sense of what he was seeing.

"For the first game," Billy said, and ran off to swarm up a rope like a monkey in party clothes.

"One which I don't think will interest you," Macafee said to Jeff. "They always start with the youngsters. The hope is that they'll be worn out and go to sleep, and then the serious games can begin."

"But what are you doing here?" It was none of Jeff's business, but his mental image of Simon Macafee did not include a taste for party games.

"Ah. You think you spot a ringer? You are quite right. I am not here to play, or even to watch." Simon nodded at the complicated web that connected floor and ceiling. "The Center was set up this way in the early days, when there was no alternative to cylinder rotation to produce a field. If you wanted to dance on the Inner Loop—and people did—you had to spin the cylinder. I've been wondering if we could use an Anadem field instead, and still keep the spirit of the games intact. What do you think? Would I be considered a heretic if I proposed changes?"

"I don't know." Jeff looked again at the mess in front of him. "I don't see anything like the games I know."

"The games of Earth? You won't find them here. I must say, I don't think that's much of a loss. They appeal to me no more than these do." While Jeff was pondering that curious comment, Simon went on, "You wouldn't recognize these games, because they are designed to be played in a low-G environment. Some of them depend on the fact that we are rotating, so things that you throw don't move in the usual way. The centrifugal force is highest near the floor, and zero on the central axis of the cylinder. That makes things do this."

He took a hoop of soft rubber from a line of them hanging on the wall, and threw it. Instead of following a straight line or falling toward the floor, the hoop floated slowly across the open space in a strange, curving path.

"Coriolis effects," Simon said. "Have you heard of Coriolis?"

"Yes. It's a fictitious force that appears in a rotating reference frame." Jeff had read about Coriolis forces, and he even had an idea how to calculate the effects. But he had never met them in practice.

"The teaching texts *say* it's fictitious, and not a real force." Simon handed a ring to Jeff. "But how can that be, when the force actually makes the path curve? Sometime—this isn't the place for it—you and I can talk about reference frames, and how with the right way of thinking about them one force is just as real as another. Try it for yourself. Throw the ring and try to hang it on the yellow spike on the far wall. You'll find it's easier if you spin it as you throw."

This sort of game was exactly the kind of exercise that Jeff was bad at. The only good thing was that there was no trembling in his hands. They usually shook when he tried something that needed physical skill, and as a result he never succeeded. Now his hands were perfectly steady. He threw the ring toward the spike, and watched it curve far out of line and hit the wall meters away. Apparently, steady hands were not enough.

"Hopeless," he said.

"Of course. It was your first shot. Are you the sort of person who has to get something right the first time, otherwise it's not worth doing? I count myself lucky if I get what I want the thousandth time I try. Do you know how many failures I had, before I found the theory that led to the Anadem field? Try again."

It was difficult to refuse. As Jeff threw again and again and achieved miss after hopeless miss he puzzled over why Simon Macafee showed so much interest in him. He found Simon and everything that the man had to say fascinating, but he couldn't imagine that the same was true the other way around. Was it the novelty of a person from Earth? He had become used to the idea that he, Hooglich, and Russo were sort of freaks to people at Confluence Center, just because of how they had come there. But Simon Macafee didn't seem the type to be interested in a freak show.

"All right." Simon handed Jeff a final ring. "You're on your own now. Remember, success is ninety-nine percent the refusal to accept failure."

Jeff saw, to his amazement, that the last two rings he had floated across the room were settling onto the yellow spike. He threw the third one, and it went wide by inches.

"You'll notice that two examples isn't enough to establish a general case," Simon added. "You'll still have misses. I have to go and meet with Administrator Cheever—I don't want to, but Connie always gets her way. But keep trying. You may want to enter the competition when the time comes."

Jeff knew he wouldn't. His horse-jumping disaster on Earth had provided enough competition to last his whole life. Even so, he went on doggedly throwing and retrieving rings until he could capture them on the yellow spike nine times out of ten. In the meantime, the Outer Loop became steadily busier. The game going on around Jeff was a kind of three-dimensional obstacle race, in which judgment and flexibility were apparently more important than strength. He saw one competitor, red-faced and bent double, stuck upside down in a narrow tube with only his head poking out. He noticed, with no great feeling of sympathy, that it was Billy Jexter. Billy's vocabulary for cursing would have done credit to someone much older.

Finally, other ring-throwers began to invade Jeff's territory. To them he was apparently not a freak, but merely another competitor. The air became filled with flying hoops.

He gave up and admitted the truth. Sure, he wanted to prove himself in Simon Macafee's eyes, by showing that he could perform this event as well as anyone. But more important, he was avoiding Myron and Lilah.

He passed the handful of rings he was holding to the girl next to him, who grabbed them eagerly, and set out for the spiral stairs that led to the Inner Loop. The higher level had filled up, too. Now the dance floor held scores of couples. He stood well back and looked them over. If Myron and Lilah were dancing, that would give him a good reason not to butt in on them.

No such luck. Even on a crowded floor he would have picked up those two, with their matching blond heads and smart outfits. There was no sign of them.

He walked toward the out-of-date autochefs, which were now going full blast. Hundreds of people sat eating at the long lines of tables. Hooglich was there, in the middle of a crowd of jinners and facing a pile of food big enough to show how she managed to remain so fat. She gestured to Jeff to join them.

"Come eat, Brother Kopal," she said when he reached the table. "You look a bit thin and peaky."

"Later. Where's Russo?"

Instead of replying, Hooglich pointed to the line of autochefs. The machine at the end was not being used. The front was wide open and a skinny backside and pair of jean-clad legs stuck out of the open door.

"What's he doing?" Jeff asked. "Cooking himself?"

"Could be. Once a jinner, always a jinner. There was something a little bit wrong with that one, and Russo says he's old enough to *remember* how it works. Don't worry about him."

"Does he really have any idea how to fix it?"

"Who knows? He won't let a Logan in to help him. He's happier doing that than anything. By the time he's done, it probably won't work at all."

"Have you seen Lilah?"

"Not for the past hour. She was dancing for a while with a blond guy." Hooglich gave Jeff a shrewd glance. "Your cousin, right?"

"Yes."

"They were over here, eating a little. And then off they went, thataway. Toward the private rooms."

"I didn't know there were private rooms. Where are they?"

"You go all the way to the end of the cylinder. You'll see these little doors around the perimeter. They take you through, each one to a different room." Hooglich pursed her lips, and her broad forehead wrinkled. "You know, Brother Kopal, I'm not sure I'm right to tell you this. Those rooms are supposed to be private, if you know what I mean."

"Is there a way to tell which ones are occupied?"

"Sure. You'll see an IN USE sign on the doors. If you see that, just be sure you don't go in and find what you might not want to find."

"I understand. Thanks, Hooglich."

Jeff headed for the great end wall of the cylinder. She was acting in his best interests, but what she said sure didn't make him feel any better. His stomach was churning in the old familiar way. Until Hooglich spoke, he'd had his mind on a meeting with Myron. Now he was thinking of Myron with Lilah, and that was just as upsetting.

He came to the first of the doors. Sure enough, it had an IN USE sign glowing above it. After a moment's hesitation, Jeff walked on around the curve of the cylinder. The second door showed IN USE; so did the third. Was there any point at all to what he was doing? Any room that was occupied was surely going to have a sign, saying that the people inside were not to be disturbed. He could barge in, but if he did, chances were it would not be Myron and Lilah that he was interrupting.

At last. A door without the glowing sign. He opened it and entered the room. It was empty. He took a quick look around and saw that it was furnished with a bathroom, autochef and serving table, chairs, table, and bed. If this was typical, someone could stay here as long as they liked—for the whole of the three days of Confluence, if they felt like it.

Jeff went back outside and continued his walk around the curve of the cylinder. He passed four more doors, all marked IN

USE. The fifth one didn't have the sign. Jeff opened the door casually and went in, convinced that he would find another empty room.

Myron was sitting at the table, his chin resting on his fists. As Jeff entered, his cousin stood up so abruptly that the chair he had been sitting on crashed to the floor behind him.

"Well. If it isn't Jefferson Kopal, the one and only." Myron's face was unusually pale and his uniform hung loose at the neck. "I wondered when you would crawl out of the woodwork."

"Hi." Jeff looked all around the room as he spoke. He could see no sign of Lilah, but the sequined scarf was on the floor inside the open bathroom door. "I was looking for you."

He sounded inane, and knew it. Myron gave a short, brittle laugh.

"After what you did, I'm amazed you have the nerve to show your face."

"I did nothing wrong."

"Oh, sure. You only failed to keep a lookout, so the *Aurora* was crippled. And then when you had the chance of an honorable escape with Captain Dufferin and the rest of the officers, you refused to go."

"That's not true. I was injured. I didn't even know that Captain Dufferin had left until days afterwards."

"That's not what I heard—and it's not what the fleet believes. I've put up with a lot of criticism the last few weeks, because of your slovenly behavior and cowardice. You are a blot on the family honor and a disgrace to the navy. You deserve a court-martial."

Myron had been pale, but now his cheeks were turning rosy. Jeff had seen the signs before—his cousin was becoming angry. When Myron was angry, he was also violent.

"Look, Myron, I'm sorry if I've caused you trouble. But if you'll just listen and let me explain exactly what happened when the *Aurora* met the sounder, you'll understand I'm not to blame.

You don't have to take my word for this. Hooglich and Russo will back me up."

"Sure. The word of two jinners—and two traitors. I'm supposed to believe them?"

"Not just them. People here will confirm it. Lilah can confirm it." Jeff looked again around the room. There was nowhere she could be hiding. "I thought she was with you. Where is she?"

"Ah, yes, Lilah." Myron was studying Jeff's face as he spoke. He turned, picked up his chair, and casually sat down on it. "You're quite right, little Lilah was here."

"But she's not here now."

"No. When we were done, I sent her away." Myron crossed his arms. "You see, cousin, your Lilah thinks she's quite the sexpot. Maybe she is—for a hick settlement out at the edge of civilization. For all I know, you were impressed with her performance, too. I can tell you, though, she wasn't a bit impressed with you. After we'd danced a little, she got excited and we came here. It was her idea. She'd been rubbing herself up against me all the time we were dancing."

"You're lying!"

"Be careful, Cousin. No one calls me a liar and gets away with it. I'll make an allowance, just this once. Anyway, it was hardly worth coming here with her. She ran through her full repertoire in about fifteen minutes. She showed me everything she had, and a pathetic performance it was. Why, even when I told her that she'd had all she was getting, she was begging me to let her stay and give her another chance to—"

Jeff didn't remember jumping. The first thing he knew was that Myron's chair had gone over backward, and his cousin was underneath him on the floor. He had his hands around Myron's throat.

Before he could exert real force, his cousin brought his folded arms wide apart and broke Jeff's grip. They both rolled over and up to face each other.

"You scrawny, knock-kneed wimp." Myron's whole face

was bloodred. His hands were at his neck, rubbing where Jeff's fingers had dug in. "That does it. What did you think you were doing, protecting the sacred honor of your little tart? I'm going to smash you to pieces. Don't forget, you started it—and I doubt if a snot brain like you will have the sense to deny that if somebody asks."

He was advancing, careful to keep himself between Jeff and the door. Jeff retreated. He knew his cousin. When Myron was in this mood, the best you could hope for was someone coming along before you were hurt too badly.

Myron jumped forward. Jeff, surprising himself with his speed, moved to one side and straight-armed his cousin in the chest. Myron grunted, more with surprise than pain, and fell back a pace.

"Rather box than wrestle, eh? Well, I can live with that. You never landed a punch on me in ten years of trying—and you'll bleed here just as well as you did on Earth. Cover your nose, Jeff!"

As Myron shouted the warning he threw a thundering right-hand punch—at Jeff's middle. If it had connected, Jeff would have been on the floor, unable to breathe. But the punch seemed to take a strangely long time to arrive. Jeff could put his hand out, intercept the fist with his open palm, and bat it away. Myron, following through, hit empty air and almost overbalanced.

His head was a perfect target. Jeff struck out at the exposed right temple—and pulled his punch at the last moment. He hit the side of the head, but too lightly to do any damage.

Myron grunted and stepped back. "Been taking lessons, have you? It won't do you any good. I'm going to see the color of your blood—and I bet it's yellow."

He came in again, more carefully this time, and aimed punch after punch at Jeff's head and body. Not one of them hit. Jeff seemed to have all the time in the world. He could slip under the blows, or take them harmlessly on his open hands and forearms, or even dance away from them completely.

After forty or fifty vain tries, Myron was panting and wheezing. He stopped, put his left hand to his chest, and shook his head.

"I don't know what's happening, but for some reason I can't hit you. And you haven't managed to land a good one on me. How about we call it evens and leave it at that? Say it's a draw, then we can go and get something to eat."

He held his open right hand toward Jeff, ready to shake.

Jeff held out his own hand. "I'll be glad to. I didn't want to fight you in the first—"

He didn't finish. While he was off guard, Myron swung his left fist and punched him hard on the cheekbone, just under his right eye.

It wasn't a knockout, but it was close. Jeff didn't have any feeling of falling, but the next thing he knew he was on his back on the floor, staring up at Myron's gloating face.

"Try that for evens, snot brain. That's fighting, you see, Space Navy style. Winning isn't the *main* thing, it's the *only* thing. And if you think you hurt now, wait a few days. The bunch of coots who run this place are too stupid to give in and hand over the Anadem field and whatever else we want. So we're going to squeeze out every last thing that's worth having, and then you're going to eat fire. The main fleet will arrive, and after we've sucked you dry we'll melt the lot of you to slag. Don't think I'll be sorry to see it happen, either. Here's a little something else to remember me by."

Jeff saw it coming, but he was too winded to save himself. Myron's boot thumped into his left side at the bottom of the rib cage. Every organ inside him burst or ripped out of position. He could not bite back his cry of pain.

Myron bent low, so his face was only a couple of inches from Jeff's. "Hurts, does it? Good. Get your fancy bitch to kiss it better. And here's something else for you to think about while she's at it: I enjoyed doing this a lot more than I enjoyed doing her."

He straightened. Jeff heard the clump of boots, then the sound of the door closing. His attempt to sit up produced an intolerable stab of pain in his side. He lay with his eyes closed, praying for it to become less.

It had to become less. There was something that he must do, soon, no matter how much he hurt.

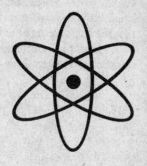

CHAPTER EIGHTEEN

THE door opened again and Jeff shuddered. If Myron was coming back to give him another kick in the ribs, that would be the end.

He heard a gasp, then the rustle of fabric. He looked up. Lilah was bending over him, her eyes wide.

"What happened to your face? And here."

"Don't touch that!"

She had been reaching out toward his injured side. She pulled her hand away.

"What happened to you?"

"It doesn't matter. Brace yourself and hold out your hand."
Jeff gritted his teeth. He reached out his right arm, took Lilah's
hand in his, and slowly raised himself until he was sitting upright. The effort made his head swim.

"I have to stand up and walk. You stand first and give me
something to hold on to. I've got to get to your mother and talk
to her. It's really urgent."

Slowly, favoring his left side and putting no weight on his
left leg, Jeff pulled himself all the way to his feet. In a stronger
field it would have been quite impossible. As it was, when he
was erect he stood swaying for a few moments before he dared
to think of moving again. With Lilah's help he edged his way to
the wall and leaned against it. After a few more moments he
waved her away and stood without assistance.

"We have to get you to a medical facility," Lilah said.
"Lean on the wall and wait there for a moment." She moved behind Jeff and went into the bathroom. The twenty or thirty
seconds that she was gone felt like an hour. When she came out
she was holding her white scarf. She showed it to him as she
threw it around her shoulders. "I was dreading the idea of coming back for this. Lucky I did, though. Can you walk? I know
where the nearest med unit is."

Jeff had taken a small, tentative step forward. It hurt less
than he had feared, but more than enough to keep his attention.
"I can walk if we go slowly. But not to the med unit. I have to
talk to your mother. I have to."

"Treatment first, then you talk to anyone you like."

"No." Jeff halted, resisting her attempt to move him
along. "We see your mother before we worry about me. This is
really important, Lilah. You don't know Myron the way I do.
When he's mad, it's like he's crazy. He doesn't realize what he's
saying. He speaks without thinking, and sometimes he says too
much."

"What *did* he say? Surely it wasn't all that important." But
Lilah was not really arguing. She had given him her arm to

lean on, and he limped along at her side. He hardly knew where he was going because his right eye had swollen until it was closed, but the path they were taking didn't feel right.

"Is this the way to your mother?"

"Sort of. I assume you'd prefer that not too many people see you, the way you are. So we're going to stay in the cylinder end. And in a little while we'll be at a place where we can meet Mother."

"Where is that?" Jeff had his suspicions.

"At the medical center. Don't give me an argument, Jeff. This is the best way to do it. I called Muv when I picked up my scarf and said we'd be going to the med center. She'll meet us there."

Jeff was beyond arguing. The real question was, How much longer could he walk before his insides fell out? Every step made him wince. "Do you know what Simon Macafee said? He said your mother always gets her way. You're just as bad." He stopped his staggering walk. "What's this?"

A machine like the cutout of a giant spider was scuttling toward them. It was flat, six or seven feet long, and no more than six inches high.

"A Logan. Mother's idea, when I told her you were in pain. You can relax. No, don't fight it!"

The machine was closing in on Jeff. He was afraid that it was going to touch his side, and he took a step back. The machine beeped, chirped, and halted. It extended a long, orange tentacle and touched his right wrist. There was a soft hiss. A feeling of coldness ran up his arm and his body went rigid. He knew that he was going to fall.

A dozen thin arms reached out from the Logan, lifted him, and placed him gently on top of the flat plane of its body. He could move his head, but he had neither feeling nor control below the neck.

"Lilah, don't let it put me to sleep!"

"All right. Do you have any problem with that?"

The question made no sense to Jeff, until he heard the

Logan reply, in a clear and precise voice, "Not initially. We may want to change our mind about that after full diagnosis. My sensors are performing an evaluation now. So far we have merely used a painkiller and movement inhibitor to prevent further trauma."

They had moved while the Logan was talking, much faster than Jeff could have walked. He heard a new sound from in front, a high-pitched whirring. Craning his neck up as far as it would go, he saw—blearily, with his left eye only—a door sliding open. In the room beyond, Connie Cheever and Simon Macafee were waiting.

"Lilah," Connie said, "this had better be serious. If you dragged me here for something minor, you're hash." She turned to the Logan. "Preliminary evaluation?"

"Layman terms?"

"Certainly."

"Evaluation is close to complete." The Logan extruded six pencil-thin legs that brought Jeff to the height of a normal bed. "There is significant tissue damage between the eleventh and twelfth ribs on the left side. The eleventh rib has a greenstick fracture. The pleurae are undamaged. In the head there is severe bruising below the right eye, but the cheekbone and orbit are intact."

"Prognosis?"

"Minimal nanny service will produce total functional restoration within forty-eight hours. Suitable nannies have been defined and will be brought here in the next few minutes."

"Hmm." Connie eyed her daughter. "Completely better in a couple of days. Sounds to me as if maybe someone overreacted when they told me I had to get here at once."

"I don't think so. Jeff sounded just like Dad, before the loss of Pezam Station."

It meant nothing to Jeff, but it must have to Connie. "My God," she said, and that was all.

Jeff took his chance. "Lilah wasn't the one who made you come and talk to me. I was. I insisted."

"Why? Did you think you were dying?"

"I felt as though I was, but that's not why. My cousin, Myron. Did you meet him?"

"Briefly."

"He and I had a fight. He did this to me, but that's not the point. When he loses his self-control, he'll blab out all sorts of vicious things. At the end, just before he kicked my ribs in, he said something awful. First the Space Navy and Sol-side will take everything they want from Confluence Center, the Anadem field and anything else. Then they will destroy you. You're going to eat fire, he said. The fleet will reduce Confluence Center to rubble—to slag. You might think he was just talking wild, but I know Myron. When he's really angry he can't think well enough to make up anything. He was telling what he had heard. I think that Confluence Center is in terrible danger."

Connie Cheever took Jeff's words calmly. She glanced across at Simon Macafee, who had been standing silently running his fingers through his long hair.

"So. It looks like we were close to the mark." She turned to Jeff. "What you told us is enormously important, but it's no huge surprise. We were thinking we might need to plan for the worst, now we have no choice. Simon? Can you?"

"How long do I have?"

"Depends how well I can stall the Sol navy people. Maybe a week. Maybe a lot less."

"Touch and go. I'll need help."

"Anything I can spare."

"As many Logans as I need, and twenty of the best jinners."

"That's too many. We'll be stretched overthin. A week like that, we'll start to see systems failure all over the place. Oh, well, in seven days there may be no systems to worry about. I'll get what you need. Don't ask how." Connie turned to Jeff. "Where do you stand on all this? It's survival for us, but you're a Space navy officer, and a Kopal. You could go back home on the *Dreadnought*, forget the Cloud, and be in the clear."

"I don't think I'd make a good navy officer. Killing people, or letting people be killed because I do nothing, is too hard. That's what Myron seems to think the navy is all about, and he's probably right. If I do get back, I'll resign."

Connie and Lilah remained silent. It was, to Jeff's surprise, Simon Macafee who said, "Ah, but if all the people of conscience leave the navy, what remains? I am sure you can work out the answer to that question."

"I can't stand the navy."

"It takes more courage to stay and endure an awful situation than to run away from it. More courage than I had, I'm afraid."

"All right," Connie said. "The two of you can enjoy the Socratic dialogue some other time. Right now, Simon, we have work to do. Lilah, the nannies will be injected in the next few minutes. Will you stay here and make sure Jeff knows what's happening?"

The hesitation was almost too small to notice, a data burst from mother to daughter and back that Jeff could sense but not read.

"Sure." Lilah pulled a chair over to where Jeff lay. "Will you have food brought in? There's no chef in here."

"What about me?" Jeff added. In spite of his numbed condition, the idea of food was making his mouth water.

"How do you propose to eat it?" Simon asked.

"Lilah will feed him." Another tiny data burst passed between mother and daughter. "Won't you, dear?"

"Sure."

"Can I at least be sitting upright?" Jeff was tired of his worm's-eye view of events.

"Why didn't you ask?" the Logan said from beneath him.

The flat surface levered up at one end, until Jeff was in a sitting position. Amazingly, his damaged ribs did not produce even a twinge. How useful the nannies would be on Earth—if only they could be imported. But before that could happen, the technology would have to be bought—or stolen?—from the Cloud. Whose side was he really on?

Connie and Simon Macafee were leaving. A smaller Logan came buzzing in with a thin bottle the size of Jeff's forefinger. "Excuse me," it said, and inserted the nozzle into his mouth. He heard a fizzing sound, but felt and tasted nothing.

"Some feeling of internal warmth may now be experienced," said the little Logan. "Pay no attention to it." Before Jeff could reply, the machine had buzzed away.

"You've explained what your cousin told you," Lilah said. She moved the position of her chair close to the left side of the bed, so that the two of them were face-to-face. "And you've explained that when he's angry enough, he doesn't think about what he's saying. But you haven't explained one thing. Why were you fighting?"

"What's it mean, 'some feeling of internal warmth'?"

"When the nannies are working, your body temperature goes up. You didn't notice it the last time, because you were unconscious. Apparently they don't propose to knock you out this time. Why were you and Myron fighting?"

"We had an argument." Jeff thought back to the fight, and the feeling that he had more than enough time to block all Myron's punches. "It was very odd. We used to fight back on Earth, and he could hit me anytime he liked. Tonight he couldn't touch me."

"No? Seems to me he could—unless you gave yourself a black eye and a broken rib."

"That happened after I thought the fight was over. Myron didn't agree. He hit me when I wasn't expecting it. But before that, I seemed to have all the time in the world to avoid being hurt."

"Have you noticed any other differences recently? I mean, differences in yourself."

"No." Jeff paused. "Except that tonight, when I was getting ready to throw rings in a game Simon Macafee showed me, my hands didn't get all shaky. They usually do when I'm in a contest and I particularly don't want them to. Would that count?"

"Of course it would. Don't you see, Jeff? It's the nannies. When they worked on you last time, they made improvements. Nothing major—that would be outside their programming. But they tinkered a little with your nervous system, for better reaction time and damping the jitters."

"I felt I could hit Myron anytime I liked. He seemed wide open." Jeff thought back, to his cousin's murderous bloodred face after he delivered that kick to the ribs. "I wish I had. Then I wouldn't be lying here dead from the neck down."

"Better than dead from the neck up. What were the two of you fighting about?"

She wasn't going to give up. Lilah was as persistent as her mother.

"He said something I didn't like. I went for him. I was the one who started it, not Myron."

"I'm sure I've said lots of things about you that you didn't like. But you didn't attack me."

"He wasn't talking about me." Jeff wished he could get up and run away. He was being forced along a path that he had no desire to take. "He said things about you."

"Oh." Lilah was quiet for a while, then she said, "What sort of things?"

"You don't want to know."

"Don't be ridiculous. I certainly do. What did he say?"

"Oh, I don't know." She stared at him grimly until he went on, "He said he got you excited, so you rubbed up against him when the two of you were dancing to try to excite him." Jeff paused. Lilah had flushed red, as red as Myron had been. "I wouldn't have hit him for that—you didn't have to dance with him if you didn't want to. But he said other things. He called you a little tart, and my fancy bitch. And he said you weren't any good at—stuff."

"And you believed what he said? I bet you did, every word of it. You may be one of the famous Kopals, but sometimes you make me wonder. Do you think I *wanted* to hang around with Myron? That your cousin is my type?" She leaned close to Jeff.

He couldn't even cringe. Myron was not there to receive her anger, but he was.

"Do you know why I was with Myron?" she went on. "I'll tell you, Jeff Kopal. Because a certain other person refused to show him around Confluence Center, and wouldn't go to Confluence with him. Mother said she asked you to do it, and you wouldn't. And you certainly hadn't shown any interest in taking me to Confluence. So guess who got stuck with the job, and was asked to be nice to Myron and show him around, and maybe see what she could learn about the fleet plans?"

"I didn't know that."

"There's plenty you don't know. But there's limits to being nice. Did you really think I rubbed up against Myron when we were dancing?"

"He said you did."

"Right. So of course you believed him. Do you believe everything your cousin tells you? Or just the things he says about me?"

"I didn't really believe what he said about you. At least, I didn't want to."

"So you started a fight with him?"

"I guess so. You see, I thought that if I—"

"Leave it, Jeff. You don't need to explain. Can't you see I'm *glad* you thought my reputation was worth fighting for? And if you want to know how much of what Myron said about me is true, I'll tell you: not a word of it. Let me tell you something about your cousin. I noticed in the first ten minutes that he never passes a mirror without pausing to admire himself. He talks and acts like he's God's gift to women. He constantly referred to you, comparing himself and pointing out how he is superior to you in every possible way. He told me about all the other girls and women he has been with—as if *that* is supposed to please me."

"He has been with others. I've seen him, at dances and parties."

"Do you think that makes a girl feel special, to be told that she's the hundredth in line? If I had done what he wanted—and he did want, and I wouldn't, I wanted nothing to do with him— then I'd just be another of his conquests. I'll tell you something else about Myron that you probably don't know. He's big, and he's handsome, and he looks great in a uniform. He's very self-confident, and he talks a smooth line. Not like you."

"Thanks."

"Don't get huffy. I'm not being horrible. I'd rather be with you any day." A Logan was arriving with a tray of food and drinks, but Lilah ignored it and went on, "I'm sure Myron has no trouble at all getting dates, or persuading girls to go off with him soon after he meets them. He wasn't lying about that. And I'm sure he has been with many girls—once, and only once. Anyone who doesn't see through Myron in the first couple of hours deserves what she gets. I bet you never saw him twice with the same girl."

"That's true. I never did."

"So why were you ready to believe I would go off with him?"

Jeff was tempted to say, "Well, it was your first date, and it had been only a couple of hours." Something warned him that would do more harm than good. "I didn't want to believe him. I didn't want him to say things about you, either. That's why I went for him."

"That's sweet of you. But you lost. And yet you say you could have hit him anytime. Why didn't you?"

"I nearly did. I had a clear target, but I pulled back at the last minute. I guess Myron is right. When it comes to fighting I'm a wimp."

"Depends on your wimp definition. People who hit someone just because they can aren't my idea of heroes. Don't move." Lilah leaned forward and touched Jeff's forehead. "How do you feel? You're very flushed."

"Like I'm on fire. It's just my head, though."

She took his left hand in hers, then reached out and placed her fingers on his leg just above the knee. "Don't get ideas. I'm checking temperatures. You can't feel it anywhere else, but you are warm all over. The nannies are starting to do their job. They use up a lot of raw materials and burn up plenty of energy. We'd better get some food into you, or they'll just take what they need and you'll crash when they are done. You'll crash anyway, once they really get going. Humans are easier to deal with when they can't decide to move around on their own."

She took the tray from the waiting Logan. "What do you want to eat?"

"Anything. Just shovel it in. You're right, I'm very tired and I don't know how much longer I'll be awake. Why did you go with Myron to a private room?"

"Oh, Jeff, let it go. Isn't it obvious that I don't find Myron the least bit attractive? I was supposed to coax him into telling me about the fleet's plans. Do you think he'd chatter on about that in public? *Yes*, I took him there. *Yes*, it was a dumb move on my part. But I do dumb things. Do you think you're the only one allowed to?"

She was forcing stew into Jeff's mouth, punctuating her remarks with spoonful after spoonful and forcing him to chew and swallow so fast that he had no chance to speak. Finally he closed his lips firmly and sat scowling until she got the message and pulled the spoon away. When he had chewed and swallowed, he said, "No more! Not until I say ready. One more question. The other day you told me that you knew what people from Earth are like. All sex-mad, you said. So why didn't you expect Myron to do exactly what he did?"

"You can blame Muv for that. The morning after you and I were in my rooms, I was really upset and Mother knew it. She asked me what was wrong. I told her what you said to me, and what I said back to you."

"I don't think I really said anything."

"That was Mother's reaction. She made me tell her everything as near as I could, word for word. She said I was emotional, and overreacting just because I like you. Then she said something I'd expect more of Simon Macafee than my mother. She accused me of 'the logical fallacy of arguing from the general to the specific.' Do you understand that?"

"It means that just because a property applies on average to a whole group, you can't assume it will apply to a particular member of that group."

"Now *you* sound like Simon Macafee. Logical to the last breath. Did you know that you imitate him all the time? I think he's your hero." She held out the spoon, and Jeff shook his head. Her outline was beginning to blur, and when she spoke again it came from a long distance. "Anyway, Muv put it this way: Suppose you say, 'Jinners don't write poetry.' On average you will be right, because most jinners certainly don't. But if you apply it to a particular jinner you could be wrong, because there are some jinners who *do* write poetry. Or, just because there are lots and lots of people on Earth, it doesn't mean that everyone on Earth is only interested in sex and breeding. Mother told me I was being unfair to you."

"I think you were." Jeff's head was swimming and he felt ready to pass out, but passion for accuracy made him struggle to go on when he knew that he ought to shut up. "But you realize that although what your mother said is true in theory, and you can't argue from the general to the specific, it's not *practically* true. I mean, arguing your way, you'll be right more often than not."

"So I ought to have assumed that Myron couldn't be trusted, because most Earth people can't? Well, I know that now." She was at the side of the bed, returning Jeff to a supine position. "But I hope you're not telling me it applies to you, too. I wouldn't be a fool to trust you, would I? Because I do. Especially since you got hurt fighting for me. I never had a champion before. Can you hear me? I hope not."

Jeff had been trying to shake his head, assuring her that he could be trusted. At her last question he tried to move it up and down, with no better success. His eyes were closing, no matter how he tried to keep them open.

Lilah peered down at him. "Hello? Anybody home? Can you hear me? I don't think so. Just as well. I think I'll just sit here and hold your hand. Then I can tell my friends that we spent the night together."

Jeff struggled to answer. He wanted to say that Lilah had the right idea, she could trust him with anything in the universe and he would spend a night with her anytime he had the chance.

Not a word came out. His last thought was one of irritation. Being unable to move a finger, and then passing out, was one hell of a way to spend his first night with Lilah.

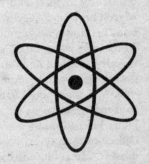

CHAPTER NINETEEN

JEFF expected to meet Myron again before the *Dreadnought* left Confluence Center; expected it and feared it, yet somehow hoped for it.

He had thought about little else but Myron and Lilah during his time in the medical center. The nannies performed their magic inside his body, his temperature rose and fell, and during his spells of consciousness the wild thoughts danced with dreams in a witch's sabbat around his head. He imagined the pleasure of seeing Myron's face when his cousin confronted a perfectly fit Jeff so soon after leaving him groaning on the floor with broken and bruised ribs and a ruined eye. There was another fight. He could see and smell it, feel and count every blow. This time Jeff could do what he had found impossible before, and he hit hard when the chance came. Myron broke into pieces. While Jeff wept over the fragmented body his cousin reassembled and came back stronger than ever. "That one was a fluke, a lucky hit," he jeered. He beat Jeff bloody as he had done so often in the past, then ssfaded away into the darkness beyond the Messina Dust Cloud.

And there was Lilah. His dreams of her were not to be spoken of, but when he awoke in the medical center she was gone. He had no idea how long she had stayed, and his final conscious minutes with her had mixed in with nanny-induced dreams. He could not be sure what was reality, and what he had imagined.

She had not been to see him since, but that was no sur-prise. Nor had anyone else except the Logans—and only one of them, the little buzzing machine that brought food and drink and checked his progress. The whole of Confluence Center must be on red alert because of the ominous presence of the *Dreadnought*. Had anyone suggested to Lilah that she should spend more time with Myron? He would like to have been there for that meeting. But when he and Lilah met would they still have that strange, delicious intimacy, the mood of the final few minutes before he had drifted into unconsciousness?

Reality was a letdown from all points of view. Jeff emerged from his two-day enforced idleness and found the *Dreadnought* prepared for departure. He was not invited to the final cere-mony and found himself obliged to watch it on a remote display in the main control room. Lilah, quiet and subdued, came in and joined him at the point where Connie Cheever was bidding the captain and crew of the visiting ship a formal and courteous farewell.

Captain Duval offered an equally restrained but flowery and friendly response.

"Words, words, words. They don't mean a thing." Lilah sounded bitter and contemptuous. It was the first thing she had said since she came in, and it hardly seemed to be addressed to Jeff. Was she referring to *her* words to him, spoken when she thought he was unconscious?

"They're only being polite, Lilah."

"People always are, before they go to war. Look at them."

Captain Duval wore a fixed smile worthy of Giles Lazenby. The honor guard at his right and left were at rigid attention. Myron, dressed to smart perfection, stood behind the captain and a little to his left. The sight of Myron produced in Jeff a flood of adrenaline—he felt equally ready to run or fight.

Connie Cheever received Duval's ceremonial bow and returned it with a rigidity that Jeff had never observed in her before.

"I don't see Simon Macafee anywhere," he said.

"You won't. He can't stand this kind of fakery. Not after what happened during the real negotiations."

"You were there?"

"No. Muv told me about them—when I pumped her hard enough. They had meeting after meeting, and we offered all kinds of concessions. The moment when mother decided that talk was useless came when Simon Macafee said, 'All right, take the Anadem field. If you want it so much, you can have it. I'll tell you exactly how it works, and how to build the generators.' That was a shocker—not only to the *Dreadnought* officers, but to our people, too. Simon has always resisted the idea of letting the field technology go to Sol. It floored Duval, and he requested a break so he and his people could huddle. When they returned he said that the Anadem field was not the only issue. There was also the question of the return of certain runaways, two jinners and an ensign, for possible court-martial. That would be a condition of any agreement. I think that's when Muv lost it. She wouldn't admit it to me, but I gather she told Duval to go and take his ship and his bargaining position and stuff them into certain unmentionable parts of himself and his crew. And Jinners Hooglich and Russo and Ensign Kopal, she said, would be welcome guests at Confluence Center for as long as they chose to stay."

The mention of his own name brought goose bumps all over Jeff. He stopped watching the display and turned to Lilah.

"We didn't run away. We were never given a choice to go with Dufferin and the others."

"I know that. I said the same thing to Mother, and she told me I didn't understand what Duval and his bosses were really doing. They are playing a double game, she says. While they tell us that you and Hooglich and Russo are runaway traitors, back Sol-side they will stir up public support by saying you were captured and must be rescued."

"Support for war?"

"That's not the words that will be used. According to Simon, who knows more than you'd think about this sort of thing, the word of choice is *annexation*. They will 'annex' the Cloud. It's a polite way of saying that the Sol fleet will invade and take us over. The logic is, the Cloud was always part of Sol's territory, and so it's not so much an invasion as a restoration of natural order."

Jeff remembered Myron's tide of anger and bloodred face. He turned again to the display and studied the image of his cousin, cold-faced and severe.

"I don't think it's just invasion. Look at Myron."

"He doesn't seem any different then he ever was. He's still a crawling hypocrite."

"You can't read his face. I can, I grew up with him. He gets that gloating look when he has you helpless, when he's going to really hurt you and enjoy doing it. If the fleet invades this part of the Cloud, they will destroy the main place of government. That's Confluence Center. Myron didn't make up what he told me. After the fleet arrives here and takes what it wants, this place will be vaporized."

"They must not realize how big Confluence Center is. It's huge."

"And you don't realize how much firepower the fleet has."
Jeff recalled the briefing materials that he had watched on the
long trip from Earth to the E-K Belt. "Don't judge Sol by the
Aurora, or the *Dreadnought*. They're like gnats. A big cruiser
can vaporize a small asteroid. Use a hundred of them, and Confluence Center would be just another hot patch of gas in the
Messina Dust Cloud."

"It's ridiculous to have anything so destructive. How can
they justify building monstrosities like that? It must cost a fortune just to maintain them, when there is nothing to fight."

"The Space Navy is so big, it has its own political lobby.
The ships are needed, they say, to protect Sol from aliens."

"But there are no aliens! Not that we've ever found—
unless you count the sounders."

"You don't need real aliens. The threat of possible enemies
is enough to keep the money flowing in." *And flowing back out
again—to industry groups, the most powerful of which is Kopal
Transportation.* Jeff, not for the first time, felt ashamed of his
own family. Most people would give anything to be a Kopal.
They didn't know the rest of the story. How, once you were
born a Kopal, you could never escape. The name alone was
enough to lock you in for life. If you didn't buy in to the cozy
navy-industry connection promoted by the descendants of
Rollo Kopal (What's good for Kopal Transportation is good
for the Space Navy!), then you were doubly damned. You were
envied or hated by outsiders for what you had from birth, and
despised by the other members of your family because you
would not fall in line. It had been that way as long as you could
remember, and it would continue for the rest of your life.

Lilah touched him tentatively on his forearm, pulling him
back to the present—and then jerked her hand away rapidly, as
if the contact had burned her. "Are you all right, Jeff?"

"I suppose so. I'm just feeling ashamed of what they are
planning to do." He gestured to the display, where the cere-
mony had ended and the group was dispersing. The ship members marched away in formation, not talking to or looking at

the Cloud representatives. "Myron told me I was a traitor. I denied it, but I'm beginning to suspect that he's right."

"If it's being a traitor to oppose something evil, then hooray for traitors. 'My country, right or wrong,' is nonsense now, and it was always nonsense. It's like everybody in the old wars claiming that God was on their side, because their cause was a just one." She laughed. "You never hear the losers explain why it didn't work. The winners write the history books."

"Don't joke about this, Lil. You may not be frightened, but I am. I've seen pictures of the fleet in action. And Confluence Center has no defenses."

"We've never needed them. God is on our side."

"Stop it, Lilah."

"I'm sorry. But we have never *needed* defenses."

"You need them now, and nobody seems to be doing a thing. I heard Simon Macafee tell your mother that it would be touch and go. He needed lots of Logans and the best jinners, and she said he could have them. On my way from the medical center I made a quick trip past the perimeter work zone, to see what was happening. I didn't find any sign of Simon, or of Hooglich and Russo. I thought they would all be frantically busy, adding drives to Confluence Center and making changes to the Anadem field rings. But they weren't there. And from what you say, Simon Macafee has been sitting in on the meetings with your mother and Captain Duval."

"Off and on. Don't assume Simon is doing nothing, even when he's sitting staring at the wall. Mother says that nobody ever really understands Simon Macafee. Have you ever noticed a faint star at the edge of your field of view, and then when you look straight at it you mysteriously find that you can't see it at all?"

"Of course. But it's not a mystery. The eye has two kinds of light-sensitive receptors, rods and cones. The rods are more sensitive to weak light—like your faint star—and the cones provide color vision. But there are no rods in the center of the retina. So although you see color and more detail when you stare straight at something, you are less sensitive to low photon levels. The faint star seems to disappear."

She stared at him. "How do you know all that?"

"I read about it."

"Do you have to find a scientific explanation for *everything*?"

"For some things, I wouldn't even try."

That seemed to fluster Lilah. She looked away from Jeff and said, "Now you've made me forget what I was talking about. Where was I?"

"Simon Macafee, and optical properties of the eye."

"Right. Well, Simon is like that faint star. You can be talking to him, and you think you understand him and know where the conversation is heading. Then you talk a bit longer and go into more detail, and suddenly he's incomprehensible. It's as though he's not there anymore. His mind has gone someplace that you can't follow."

Jeff didn't agree. Simon Macafee might be disheveled and scruffy, but everything he uttered through that jungle of facial hair made perfect sense.

"I'd like to talk to Simon myself. Do you know where he is?"

"He wandered off early, so he couldn't be dragged into the formal farewells. He's not here, and you say you didn't see him at the perimeter work zone. We'll check there again, but if we don't find him I know only two other possibilities. Either he's in his secret den, or he's not on Confluence Center at all. Come on."

Jeff thought he knew the way. Lilah headed in a totally different direction.

"Farther but quicker," she said. "Of course you don't know it, you're a quick learner but you've only been here a week. Give it six months, and you'll be able to scoot from place to place without bothering with a route finder."

"Six months! Lilah, no matter what happens I won't be here in six months."

She halted and stood rigid. "You won't? Why not?"

"Suppose the fleet doesn't kill all of us—which is what I'm most worried about. I'll still have to go Sol-side, back to Earth, to try to clear my name. It's not because I'm a stupid Kopal, if that's what you're thinking. It's because I have a sick mother back there. I can't leave her thinking that I messed up my job on the *Aurora*, ruined the ship's drive, and then deserted. No matter what they do to me afterwards, I have to go home and explain."

"I suppose so." Lilah started moving again, much more slowly. "Back to Earth. The way you say it, it sounds like Hades. I know you don't think you're lucky to have been raised there, but I do. Did you ever have a parakeet, or a canary? I've always wanted one."

"No. Mother didn't approve of birds being locked in cages. When she first told me that, I thought to myself that I was one."

"No pets at all?"

"I had a pet rat once."

"Yecch. Gross. What happened to it?"

"I'm not sure. I think Uncle Fairborn's terrier got him. She was supposed to be a great ratter, out in the barns."

They were approaching the last ring of chambers before the perimeter and the catwalk. Lilah had never regained her first pace, and as they went on through the air-filled space between the hulls she went slower and slower.

"This is really odd."

Jeff looked around him. "I don't see anything."

"That's because you're not familiar with normal operations. After you've been at Confluence Center awhile longer. . . ." She paused and shook her head. "Sorry, I know you have to go and I understand why. I have to get used to the idea. But it's what we're *not* seeing that's peculiar. It's far too quiet. We haven't encountered a single jinner, and I have seen only a couple of Logans. This area should be swarming with them. So where are they?"

"Working deeper in the interior?"

"We didn't meet them on the way. In fact, I don't recall seeing a jinner all day."

"Then your mother gave Simon what he asked. The jinners and Logans are with him."

"Maybe they are. But that takes us full circle. We don't know where *he* is, and he's the one we started out to find. No point in wasting more time here. Let's try his hideaway. We start from the Ninth Sector, Fifth Octant. Do you know the way?"

Jeff shook his head. But two minutes later he realized that he knew where they were. Once again they were passing through the chamber with the dinosaurs and spaceships and the giant face on the walls. Today the smaller face that formed the nose had the eyes blank, and this way it somehow looked even more hideous.

He thought he knew what came next. When Lilah moved away in a different direction, he halted her with his hand on her arm. "Isn't the other direction the way to go?"

"If you want a good crawl through ventilator shafts, it is. Not otherwise." She started forward again. "I've learned a few things about this part of the Center since last time we were here. This is a lot easier."

Lilah's new route brought them to Simon Macafee's hideout from a different direction. All the lights in the great room were full on, and the silver cylinder, with its halo of orange light, stood by the entrance. Beyond it was the miniature Anadem field generator, filling the air with a bass drone, and on the other side of that hulked the black cube. The cube seemed even darker than before, sucking in and destroying the light around it. Next to it sat Simon Macafee's great padded chair.

"Oh, damn," said Lilah suddenly. "I thought that with all these lights he had to be here."

Jeff didn't know what she was cursing at—until he saw a pair of little legs sticking out beyond the chair seat.

"Billy!"

The legs wriggled forward, and Billy's head came into view.

"You're too late," he said. "They left hours ago." He stared at Lilah with a mixture of disgust and satisfaction. "So they wouldn't let you go, either."

"Simon Macafee?" Jeff asked, while Lilah swore again.

"Him, and loads of jinners, and more Logans than you've ever seen in one place."

"Where did they go?"

"I don't know. It was somewhere outside Confluence Center, but they wouldn't tell me where. Everybody was acting all mysterious—even Simon. He said I had to stay, because I had a job to do. I was to wait here until you two came along—"

"How did he know we would?"

"He didn't tell me that. But he said that you, Jeff, are so nosy to find out everything that you'd be here with a hundred questions." Billy held out his hand. "He left this for you. He said it was in case things went totally wrong with what he and the jinners are hoping to do. If that happened, you were to hold on to this and never to lose it."

It was a small plastic card, about three inches by two.

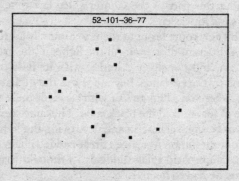

Jeff bent over it eagerly. After a few seconds he shook his head. "Are you sure he said to give this to me?"

"Certain sure."

"I don't see why. It has nothing to do with me." Jeff handed the card to Lilah. "What do you make of it?"

"Well, it looks old. You can see where the edge has worn away." She touched the top of the card. "What about this number, 52-101-36-77? That could be a personal ID."

"It could. Or it might be a serial number, or coordinates, or all sorts of things."

"And there's this." Lilah was not looking at the card, but feeling it. She lifted and tilted the plastic. "If you hold it at the right angle to the light, you can see them. Dots."

"I see them. But what are they? They don't make the shape of anything."

"I know. Just sixteen isolated little dots. Billy, did Simon say anything else?"

"Only that he'd skin me alive if I forgot to pass it on to Jeff. And I didn't."

"I'd like Mother to see this." Lilah ran her fingers again over the surface of the card. "She's usually full of ideas. Let's go find her. Billy?"

"I'd rather stay here. This place is fun."

"Don't ruin anything."

"Simon says it's foolproof."

"Just as though it was designed for you. If he comes back, Billy, let us know. And we'll ask Muv what's going on with Simon and the jinners."

"Do you think she'll tell you?" Jeff reached out his hand to take the little card from Lilah as they started back toward Control, then restrained himself. He felt obliged to add, "Show it to your mother, but whatever you do, don't lose it." He trusted Lilah, but he was the one Simon Macafee had told to hold on to it.

"I'll guard it with my life. And if I nag her, she'll tell me." Lilah spoke as someone with many years of experience. "Don't worry, it's like wearing down a stone. Provided I go on long enough, and moan and groan and plead and whine hard enough—she'll tell me anything."

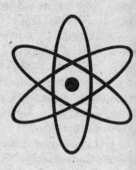

CHAPTER TWENTY

IN normal times, Lilah was surely right; but these were not normal times.

The first evidence of that was provided before they reached the control area. It came in the form of a sound, a deep humming that resonated in every bulkhead and floor and corridor of Confluence Center.

"What's *that*?" Jeff stopped dead. The vibration was so strong, the structures around him seemed ready to shake apart.

"Emergency energy generation." Lilah didn't sound alarmed, but she moved faster. "They are pumping up the big storage rings. It's happened before when a big power draw was on the way, but I don't remember it ever being this strong."

"Why do we need emergency energy?" Jeff was hurrying along after her, entering the final corridor that led to the control room. "The jinners haven't added a drive, this place can't go anywhere."

"I guess that's another question we have to ask—we're getting quite a list. Mother!"

She had caught sight of Connie Cheever, hurrying along the corridor ahead of them. As her mother stopped and turned, Lilah called, "I'm glad to see you. We have all kinds of questions for—"

"Not now." Connie cut her off in midsentence. "Jeff, I'm glad to see you. I have a job for you."

"For me? What happened?"

"Treachery is what happened." Connie was shepherding Jeff and Lilah ahead of her into the control room. "The *Dreadnought* left half an hour ago."

"We know, Mother. We saw it leave."

"All the time they were here, we took our meetings with them seriously and did our best to be good hosts. We made it clear that we don't want trouble with Sol and we'll do anything we can to avoid it. Now I've had reports in from rakehells and harvesters at the other side of the Cloud, close to the node. The Space Navy fleet left there long ago, they're not sure when, but certainly well *before* the *Dreadnought* left here. All the ships are heading this way. It's obvious, no matter what we said, Duval would have found a reason why our promises were unacceptable. He was just trying to distract our attention from what they were planning. Thank God for Macafee. Simon knew. I don't know how, but he did. We'll have to scramble, but there's still a chance that we can be ready." She ushered Jeff forward to a seat in front of a big three-dimensional display. "Do you see that?"

"Of course." It was impossible to miss the image of the ship, hanging in black space apparently right in front of Jeff.

"Do you recognize it?"

"I recognize the type. It's a cruiser, Achernar class. We were briefed on all the Space Navy flotilla."

"Good. That's what I hoped. According to the reports I'm getting, that ship will be here in two days at the most. I want you to tell anything you know about it—weapons, power systems, drive, peculiar features, anything at all. Don't worry about repeating yourself, or the order that you say things. Everything will be recorded, and a Logan will put it all together. And don't be upset if you don't know something, either. We'll be merging your data with what we already have in our databases—not nearly enough, I'm afraid. It's not the sort of information we've worried about before."

"I'll do what I can."

"Have a break when you really need one, but don't stop. I need this information for every vessel heading our way, as soon as I can get it."

"How many are there?"

"At the last count, sixty-four. Those are the ones on the way here now. If anything else comes through the node, we'll worry about that later. Do your best, Jeff."

"I will."

"And you, Lilah, come with me. He can't afford to have distractions."

Something in her mother's voice told Lilah not to argue. Jeff hardly noticed them leaving. He was staring at the display, trying to use what he saw to provide an exact recall of the fleet data he had seen or heard.

"Cruiser, Achernar class. Net mass, forty-eight thousand tons. Average crew, seven. Drive, Mark Six Diabelli Omnivores, maximum burst acceleration, eleven Gs. Main weapons: vacuum energy tap, field resonance, computer decoherence."

Ominous thoughts accompanied his words. This was just one ship, but it, alone, had enough firepower to destroy Confluence Center. There were sixty-three more, many of them far more powerful. It was all very well for Connie Cheever to make plans for what to do when the Space Navy flotilla arrived, but those plans would be useless if the fleet decided to attack.

The people in the Cloud simply had no idea what forces were on the way.

He spoke again into the recorder.

"I don't know of any vulnerabilities possessed by vessels of the Achernar class. Next ship: battle fort and launch platform. Exeter class. Net mass, ninety-four thousand tons. Average crew, twenty-seven. Drive, Mark Seven Omnivores, maximum burst acceleration, sixteen Gs. Main weapons: . . ."

Another depressing thought. He knew much of this without thinking. He had picked up masses of information from the navy briefing materials almost unconsciously, and on subjects of no interest to him. It would be nice to think that, for a change, that dreary catalog of weapons might have a use.

"Supercruiser, Monitor class. Net mass, sixty thousand tons. Average crew, five. Drive. . . .".

But of what use was any listing of weapons, unless it persuaded the people of Confluence Center that their only hope was flight? Energy buildup in the storage rings, no matter how much it might give Connie Cheever the feeling of doing something, was a waste of time. Energy alone could not protect them from the weapons of the approaching fleet. In a day or so, the bearers of destruction that he was detailing so intently would be here. Flee, then, as far and as fast as possible. Surely no one still believed it was possible to *negotiate* with Mohammad Duval and the Space Navy leaders? Jeff didn't. But he had the personal memory of Myron's vengeful face to guide him.

"Space frigate, Mirage class. Net mass, fourteen thousand tons. Crew of two. Experimental isomer drive, burst acceleration twenty-two Gs in kamikaze mode. Weapons. . . ."

All the time, in the background, driving him along and encouraging him to stick at his task, he heard that deep organ tone of the emergency energy system. Whenever he took a short break he felt the vibration, beneath his feet, in the air around him, grating in his very bones.

How many more? He was avoiding looking at the

counter—it might be too discouraging—but he had described what felt like hundreds of different vessels. Finally, though, he was getting repeats. Cruisers of the Alpheratz and Altair classes were different only in crew complement from the Achernar that he had started with, while the Ajax and Achilles battle forts were simply smaller versions of the Exeter. But one thing was certain: This was no fleet designed for a border skirmish. The most powerful vessels of Central Command were here. It was proof that more was involved than any negotiation. Myron had spoken in anger, but he had spoken truth. The plan was to plunder the technological assets of Confluence Center, starting with the Anadem field, and follow with total destruction.

Without warning, the image that he had been describing vanished from the display. Nothing replaced it. Jeff glanced to the vessel count. Sixty-four. He was done. At last.

He sighed, stretched, and realized that Lilah was sitting at his side. When had she arrived?

"What's wrong, Lilah?" She had said not a word, but he was learning. She was upset, and she was angry.

"Nothing you did, Jeff. It's Muv."

"She wouldn't tell you what Simon's card meant?"

"Not that. She took one look and said she had no idea. I'm sure she was telling the truth. But when I asked her where Simon Macafee and the jinners were, and what they were doing, she said she couldn't tell me. And she told me not to ask her again—she *never* does that."

"If it's some kind of military secret. . . ."

"No. She said she couldn't tell me *because of you*. That's when I got mad."

"I haven't done anything."

"It's not what you've done. It's what you might do. Muv says that no matter how we think of you, you're still an ensign in the Sol Space Navy. She has no idea what oaths and vows you may have taken. If she were to tell you important secrets, you might find yourself in a position of divided loyalty. That would put unfair pressures on you."

Jeff stared at the vacant display region. "It's a bit late to tell me that. I've just finished hours and hours of work, describing the capabilities of fleet vessels. Your mother wants it both ways. She uses me when it suits her, but she won't trust me."

"I told her that. She agreed, but she said this is one case where the end justifies the means. She wants to avoid killing, and the more we know about the Sol fleet, the better. But she wouldn't tell me any more than that."

"You could have promised not to tell me whatever she said."

"I tried that, too. She said that I could be trusted with most things, but not when it came to you. If I knew something that you wanted to know, you could talk me into telling you, no matter what. That's when I really lost it."

"Is it true?"

"I don't know." Lilah studied Jeff for a few seconds, and at last shook her head. "I told Muv that she was being ridiculous, but now I'm not so sure. She's right an awful lot of the time."

"So maybe she's right about me." Jeff wondered if he had done the right thing, describing the fleet ships in such detail. If he were asked to do it again, would he?

Probably. He trusted Connie Cheever, apparently a lot more than she trusted him. Either he was a great judge of character, or he was stupid. He would find out, soon enough.

"Twenty-four hours, at the most," Lilah said. Jeff wondered if she could read his thoughts, until she went on, "Then Muv promised she'd tell me. She asked you to wait, and give her the benefit of the doubt."

Twenty-four hours. Jeff again glanced to the vacant display region, but now his imagination saw it filled with every one of the ships that he had carefully described. He had never estimated their combined firepower, but it was overwhelming. In twenty-four hours or less they could all be here. And then. . . .

The deep diapason tone throbbed through Confluence Center, sounding more threatening than reassuring. Connie

Cheever might feel that the spare stored energy helped, but Mohammad Duval would sneer at that idea.

The fleet captain had been here, he had toured the Center. He knew that the place had no defenses. In another day, if Duval felt so inclined, Confluence Center could be an expanding sphere of hot gases.

And then all explanations would become irrelevant.

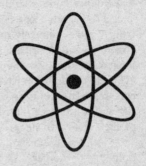

CHAPTER TWENTY-ONE

IT might have been nervousness, wondering if this was one last night before an eternity of darkness. Or maybe it was the vibration that shook every corner of Confluence Center and grew stronger with every passing hour; or perhaps even the suggestion planted in Jeff's head by Connie Cheever that by his action in describing the navy vessels for her he was guilty of treason—though he had sworn no oath to seek the destruction of peaceful people, in the Messina Dust Cloud or anywhere.

Whatever the reason, sleep proved impossible. Jeff lay restless, flat and curled up, on his back or side or stomach, covered or uncovered. Long before the usual waking time he abandoned the attempt to sleep and went wandering through Confluence Center to find a quieter spot.

His search was a failure. The sound followed him everywhere; always he felt that he stood at its exact center. The control-room door was, for the first time in Jeff's experience, locked. In any case, the noise level there seemed higher than ever. He tried Simon Macafee's hideout, hoping less to find escape from the vibration than to find Simon himself. The chamber was empty except for Billy Jexter, curled up in Simon's great padded chair and sleeping soundly.

Jeff was filled with envy. Oh, to be seven years old, and oblivious to danger.

At last he decided that the most peaceful place ought to be outside the main body of Confluence Center. That meant he must travel beyond the influence of the Anadem field, to an environment close to free fall. He could take that. Any amount of discomfort in his insides was preferable to the resonance that shook his bones and set his teeth on edge.

He called for a route guide. After examining the layout of Confluence Center, he set off for the farthest chamber of the longest extension corridor. On the way he passed the double torus of the Anadem rings. The air of the region smoked and shimmered. He knew from Lilah that the field could be used to store vast amounts of energy. How much? What happened if you tried to exceed that? And what did Connie Cheever and Simon Macafee hope to do with all that stored power when they had it?

The extension tube was not air-filled. Jeff logged out a suit, cycled through the lock, and entered the long arm of the corridor. The cylindrical dimly lit tunnel stretched off into the distance, as far as he could see. He headed out along it, feeling himself grow steadily lighter as he moved away from the zone of influence of the Anadem field. For the final half kilometer he floated, using only an occasional touch on corridor walls to make small corrections to his motion.

The arm ended in a launch facility and observation bubble. He spent a few moments examining the ships standing ready for launch, and wondered if Confluence Center had enough lifeboat capacity to evacuate everyone in case of emergency. Surely they must; space colonies had to be prepared for any disaster. But no one ever said a word about emergency procedures. "Abandon Confluence Center" was an unlikely command. The inhabitants of the Center had too much faith in their own creation. The idea that something could completely destroy their home probably never occurred to them.

Jeff moved into the observation bubble. He ordered the sensors to display the direction of the entry node from Sol. He didn't expect to see the node itself, and he knew there was no chance of detecting the approaching fleet until it was much closer. The displays showed only the vast, multicolored face of the Messina Dust Cloud. But he was clear of the nerve-tingling throb of power that filled the inner regions of Confluence Center, and looking out on the Cloud might help him to relax.

He went over to the clear window of the observation bubble. Electronic enhancers saw much more detail than human eyes, but there was something special about direct viewing.

The Cloud filled the sky. With plenty of time for examination, he could at last see logic behind the fanciful names that Lilah had offered. The Treasure Chest was an easy one, knotty strands of lustrous gas coiled and tangled in a jeweled rectangle defined by four bright supergiant stars. The Blind Man's Eye, off to the right, was a clouded oval of white light, like a cataracted pupil sitting at the center of a larger iris of royal blue. The Sisters were three tall columns of gas, bonded at their lower ends as the streams comprising them twisted and turned in response to local magnetic fields. The Snake formed a single luminous river of green, a colossal sidewinder coiling and wriggling its way across a third of the sky.

The Horsemen required more imagination. If you were generous and did not focus too hard, those four blocky islands of light might become hooded figures, galloping across the sky on spectral steeds of magenta and gold. But when you looked harder, those shapes, like Lilah's impression of Simon Macafee, would fade before your eyes.

Snakes, Horsemen. It was strange to find elements of far-off Earth named here. The labels must be old, established when Cloud residents still came from and knew well the worlds of Sol. It answered another of Jeff's questions: How permanent were the structures drifting before his eyes? Like the stars seen from Earth, the great dust rivers must endure over many centuries, otherwise the names would lose meaning within a person's lifetime.

Jeff's mind was wandering, well into the hypnotic stage that comes just before sleep, when he felt a gentle touch on his shoulder. It brought him to nervous, heart-pumping awareness. He turned violently, forgetting that he was in free fall, and found himself floating away from the wall of the bubble.

A suited arm reached out to hold and steady him.

"It's all right, Jeff." Lilah's voice sounded on his helmet channel. "It's only me."

He took a deep breath and tried to speak normally. "How did you know I was out here? I didn't tell anyone I was going."

"I tried your room, and you weren't there or anywhere else I thought you might be. I queried the general database as a last hope. I learned that you had checked out a suit for vacuum use, and where you did it. This was the only logical place you could be, with that exit point from the Center."

"What do you want?"

"Calm down. Maybe I couldn't sleep, either. Or maybe I just wanted to see you."

"I'm sorry." His question had been abrupt, betraying his nervous condition. "It was a shock, because I wasn't expecting anyone. I've been floating here for ages by myself, just looking at the Cloud. You're quite right, when you stare for a while you start to see all the shapes you told me about."

"Shapes. That's why I came looking for you." Lilah took his arm and urged him to move along the corridor toward the bulk of Confluence Center. "Simon Macafee isn't back yet, but Hooglich came dashing through the Inner Level. She wouldn't tell me what they were all doing, and she was in a terrible hurry. But I sketched her the pattern of dots on Simon's card, and she recognized it."

Jeff felt the hair-bristling mood return. "What is it? Some kind of code?"

"Easier than that. It's a constellation—a star pattern."

"I know what a constellation is. Was Hooglich sure?"

"She seemed to be. She said at once, 'I know that, it's the Dragon.' "

"But your mother didn't recognize it, and she used to be a Cloudship captain. She ought to know the constellations better than Hooglich."

"I think she does. But she knows constellations as they look from *here*, in the Cloud. You're forgetting, we're twenty-seven light-years from Sol. Lots of the bright stars are different, so the constellations change. Hooglich says that the dot pattern on the card is the Dragon constellation, *as it looks from the region of Sol*. You must have seen it when you were on Earth."

"I thought the pattern looked kind of familiar. But what does it mean? Why did Simon Macafee put it on the card?"

"I don't know. I was hoping you could tell me."

Helmet to helmet, they stared at each other in silence until Jeff at last shook his head.

"It's no use. Even if Hooglich is right and it's the Dragon constellation, that doesn't give me anything new." They were making easy progress, gliding side by side along the corridor toward the main bulk of Confluence Center. Even from a kilometer away, Jeff could feel the thrum of energy generation whenever his hand or foot touched the tunnel walls. "Did you tell your mother what Hooglich said?"

"I can't get near her. Everything in Control is locked up

tight and has been for hours. I'm not sure that the messages I leave for her even get through. You thought she wasn't taking the danger from the Sol fleet seriously enough. Well, I can tell you, if that was true before it's not true now. I've never known Confluence Center to be wound up like this."

"So what do we do? We can't find Simon Macafee, we can't get to your mother, and the Space Navy will be here to-morrow."

He turned to face Lilah. She had stopped and was holding her gloved hand against the wall of the tunnel.

"Tomorrow?" she said. "Are you sure? Feel, Jeff. It ended."

He reached out his own glove. There was no longer a vi-bration, passing along into his whole body through his finger-tips. The wall was dead to his touch. "They've stopped the power generation and storage. What does that mean?"

"It could mean we have all we need. Or"—Lilah was mov-ing again, speeding along the corridor to and past Jeff—"maybe we ran out of time. You can't pump energy into the Anadem field rings and take it out at the same time. What's the *earliest* that the Sol fleet could get here?"

"At full speed? If it started not long after the *Dreadnought* arrived, the fleet could be here now. The *Dreadnought* would have mapped a fast and safe route."

"Then I think they arrived. Come on, Jeff."

She was moving fast, propelling herself along the walls with a skill and efficiency that he could not match. He caught the urgency in her voice and followed pell-mell along the cor-ridor. He came to the airlock, already opened by Lilah, with his arms and legs flailing in all directions. He could not stop, and sailed across to ram into the far wall. By the time he got his breath the lock was already cycling.

"Suits off," Lilah cried. "Let's go, Jeff."

"What's the big hurry?" He followed her method and started to remove his suit from the bottom, so that his body was free while his helmet was still in position and he could breathe its air while the lock was working.

"You'll see." Her helmet was off, and she helped him with his. "If we're not careful, we'll be locked out of the interior."

He didn't have time to ask how that might happen. They had weight again, and he could keep up with Lilah as she dashed inward. Within seconds he could see the two great rings of the Anadem field.

As they approached the catwalk between the rings, a loud voice blared out: "FIELD PREPARING FOR POSSIBLE DISCHARGE. LEAVE THIS REGION AT ONCE."

"Keep going!" Lilah shouted. "We have to."

They were right between the rings, and Jeff could see a violet blue discharge in the air. They were running toward a vertical curtain, a smoking nimbus of ionized air. He could smell ozone, and he might have paused and turned around, but Lilah had him by the arm. She dragged him forward, into and through the shimmering screen.

He felt his weight double, then increase again. He staggered and nearly fell, but regained his balance at the last moment; then it was his turn to pull Lilah onward as her knees buckled under her.

They crawled the next ten yards side by side. Jeff felt his weight gradually return to normal. Behind him, the blaring voice announced: "THIS REGION CLOSED TO HUMANS WHILE FIELD DISCHARGE IS PREPARED. ENTRY IS PROHIBITED."

"It's all right." Lilah climbed awkwardly to her feet, stooping to rub her bruised and scraped knees. "We're safe now."

Safe, with a Space Navy fleet perhaps within firing range? Maybe they would have been better off to head outward, using their suits to jet as far away from Confluence Center as they could get. Jeff didn't pass that thought on to Lilah. It was too late to act on it anyway. He said, "We have to get to where we can see the displays. If the navy is arriving I may be able to guess what they are going to do from the positions they take up. Standard formations are designed for use in particular types of engagement."

"The control center—if we're not locked out of it. There are other display points, but they're not as good."

They were hurrying inward, toward the middle regions of Confluence Center. Another steady hum filled the air. Jeff glanced at Lilah, but she shook her head. "Nothing to do with energy storage or use. That's the general-address system. Everyone will want to hear what Control says to the fleet, and what the fleet says back. Think lucky, Jeff. We're almost there."

Even before she finished speaking, Jeff could see that the sliding door at the end of the corridor was open. Was that the luck that Lilah was talking about, that the control center would not be closed to them?

Before the day was over they would surely need a lot more luck than that.

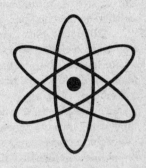

CHAPTER TWENTY-TWO

LILAH slowed to a walk as she reached the open door of the control center and strolled through, as though this were the perfectly ordinary morning of a perfectly normal day.

At first sight it was. The control room was quiet and uncluttered. Connie Cheever sat at a communications console, apparently relaxed. Half a dozen senior staff members surrounded her. Only the displays, set to show the sky in every direction from Confluence Center, told a different story.

Scores of ships were displayed there, four or five on every screen. They were moving into position, slowly and deliberately. The fleet had abandoned the hollow-cone formation used on long journeys, and was regrouping to form a great hemisphere with Confluence Center at the center. Once a ship reached an assigned position, it remained there.

"You know what that means?" Jeff said softly. "If they just wanted to keep us from escaping, they would deploy around the whole sphere. Ships form a formation like this when they want to be sure they can't fire past the target—us—and hit each other."

"I guessed that." Like Jeff, Lilah spoke in a whisper as they edged into the room. "Bad sign."

"But a good sign, too." Jeff added. "They aren't going to fire at once. Before they do that, you'll see them turn to face us head-on. As long as you see the ships in profile, you're all right."

Low as they had kept their voices, they had been noticed. Connie Cheever had her back to them, but she turned and pointed to Jeff. "You stay. But I don't want a word from you unless you see the fleet doing something that you think I'll miss. Then you pipe up at once. Don't worry, no one in the fleet will be able to see or hear you. Lilah, you can stay, too—but not a peep, no matter what."

Lilah did not risk a reply. She came forward and settled down cross-legged by her mother's chair. Jeff, not at all sure what Connie Cheever might notice or overlook in the actions of the fleet, moved forward and stood by Lilah's side. As soon as he was settled, Connie Cheever touched a pad on the console and said to the air in front of her, "Go ahead."

The face of Captain Mohammad Duval appeared. Jeff started to say to Lilah, "The *Dreadnought* never left! They just pretended to!" He bit back the words.

"Administrator Cheever." For a change, Duval was not smiling. "Following our last conversation, I have had the opportunity to consult with the Sol authorities."

Lilah gave Jeff's leg a great jab with her elbow. He could guess what she meant. *He's a bloody liar. You can't talk to Sol authorities without going back through the node, and we know he hasn't done that.* He nudged his calf back at her arm, looked down, and winked in agreement.

"I see." Connie spoke slowly, and only after a long pause. "Are you permitted to tell me what the Sol authorities told you?"

Not a word about the sudden appearance of the fleet. No mention of Mohammad Duval's obvious deceit the last time that they met. Jeff decided that he had no idea what game Connie was playing.

"I relayed to them your proposed terms, including your offer to provide the Anadem field and all associated technology. Unfortunately"—Duval offered his flawless and humorless smile—"those terms are judged unsatisfactory."

Again Connie delayed before she answered. "I am sorry to hear that," she said slowly. "Was there a suggestion for more acceptable terms?"

On her final words, Hooglich came hurrying in at the other side of the control room. She was wearing a space suit. She nodded vigorously, gave a thumbs-up sign, and was away again without a word.

"Because, of course," Connie went on, at more like her normal rate of speech, "we are anxious to reach agreement with you. We prefer to enjoy a mutually beneficial trade relationship with the Sol worlds, rather than engage in disputes."

Instead of answering, Duval vanished from the display. He was back in a few seconds, and now he was not smiling at all.

"Administrator Cheever, my technical staff report that a powerful, very low frequency electromagnetic signal is emanating from your facility. If you imagine that this somehow shields you from the weapons of my fleet, let me assure you that is very much a mistaken notion."

"I never held any such illusions, Captain Duval. The long wavelength radio signal that you refer to is simply a part of our communications system. Let me say again, we would like to hear the terms that Sol would consider acceptable."

"Very well." Duval glanced to one side, seemed reassured

by what he saw or heard in his own ship, and went on. "As you know, the Sol central government regards the Messina Dust Cloud as historically part of the Sol domain. All technological developments made in the Cloud therefore legally belong to Sol, as do any and all materials and natural resources found in the Cloud. I am directed to perform annexation of the Messina Dust Cloud in the name of Sol. You are to turn over to me, and to my fleet, control of Confluence Center. You will also direct all harvesters and rakehells operating within the Messina Dust Cloud to report to me."

Jeff felt Lilah jerk on the floor beside him, and heard her stifled snort of disbelief. The independence of the crews of harvesters and rakehells was legendary. How could Connie Cheever make them report to Duval and the Sol fleet, when they never acknowledged any government?

Jeff had his own worries. He was watching the ships on the screen. One by one they were turning to point directly toward the Center. Firing position.

"And, of course," Duval was continuing, "your submission to us must include turning over to my custody the renegade jinners and ensign of the *Aurora*, so that they may be delivered Sol-side for trial."

"The ships," Jeff whispered. "The fleet ships are getting ready to fire."

Connie turned at once. Out of sight of Duval, she spoke into the general-address system. "All personnel into suits." And to Jeff and Lilah, "You too!"

While Lilah went scrambling toward a control-room locker that Jeff had never even noticed, Connie returned to her position and nodded to Mohammad Duval. "Let me make sure that I understand this, Captain," she said calmly. "You lay claim to all of the Messina Dust Cloud, including Confluence Center and its contents. The Cloud will become an occupied territory, taking direction from Sol. You further require that all harvesters and rakehells submit to your orders. And we must hand over to you Jinners Hooglich and Russo, and Ensign Kopal."

"Correct."

"And if we refuse to do so?"

"I suggest, Administrator Cheever, that refusal is not an option for you. Perhaps I was not clear. Let me say this now in such a way that you cannot possibly misunderstand me. My orders are quite explicit. We are not here for *negotiation*. We are here to accept your surrender."

"Yes, that's clear enough. And if we do not surrender?"

"I repeat, that is not an option. I am empowered to use all necessary force to make you comply. If you do not surrender, I will be obliged to use whatever weapons are needed to subdue you or destroy you. I suspect that you do not comprehend the forces at my disposal."

He gestured offscreen. Where he had been standing, the display now changed to show an image of Confluence Center, floating free against the glimmering backdrop of the Messina Dust Cloud.

"Watch closely, Administrator," said Duval's voice. "This does not show the strength of my fleet—rather, it demonstrates the power of one weapon of a single midsize cruiser. Now!"

At his final word, the control room of Confluence Center shivered. The displayed image of the structure blazed with light, then cleared to show that the longest extension arm of Confluence Center was gone. It had not been sheared off, to hang loose in space. It had vanished in a puff of incandescent gas.

Jeff felt a knot in his chest. He and Lilah had been in that very arm less than a quarter of an hour earlier. But for her arrival, he would have stayed there and been vaporized. If the fleet fired at Confluence Center, the suits that Lilah had brought and they had just put on would do nothing to protect them.

"Do you need further proof, Administrator?" Once more, Duval occupied the display region, and the smile was back on his face. "I am sure that you will agree you have no alternative. Nor, in fact, do I. I must demand your surrender."

Connie, without looking down, touched the control pad in front of her. Jeff heard—or imagined, it was so deep and faint that it was hard to tell which—a subsonic murmur in and around him.

"You make matters very difficult for me, Captain Duval. I do not wish to endanger my people, or seek to harm yours. I ask again, Is there any way that we can negotiate a peaceful resolution? As you know, we are willing to make concessions."

"You heard my terms. I cannot change them, even if I wanted to. As for your ability to harm us, that is ludicrous. You must surrender. After that, we will see."

"We will not surrender, Captain. The terms that you state are totally unacceptable. In fact, they are insulting."

Duval stared back, tight-jawed. "Administrator Cheever, you are insane. You must accept our terms. Didn't you hear what I said? I am empowered to use *all necessary force*. If you resist, I have no choice. You face total destruction."

"You believe that, Captain. We—and I speak for all senior members of Confluence Center and the Cloud government—feel differently."

The background murmur was stronger, increasing steadily in pitch. It was now unmistakable, a low rhythmic whine as loud as speech. Connie Cheever raised her voice to speak over it. "I say again, we reject your proposed terms. Moreover, I urge you and your fleet to leave the vicinity of Confluence Center at once, and as fast as possible. If you refuse to do so, I cannot be held responsible for the consequences."

Duval's face reflected his disbelief. "*We* are in danger? From your stupid, do-nothing radio signals? I don't know what your scientists told you, Administrator, but it's nonsense. The low-frequency field you are generating does nothing to us, and it will not protect you from our weapons. Surrender immediately—or suffer the consequences."

"You have it the wrong way round, Captain. *You* must

surrender to us. Do so at once, and formally, and you will not be harmed. Fail to do so, and I cannot say how many of you will be alive one hour from now."

"That was your last chance." Duval glanced beyond the display region to left and right. "Gunners, prepare to fire. Cheever, you do not have an hour. You have exactly half a minute. Surrender within that time—or die."

"We will not surrender. We will *never* surrender. Captain, I beg you, for your own sakes, leave here—and leave *now.*" Connie Cheever glanced down, and Jeff caught her muttered words. "Simon Macafee, you had better be right."

The whine became a scream. As it moved higher in pitch, it also became familiar.

Shreep-shreep-shreep-shreep.

Jeff covered his ears with his hands and crouched down beside Lilah. To his surprise, Connie Cheever left her position at the control panel and joined them on the floor. She worked her way rapidly into the suit that Lilah had brought for her. When that was done she put her arms around her daughter and Jeff. She pulled them to her, huddled their heads close together, and said, "It's out of my hands now. God help us, no matter who wins."

A moment later, Lilah broke her mother's order to remain silent. She cried, "The displays! Look at the displays!"

Jeff raised his head. He had never seen an actual space battle, but no one born a male Kopal could spend his boyhood without being forced to watch scores of simulations and reenactments. He was looking at a classical pattern. The ships of the Sol fleet showed on the screens in a great hemisphere, poised in formation and ready to fire on Confluence Center. The glowing mass of the Cloud sat behind them, its rivers of neutral hydrogen swirling with plasma streaks of ionized carbon and oxygen and salted with pockets of stable transuranic elements.

He had stared at the Cloud a hundred times in the past few weeks, but it had never been like this. As he watched, the smooth dimly lit face sparked and scintillated with a million scattered points of light. Pinpricks of orange and gold flared bright and then as quickly faded. Where they had been, space held a curious empty clarity. Jeff felt that he could see all the way to the edge of the universe.

The luminous clarity lasted for only a few seconds. Then black marks pocked the delicate lilac-and-pink background. At first they appeared as little more than tiny dark tadpoles, but rapidly swelled to more ominous shapes.

Sounders—and sounders in numbers that Jeff had never dreamed of. They were appearing from nowhere, more and more, in their hundreds and in their thousands. Every one came racing in, rushing straight at Confluence Center. *Shreep-shreep-sh-r-e-e-e-e-p.* The ear-piercing signal generated within the Center faded. As it did so, a thousand answering calls poured in from space, *shreep-shreep-shreep-shreep.*

The infalling wave of sounders came toward Confluence Center like the rush of night, a closing wall of darkness oblivious to the loss of the outgoing signal. Between sounders and Center stood the ships of the Sol Space Navy. They had certainly detected the presence of the sounders—the calls resonated in every electromagnetic circuit within thousands of kilometers. For a few moments navy discipline held, all ships maintaining their positions. Then, one by one—with permission from Duval, or without it; there was no way that the watchers on Confluence Center could tell which—the ships turned.

Half of them fled, streaking toward and through the sphere of sounders at maximum acceleration. The rest, confident of the power of their weapons, held their ground. As the sounders closed and closed, space filled with the infernal flare and sparkle of Space Navy might.

The brilliance was too much for the display screens. They overloaded. When they flickered back into service, the scene had changed. Sounders closest to the ships were homing in on them, apparently little damaged by the first attack of navy weapons. The dark maws were stretching wide. Jeff saw a cruiser, its weapons firing right into the open gullet of a

sounder, engulfed by that dilating hole in space. As the cruiser
was swallowed down, the mouth closed. The sounder appeared
to shimmer and dissolve, and then was gone.

The set piece of navy formation fractured into dozens of
separate engagements. Jeff realized that he was in the middle
of—and part of—a full-scale naval battle. Even if the ships were
not firing at Confluence Center, in the heat of conflict they
could easily hit it by accident. He also knew what perhaps Lilah
and Connie did not: The weapons of the fleet were either pulses
of neutrinos and radiation, traveling at light speed, or they were
highly relativistic particle beams, moving only slightly slower
than light. In either case, Confluence Center could have no
possible warning before a weapon struck.

The sky became a wild tangle of ships and sounders. A
few vessels, learning from the experience of their fellows, directed their salvos away from the maws and struck at the sides
of the sounders. Each time, the wounded sounder either vanished in a spangled glitter or spun to take the attack on its open
maw. Power directed there was absorbed with no apparent effect. The navy ship had a simple choice: Try to flee, or hold position and be swallowed up. Of the dozens who engaged the
sounders, only a handful were clever or lucky enough to escape.

Jeff, trying to look everywhere at once to follow the bright
kaleidoscope of discharging weapons, felt but did not see the
thunderbolt. The floor of Confluence Center shook beneath
him, sending all three people sprawling full-length on the floor.
Moments later an urgent and unfamiliar voice spoke over the
address system: "Sector Four is breached. We have casualties.
We need help."

Connie struggled to her feet and moved to the control
chair. She had not quite reached it when the second hit came.
This one was nearer, so close that the chamber walls buckled.
Air screamed out through fractured seams. Connie went spinning away across the room, while Jeff and Lilah skated across
the floor and ended underneath a table. He was behind her,

and his weight drove her body hard against one of the table legs. He heard her cry in pain.

"Sector One is gone," said a breathless voice. "Adjoining bulkheads have failed to close. This is Sector Two. We have many casualties."

Jeff struggled out from under the table. He saw Connie lying against the far wall. He felt sure that she was dead, until he saw her roll over and crawl doggedly back to the control panel.

"Maintenance Logans to Sectors Two and Four," she said through clenched teeth. "If necessary, seal off Sector One. All others, hold position pending instructions."

Jeff pulled Lilah out from beneath the table. She was still and silent. He was enormously relieved when at last she whimpered, shivered, and put her hand on her right side. He turned again to the displays. They had blanked out when the second impact came, and now they were flickering back, one by one.

The battle continued, but its character had changed. The remaining navy ships had realized that their weapons could not destroy all the sounders. Some tried a late escape, drives flaring at maximum acceleration. A few broke clear. Others, despite the thrust of their drives and the inferno of their discharging weapons, were drawn helplessly toward and into the sounders' dark throats. As the ships were absorbed, the sounders shimmered, called across space, and vanished.

Finally just one vessel remained. It was the flagship of the Central Command fleet, a battle fort of the Thor class. Captain Duval himself commanded the half-kilometer sphere and its bristling array of weapons. According to navy publicity, a vessel of this type was invincible and indestructible.

The fort faced one of the largest sounders. The two approached each other, the fort firing all weapons, the sounder shivering and shuddering under multiple impacts to sides and head but not slowing its advance. The maw opened and opened, a chasm in space. By the time that the orbital fort changed tactics and turned to escape, it was too late. Slowly, weapons firing everywhere, the fort was engulfed. Bolts of random energy lit up the sky. The sounder called, high and loud, *shreep-shreep-shreep*, and disappeared.

The battle involving Sol's navy was over. But hundreds of sounders remained, undamaged and still heading toward the crippled Confluence Center. Jeff felt Connie Cheever's arm tightening convulsively around him. She had moved back to sit on the floor between him and the wounded Lilah.

"Now we'll find out," she said. "Oh, Simon, Simon, Simon. You'd better be right."

The sounders came on like a black tide. In ten seconds they would reach Confluence Center. Jeff could see beyond the maws the long, dark sides, stretching away into the distance and marked by patterns of lighter dots and swirls. He could see the eight tendrils, their blue-white and green-white whiskers distorting space around them. The nearest sounders were so close, he could look down the open gullets to a region of obsidian blackness, and see within them occasional glints of faint iridescence.

The nearest sounder was another giant. It raced in, all dilating mouth. And then, after a few long seconds, it began to slow. For a while it held steady, tendrils extended as though tasting the space around it. At last, when Jeff felt he had to breathe or burst, the sounder turned. He saw its vast sides, mottled and scaled and marked by strange spirals. And then it was retreating from Confluence Center.

Connie Cheever took a long, deep breath as though she, like Jeff, was learning again how to work her lungs. "Hats off to Simon," she whispered. "He was right, they don't like a low-frequency electromagnetic field. Look at them."

Sounder after sounder was approaching Confluence Center. When they reached a certain distance, one by one they slowed and tasted space with those long, impalpable, whisker-like tendrils. And, one by one, they halted, turned, and made a stately departure. Far from the Center, the backdrop of stars and Cloud around each sounder would shiver and twist. A moment later, the sounder called and vanished. The clarity of space faded; there was soon no sign that a sounder had ever been.

Within Confluence Center it should have been a time for relief. Jeff saw no hint of that. Connie sat again in the control chair, fielding a dozen urgent messages from the damaged sectors. A hole, twenty-five meters wide, had been punched right through Sector Four. Forty people had disappeared without trace, and another hundred were badly injured. Sector One had fared even worse. It was simply gone, together with all its equipment and hundreds of colonists. Five adjoining levels had been badly damaged by the same searing blow, and Sector Two was still trying to discover the extent of its loss.

Jeff watched and listened to the reports that streamed in, but he felt only half there. He was numb and exhausted. Lilah was worse off, it hurt when she breathed and she would not let him touch her ribs. But they were the lucky ones. Were Hooglich and Russo alive? Was Simon Macafee, and Billy Jexter? It might be hours before anyone knew.

Confluence Center had survived the battle with the Space Navy fleet; maybe it had even "won." But at a terrible price.

To Jeff's relief, Hooglich entered the control room. She had removed her suit, and her black face and arms were streaked with grey powder and what looked like drying blood. She came forward, slumped into a chair, and shook her head. "Hundreds or thousands of people lost here, and on them ships. Some of my best jinner buddies."

"I know." Connie Cheever broke off from rapping out streams of terse instructions. "It's an appalling tragedy. There were good officers and people in the Sol fleet, good as our people here. Most of them were just doing their jobs. Any feedback?"

"Not yet. Too soon. Lures may be working, but we won't know for a day or two. Macafee says—"

"He's alive? You're sure of that?"

"Sure am. I saw him, cool as liquid helium. Takes more

than a battle to rattle him. He says the lure we set here would only have had time to call locally. If the sounders go back where they came from, or to one of our other lures, they'll be near a Cloud reef. But if a sounder made an interstellar hop, or decided to go extragalactic. . . ." Hooglich blew out her fat cheeks and wriggled her shoulders against the chair back as though they were paining her. "The only hope would be to pump up Confluence Center again to high energy, and see if we can call 'em back."

Jeff had an awful thought. "Myron. My cousin. He was on Captain Duval's ship. . . ."

"We don't know that," Connie said. "He came here on the *Dreadnought* with Duval, but then Duval switched to the orbital fort. Maybe your cousin switched, too. He could be on one of the ships that escaped. I'll try to find out for you. We have to open communication with them anyway, see which of the survivors need help. Most of them took off at accelerations enough to burn out the drive. They'll be hanging helpless."

"Like we were, on the *Aurora*." Hooglich stood up. "Seems like years ago. I ought to say, let 'em rot. But I can't. I'd like to help them. Maybe we can jury-rig something, enough to let them crawl back to the node."

"No." Connie Cheever stood up also. "I know how you feel, you want to help your friends. But we are still at war with the Sol government. They did terrible damage to us, while we didn't want to hurt them in any way. Until that's resolved, I am going to blockade the node. Nothing comes through from Sol without our permission. No ship of the fleet will go back."

"But people on those ships may be badly hurt. They may be dying."

"I didn't say we wouldn't help them. We will. As soon as we've done what we can for our own, we'll provide humanitarian and medical aid to them. Nannies, too, if they'll agree to it. But their drives stay dead. The node will be guarded with a sounders' lure. So far as Sol is concerned, the Central Command fleet was routed, demoralized, and captured. If we choose to do so, it can be annihilated. I'll take a couple of navy eyewitnesses with me, who can vouch for all of this."

"*Take* them?" Lilah asked. She spoke in a weak, pained voice, but at least she spoke. Jeff felt his spirits rise. Maybe she had nothing worse than bruises.

"To Sol." Connie met her daughter's gaze. "That's where I have to go."

"But it's dangerous."

"I don't think so. Not when we have half their fleet as hostages."

"Why can't you negotiate here, with Duval or whoever will take over if he's gone?"

"Because Duval isn't the key. He was only following orders, and I'm sure those came from Sol-side. That's where we must do our talking. And as soon as possible. I can't hold a Central Command fleet—what's left of it—forever. We have to reach an agreement with the Sol government. And since I won't let them through the node to come here, someone must go there. Someone who can speak for the Cloud."

"Mother—" Lilah began. But Jeff cut her off.

"You have to go." He moved to stand between Lilah and Connie. "I have to go, too. Back home I've been branded a renegade and a traitor, guilty of negligence on the *Aurora* and of desertion from the navy."

"Certainly." Connie nodded. "After the negotiation is completed, when it's safe for you—"

"No." Jeff interrupted the general administrator of the Messina Dust Cloud without hesitation. "I must go as soon as possible. My mother is on Earth, alone and maybe desperately ill. The reports accusing me of treason could be killing her. I have to see her and explain what really happened."

"It won't work, Jeff. Suppose you did go with the negotiation party. You can't just arrive in the Sol system and demand transportation to Earth."

"Yes, I can." Jeff gave Connie and Lilah a grim and

humorless smile. "Though I agree that you and Hooglich couldn't." He turned to the jinner. "Could you?"

"No way. Try it, and I'd be straight in the can."

"But I can. Remember who I am. I'm Jefferson Kopal, one of the almighty Kopals who run Kopal Transportation and half the Space Navy. Maybe I'll be court-martialed when I reach Earth; for all I know they'll want to execute me. But until I'm tried, and until I'm found guilty, I'll be treated like royalty. I can make things easier for you when you get Sol-side. I'll make sure you are talking to the right people. I can tell you who you can't trust, who the snakes are—I'm afraid it's mostly my own family."

Connie's eyes locked onto his, and he did not flinch. "I see," she said at last. "We'll have to discuss this. But not now. There are more urgent items on my agenda. Go with Lilah, and we'll talk later."

Jeff nodded. He held his arm out, so that Lilah could hold on to it and limp alongside him. He would settle for Connie's promise of future discussion. She was going to give him an argument, he was sure of it. No matter when that began or how long it took, he would be ready.

Being born a Kopal was a nuisance, a burden, and a torment that no one in his right mind would ever choose; but sometimes, just when you felt ready to curse your name and household and all that they stood for, the name might prove a blessing and a boon.

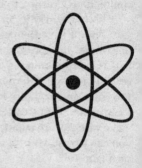

CHAPTER TWENTY-THREE

JEFF was in the study center when Lilah brought him the news. Told to stay out of the way while the cleanup and repair work were going on, he had been sweating over the design of Logan empathy circuits. Somehow they used a combination of quantum effects and probabilities to produce classical logic. He had been going crazy trying to understand how they did it, and the interruption was welcome.

"Yes!" He smacked his fist onto the desk when he heard Lilah's news. "I'm going! I wonder what I said that persuaded her? In our last meeting she was like a stone wall."

"Sorry, superman, but you had nothing to do with it. In

fact, an hour ago Muv still seemed determined that you wouldn't go."

"Why? She knows I could be useful."

"Useful? Neither useful nor ornamental." Lilah stuck her tongue out at him. She was hyper, a side effect of the nannies that were still doing repair work on her ribs. "It would be too dangerous, Muv said. Too dangerous to *you*. That's your own fault. You were the one who told us that you were supposed to die when the fleet came."

"That was Hooglich's theory, not mine. I think I was more like bait, to persuade people on Earth that a fleet had to be sent to the Cloud to bring me back. But that's all over, since they surrendered."

"Some people Sol-side may not agree. The story you have to tell could still hurt them."

"It could. And it will. But if your mother insisted that I *couldn't* go, and now I can. . . ."

"Don't thank her, or me. Thank Simon Macafee."

"You've seen him?"

"I sure have. He wandered in when Mother and I were eating breakfast, and announced that he ought to head Sol-side, and you should go with him."

"But he's the one they were after in the first place. He's the key to the Anadem field, and he's halfway to understanding the sounders."

"Exactly what Muv said. If he goes, how do we know they won't keep him and pick his brains forever? Simon didn't turn a hair. He said he'd be perfectly safe, and so will you. But when Muv asked him how he could be so sure, he just gave her that patented blank look. You know the one."

Jeff, recalling those distant, pensive eyes, nodded. "Why does he want to go?"

"He didn't say. But when Muv told him, no, definitely no, he shouldn't go and couldn't go, he looked at me in a pointed sort of way and asked for a private two minutes. Then they threw me out—halfway through my meal. Two minutes, it took more like half an hour, and when I was finally allowed back in my food was cold and everything had changed. Muv still seemed doubtful, but she agreed that if Cloud technology becomes part of a negotiation—and they think it will—she won't be able to handle it. Nobody can but Simon. Nobody else comes close with that scientific gobbledygook you two love so much."

Jeff felt sure that the last comment came from Lilah, rather than her mother. But he was feeling too pleased to protest, or to worry much about the reasons for Connie Cheever's change of mind. "I'm going," he said again.

"I know you are. Lucky beast, you don't have to rub it in. But you have to make me a promise—two promises."

"Sure. Anything." In his present mood, he meant it.

"First, promise that you'll come back."

"Of course I will."

"Good." Lilah grabbed his arm and started to swing herself around him, then grabbed at her rib cage. "Oof. Can't do that yet. And promise that when you do come back, next time you go to Earth you'll take me with you."

"It's a promise."

The pledge came out easily, and Lilah's answering smile was like the sun; but as Jeff spoke, he felt the chill of doubt. In a day or two he would be shipping back to the solar system and to Earth, to clear his name. He was certainly innocent. But suppose that he was not believed—that it came down to his word, alone, against the combined accusations of Eliot Dufferin and Cousin Myron and Uncle Giles?

Then he would face, at best, a court-martial and a dishonorable discharge from the navy. He would not be going to the Messina Dust Cloud—or anywhere else—for a long time.

That had been eight days ago. On the flight from Confluence Center to Node 23, Jeff's worries about what lay ahead strengthened. Once, his biggest worry in life had been acceptance into the Space Navy. The idea of dishonorable discharge—to a Kopal, the ultimate disgrace—had never occurred to him.

Now he had to fight to prevent it.

Again and again, he went over in his mind the statement that he would make at his hearing. He did not propose to offer one word more or less than the truth. But how would his accusers testify? Captain Dufferin would certainly present his own actions in the best possible way. That meant he would blame Jeff for what had happened to the *Aurora*, while the only people who could refute that and support Jeff's version of events were Russo and Hooglich—neither of whom would be present.

It did not help that Jeff was left to himself for most of the journey. Connie Cheever and Simon Macafee were on board, but they barely acknowledged his presence. They huddled aft in private meetings, only emerging for food and sleep. On the one occasion when Jeff caught Simon alone, he held out the card left with Billy Jexter and tried to ask what it meant.

Macafee was clearly in a hurry. He cut Jeff off in midsentence and grabbed the little oblong of plastic from his hand. "I wanted you to have this in case I didn't come back. I did come back. So now you don't need it. I'll take it."

"But what was I supposed to do with it? And what does the card mean?"

"Nothing important."

Simon stared right through Jeff as though his mind was already elsewhere. He pushed on past.

"That's a constellation on the card, isn't it?" Jeff bobbed around again in front of Simon. "The Dragon, as it's seen from the solar system."

"Oh." Simon halted. "You know that, do you?"

"Hooglich told me."

"Well, then." The eyes focused, and Simon's mouth took on a shy smile. "You have everything. You just need to think about it."

"But I don't know—" began Jeff. Simon slipped around him and hurried along the corridor, at a pace that suggested he would not tolerate more delay.

Jeff gave up. Now he had neither understanding nor the card. He headed in the opposite direction from Simon, to the forward observation bubble. The ship had completed its deceleration from Cloud travel speeds and was creeping toward the node. Jeff stared impatiently ahead at the shimmering orb.

When they finally matched position and velocity, he did not dread the disorienting spinning and stretching that would accompany the node entry. He welcomed it, as evidence that eight days of nagging worry were soon to end.

His own top priority was clear. As soon as they emerged into Sol space he headed for the communications center. Trying to send messages to Earth from the Messina Dust Cloud was a waste of time, a signal took twenty-seven years to get there; but now they were in the Kuiper Belt, Sol was visible as a bright beacon in the sky ahead, and a signal would reach Earth in less than half a day.

He had worked hard on the message and cleared it with Connie Cheever. It was going to his mother, but Connie was sure that others would also see it—every word from the ship would be analyzed by the Sol authorities, in preparation for meetings with the Cloud representatives. Even if Jeff swore that he had nothing to do with those meetings and would not be allowed to attend them, no one would believe him.

His brief message said only that he was well, that he hoped Mother had recovered from her operation and was feeling better, and that she was not to worry about him no matter what she might have heard. When she knew the full story she would realize that he had done nothing to bring dishonor to the family name.

He hoped for a reply, but he told himself not to expect one. Earth communications with the arriving ship would surely be tightly censored. It was a shock and a wonderful surprise, three days later, to hear over the ship's general-address system that a message for him had been received from Earth.

He was sitting again in an observation chamber, this one close to the rear of the ship. After they reached a point inside the orbit of Mars, the vessel had turned for its final deceleration and insertion into Earth orbit. Earth and Moon were already visible, a brilliant pair of mismatched sister worlds.

The recorded message carried video as well as audio signal. Jeff asked the communications system to pipe it through to the observation chamber's display, and waited anxiously and impatiently while that was done.

When his mother's face appeared, he felt a double shock.

It was great to see her again, but he remembered her as she had looked when well. With her lung operation over, he had hoped to see her that way again. He was forced to remind himself that although he felt like he had been away for years, only a couple of months had passed. Florence Kopal's scarred face was as pale and drawn as when he saw her last, and now it bore a new nervousness and intensity.

"I am at Kopal Manor." She began abruptly, without a word of greeting. He wondered, Had the message been edited?

"Jeff, I am very, very sick." Her voice sounded weak and full of self-pity. "I don't know how long I have. Please come and see me. Come as soon as you possibly can—or you may be too late."

She opened her mouth to speak again, but the screen went blank.

Jeff ordered the message to be played again, and then a third time. He watched and listened closely, but could draw few conclusions. His mother did not look well, that was true enough. On the other hand, she was clearly much better than when he had seen her last. Earth's surgical procedures could not compete with the nannies of the Messina Dust Cloud, but Florence Kopal was no longer struggling for breath. Her pallor suggested tension and worry more than terminal illness.

He needed a second opinion. He went to the cabin where Connie Cheever and Simon Macafee held their meetings, and sat down cross-legged on the floor in the passageway outside.

He was prepared to wait as long as necessary, but after only a couple of minutes the cabin door slid open.

"What do you think you are doing?" Connie Cheever stood staring down at him.

"Waiting." Jeff scrambled to his feet and noticed for the first time the tiny monitor that sat above the door and scanned the whole passageway. Connie probably had continuous reporting of anything that happened, anywhere in the ship.

"I wasn't trying to listen in on your meeting," he added, and decided as the words came out that only someone who *was* trying to eavesdrop would say that.

"I don't care if you were or you weren't," Connie said. "I don't like you sitting there, you're a distraction. What do you want?"

"I had a message. From my—from Earth. It seems straightforward, but I don't think it is. Can I show it to you?"

Connie said nothing, but motioned him into the cabin. Simon Macafee was leaning against a bulkhead, eyes closed. With anyone else, Jeff would have assumed that he was asleep. With Simon, it could mean anything.

Still without a word, Connie gestured to the wall display. Jeff called for the message, Simon at last opened his eyes, and the three watched in silence as Florence Kopal's short message was repeated.

"That's all?" Connie said at the end. She was frowning.

"That's the whole thing."

"Again."

Jeff played the message over. At the end Connie said, "Simon?"

Macafee had closed his eyes again and had apparently lost interest. "Obviously edited," he said dreamily. "But I think she did something very clever. My guess is that right after what we heard, she deliberately said something that she knew would never be allowed to get through to this ship. It concentrated the censor's attention on that."

"And they cut out the wrong bit?" Connie said. "In any case, there's no point in puzzling over what isn't there. Let's think about what is." She turned to Jeff. "You know your mother, we don't. But you saw something wrong with her message. What was it?"

"Mother was whining. She *never* whines, no matter what happens to her or how much she hurts. She said she was very sick and hinted that she is dying. But she looked a lot better than the last time that I saw her."

"Then we'll discard that part of the message. Is your mother smart? Don't be nice to her, be objective about it."

"She's very smart."

"The way she handled the message censors supports that," Simon added.

"So what are we left with? Do you think it might be a trap set by your aunts and uncles, Jeff?"

"I don't think so." Surprisingly, it was Simon who answered. "They know we hold Myron Lazenby, the son of Giles Lazenby, captive on a navy ship in the Cloud."

"True." Connie turned to Jeff. "Let's hear it one more time."

He played the message through again, and she nodded.

"Leaving out the tone of the message, which you say rings emotionally false, we are left with something very simple. It is important that you, Jeff, go to Kopal Manor—and as soon as possible."

"What do you think is happening?"

"I have not the slightest idea. But if you want a guess, I'd say that the news of our arrival in the solar system, with you aboard this ship, might be a key factor."

"Will I be *allowed* to go to Kopal Manor?"

"I see no reason why not. Your hearing before the navy board won't take place for several days. You can't run away, and if you had wanted to, you would never have left Confluence

Center. If anyone asks questions you can wave your mother's message in their face. Ask them if they want to deny a dying mother's last wish to see her only child."

"When can I leave?"

Jeff expected Connie to answer, but to his surprise she turned to Simon. He nodded toward another of the cabin displays. It showed that the ship was closing fast on Earth, the pattern of Africa and Asia already visible as brown smudges on the blue-white globe.

"Four more hours. Then we'll be parked in low Earth orbit and you can take a shuttle down." Simon turned back to face Jeff. "Any objection if I go along with you? When you live out in the Cloud, Earth seems like a kind of fantasyland. I'd like to pay a visit."

Jeff didn't mind at all, though he felt sure that Connie would object. But here was another surprise. She was nodding agreement.

"I only wish I could come with you and wander around," she said. "Everyone in the Cloud is curious to know what Earth is like, and we don't often have a chance to find out. But I'm the formal head of the party. I'll be visiting Earth, and my movements have been orchestrated. Official functions and boring dinners, no fun at all. But Simon ought to take the chance while he has it—everything will turn hot and heavy once the real arguments start."

Jeff was convinced that he was missing something. Connie was agreeing with every one of Simon Macafee's suggestions, when common sense insisted she should veto any proposal that Simon wander around freely on Earth. After all, this was the same man who had been so uncontrollable in the Cloud. He might say and do anything.

Connie's next statement added to the feeling of topsy-turvy logic. "I think," she said, "that it would be a good idea if the two of you stayed together. At least at the beginning."

Which meant, of course, that they would travel together to Kopal Manor.

Jeff regarded Simon and saw him with new eyes. Dress code and grooming in the Cloud were, to put it in the nicest way, of low priority. But even there, amid the grimy jinners, the dusty and disheveled Simon Macafee stood out as an eccentric. How would the long hair, casual clothes, and tangled beard fit into the elegant and polished—and, let's face it, terminally snobbish—ambience of Kopal Manor?

No need to speculate; a few hours from now, Simon and Jeff were going to find out.

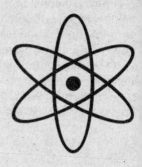

CHAPTER TWENTY-FOUR

HALF a mile from Kopal Manor, Jeff asked the car to stop. He told it that he and Simon Macafee would walk the rest of the way.

In principle, that was to allow Simon to sample another aspect of alien Earth. Jeff knew that nothing in the Cloud remotely resembled the long avenue of oak trees leading to the manor, the carefully tended acres of grassland stretching off to the horizon, or the formal flower beds and shrubberies.

In fact, it was Jeff who felt like an alien. He had seen all this as baby and infant and growing boy, so many times that he could not count. Yet today every sight was like the first time. He found himself marveling at the way grass fought a constant

battle to invade the flower beds, at wheeling flights of starlings
in the fall sky, at the intricate and delicate structure of late roses
and chrysanthemum blossoms, and at leaves, red and brown
and yellow, fluttering to earth with the touch of frost.

Simon, on the other hand, hardly glanced to right or left.
He jerked to attention only once, when a pair of small bushy animals scurried across the road in front of them.

"Squirrels," Jeff explained.

"Yes." But Simon seemed to have no interest in the flora
and fauna of Earth. He walked with head bowed, two fingers
scratching absently at the chin beneath the long beard. Jeff
saw—or imagined—a fine rain of dandruff. Simon had taken no
hint from the splendidly dressed and coolly courteous officers
who had greeted them and shepherded them down to Earth.
He wore a uniform of sorts, but it was faded, patched, and non-
descript.

Jeff wondered if it were deliberate, a subtle message to
the Earth authorities that said, "You can't impress us, you know.
We have your fleet. Who do you think has the stronger position?"

Jeff decided that the casual appearance was not deliberate.
Simon was just being Simon.

But Jeff was not, most decidedly, just being Jeff. Before entering the shuttle he had burnished to a fine brilliance everything on his ensign's uniform that would take a polish. His hair,
cut short, was as neat as he could make it after weeks of casual
care. He could not see his own insides, but from the feel of
them they stood to attention and were wound up as tight as
they could get. He had a great urge to hurry, and an equal urge
to put off their arrival at Kopal Manor for as long as possible.

What did his mother's message *mean*? There had been
nothing more from her, and Connie Cheever had urged Jeff
not to send another message.

"You'll see for yourself in a few hours," she said. "You can
wait that long. Be patient."

Easy to advise, hard to do. Jeff moved his eyes away from

the lawns and gardens to the road in front of him, where Kopal
Manor lay less than a hundred yards ahead. Not much to see
from the outside, except four air runabouts parked on the circular driveway. Every one was brand new.

Jeff and Simon moved from the paved road onto the circle
of the drive, and their boots crunched loud on the gravel. Still
no one was visible, but the big double doors silently swung
open in front of them.

"Just follow me." For some reason, Jeff felt he had to speak
in a whisper. He went inside, from bright afternoon sunlight to
the shaded gloom of the paneled entrance hall.

Midgeley stood within, partly shielded by one of the open
doors. He nodded to Jeff, as though the arrival of a renegade
from the Space Navy was a perfectly normal part of his day.

"Who's here?" Jeff gestured to the parked aircars.

"Your mother, and your uncles and aunts with the excep-
tion of Commodore Fairborn Lazenby. He was unexpectedly
delayed, and is expected within the hour. Lady Florence Kopal
is still in her suite, but her departure for the spaceport is imminent. She is most eager to see you and extended her stay here
for that reason. The others are all in the big conference room."
Midgeley said nothing more, but he stared at Simon with
slightly raised eyebrows that asked their own question: And
what is *this* that you have brought with you?

Most visitors who came through the front entrance of
Kopal Manor were highly placed officers of the Space Navy or
powerful business executives. Midgeley's expression suggested
that Jeff's companion belonged around the rear, at the trades-
men's entrance.

"Thank you, Midgeley," Jeff said as he went inside. "This
is Simon Macafee, a visitor to Earth from the Messina Dust
Cloud. He will accompany me."

Not his idea, but Connie Cheever's. She had insisted on it.
"Another pair of eyes and ears. Where your family is involved,
it will be hard for you to evaluate what they say as an impartial
witness."

Midgeley's opinions needed no evaluation, since he would never express them verbally. He nodded politely to Simon and said, "Welcome, sir, to Kopal Manor."

"Come on, Simon." Jeff was already running up the broad staircase. "I want Mother to meet you."

Uncle Lory was lounging at the top of the stairs. It was no surprise to Jeff that Midgeley had not thought to mention him. Uncle Lory was *always* at Kopal Manor, as much a fixture as Midgeley himself. Lory gave Jeff a surprised nod as he ran past, but he stared with a good deal more interest at Simon Macafee.

"Hey!" he said. "You—" Jeff heard nothing more. He was already dashing along the corridor to the east wing, Simon close behind.

The door to Florence Kopal's suite of rooms was ajar. Jeff burst through without knocking. She was sitting in a chair over by the north-facing window, gazing out over the slowly darkening sweep of lawn.

"Mother!"

As he ran to her she spun around and stood up. A good sign—she could not move so fast and easily when he left. But her first words renewed his fear. "Jeff! Oh, Jeff. It's great to see you. But you're too late!"

"What is it?" He put his arms around her. "Are you getting worse again?"

"No. I'm improving. And when I start physical therapy I'll be better yet. I'm scheduled for treatment in the orbital medical facility tomorrow, and I ought to have left for the spaceport hours ago. But I hung on here to the last minute, hoping you would come."

"Why didn't you just tell me to meet you at the spaceport?"

"Because you had to come here. It's your uncles and aunts; they've found a way of taking over Kopal Transportation. I couldn't stop them, and you're too late. If only—"

She paused. She was staring over Jeff's shoulder. He turned and realized that she had noticed Simon Macafee.

He was certainly something to notice. His arms hung loosely at his sides, his mouth drooped open, and his wrinkled uniform and unkempt hair made him a walking parody of a navy man.

At last he raised one hand to shoulder height, palm outward, and said, "Hi."

"This is Simon Macafee." Jeff was tempted to add, "The leading scientific intellect of the Messina Dust Cloud," but he didn't think his mother was likely to believe him.

It didn't matter, because after a first startled glance she had turned back to Jeff. "You're too late," she said again. "When the *Aurora* was lost and Captain Dufferin came back, you were charged with dereliction of duty and desertion—"

"That's not true!"

"I never believed it was, Jeff, not for a moment." Florence Kopal tried to smile at him and did not quite succeed. The scars on her face became more noticeable. "I swore that when you came back, we would learn what really happened and you would be exonerated. But since you left, everything seems to have gone wrong. Uncle Giles moved at top speed, and his petition to declare the official death of your father was approved a month ago. After that, you were all that stood between the board members and their freedom to do what they liked with Kopal Transportation. Then the crew of the *Aurora* came home without you. Desertion is grounds for a court-martial—and a court-martial from the Space Navy means disgrace and disinheritance."

"Hold on. I haven't been court-martialed. My hearing hasn't even *started*."

"I know. It doesn't have to. Uncle Giles somehow obtained a full statement of the charges against you."

"I can guess how. He's a snake who wriggles through the whole navy."

"Based on those charges he can offer a board resolution removing you from any management role in Kopal Transportation. He scheduled the resolution for a board vote this afternoon. And you weren't here. If you had been. . . . It's no good, Jeff, you're just too late. And I have to leave, I can't even stay to try and help."

But her final words were spoken to his back, as he dashed past Simon Macafee and out of the door.

"Go to the spaceport, Mother," he shouted as he ran. "Start your therapy. Maybe I'm not too late. Uncle Fairborn was delayed. If they need all the board members, and he didn't get here yet. . . ."

There was no point in any more shouting. He was out of earshot, racing past a startled Uncle Lory and hurtling down the staircase to the ground floor.

The double doors beyond the two antechambers were closed but not locked. Jeff threw them open and burst inside in one movement.

"Here at last!" said a familiar voice. "Now we can get on with—good Lord!"

It was Uncle Giles, in his usual seat at the head of the table. Uncle Terence and Aunt Willow sat to his left, Aunt Delia on his right. It was the same arrangement as the last time that Jeff was in the room, with one blessed difference. Uncle Fairborn was not present!

"No, I'm not Fairborn." Jeff advanced slowly to the end of the long table, moving through a dead, unnatural silence. "I'm Jeff, back from the Messina Dust Cloud. I didn't die, and I'm not too late. You haven't voted on the board resolution to take over Kopal Transportation, have you? Because you can't do that without Uncle Fairborn."

His uncles and aunts stared at him with a mixture of astonishment and cold dislike. The silence continued until at last Giles Lazenby said softly, "Hello, Jefferson. I can't say I'm too surprised to see you, even if the rest of us are. I knew that you were heading down to Earth. And you are quite right, there has been no vote. Thanks to Fairborn. Your uncle"—his mouth twitched—"was delayed by, and I quote, 'personal business.' We had words, and he finally abandoned his perfumed pleasures. He will be here in less than half an hour."

"Good. When he arrives, I demand the right to tell you what happened in the Messina Dust Cloud. It's nothing like the report that was filed by Captain Dufferin."

"I am prepared to believe that your version of events is at variance with the official report." The others at the table were still scowling, but Giles Lazenby was under control. He was even smiling at Jeff. "When you appear for the official navy hearing, you will be provided with an opportunity to state your case formally. However. . . ."

His voice trailed away. Giles was frowning, not at Jeff but right past him.

Jeff hardly needed to turn. This seemed to be his day for explaining Simon Macafee.

"Who the devil are you?" Giles continued in a colder tone. "And what are you doing here? This happens to be a private meeting, in a private house."

"He's with me," Jeff said. "His name is Simon Macafee. Maybe you've heard of him?"

It was a question that didn't need an answer. Aunt Willow seemed baffled, but the startled faces of Aunt Delia and Uncle Terence spoke for them. Only Uncle Giles had the presence of mind to put the smile back on his face. "Simon Macafee? Yes indeed, I have certainly heard of you. And under normal circumstances I would be delighted to welcome to Kopal Manor the inventor of the Anadem field, and hope to enjoy the pleasure of your extended company. But for the moment I must ask you to leave. We are engaged in private family business."

Simon returned the smile, but he did not speak. He seemed to be waiting for something. After a few silent seconds he nodded, turned, and left the conference room without a word.

Giles stared after him, his brow furrowed. He put his hand to his forehead. It took Aunt Willow to recall his attention, with an acid, "What a disgusting person! I am astonished, Giles, that you would even pass the time of day with such an interloper, still less be polite to him."

"You *would* be astonished." Giles turned on his sister. "Willow, you are an ignorant fool. When you have no idea what is going on, you might at least learn to be quiet."

"Giles! I will not permit you to—"

"Shut up. The man who just went out is the reason we lost a whole navy fleet in the Messina Dust Cloud. He could also be the man who destroys Kopal Transportation. With his damned invention, he is in a position to ruin us."

For a split second Jeff saw a different Giles in the tight jaw muscles and corded neck veins. He shivered; but the next moment the smile was back and the soft voice was continuing, "However, let us not permit this meeting to be distracted by matters over which we presently have no control. I will explain the possible importance of Simon Macafee to the future of Kopal Transportation, my dear Willow, on another occasion. Just now I must explain something else to our young nephew, Jefferson."

The smile turned Jeff's way. Now that he had seen the other Giles, Jeff recognized the venom behind it. He forced himself to stand to attention and wait.

"You see, Jeff." Giles spoke mildly, with none of the contempt that he had displayed toward Aunt Willow. "Your education has been deficient in a number of important areas. You do not understand the difference between *formal* and *informal* reports and hearings. *This* is formal." He picked up from the table a thin packet of papers and waved it toward Jeff. "It consists of Captain Eliot Dufferin's sworn statement as to the events occurring on the navy ship *Aurora*, from the time that it passed through Node 23 and entered the Messina Dust Cloud. The captain's statement is supplemented and supported by the statements of other members of the crew."

"It's all lies! He was trying to save his own reputation, and they were afraid to disagree with him."

"Perhaps so. But this is the evidence on which the charges of desertion and treason against you were based. And these, as I say, are formal, official documents. Now, in a few days you will appear before a navy tribunal. You will be given a chance to offer your version of events. That, too, will become an official document. Do you understand?"

"Of course I do. I've been working on my statement for days."

"I'm sure you have. Your future navy career could depend on it. Then there are *informal* reports. You may have told your side of the story already to dozens of people. But that was not under oath, and it does not form part of the official record. It therefore carries no legal weight. Now, you wish to present that story to the board. We will certainly not deny you that right. You will be given the opportunity, as soon as Uncle Fairborn arrives."

It sounded reasonable—too reasonable. But Jeff had grown wary.

"And after that?"

"After that, the board meeting will continue. Of course, it will do so with only the board members present."

"Without me. And only formal evidence will be considered."

"I did not say that. Of course, the board will balance formal sworn statements, with impartial witnesses, against informal statements by someone with a strong personal interest."

"You're saying that you'll ignore what I say."

"Not at all. I am telling you that our official responsibility as board members demands that we weigh everything we hear, and judge accordingly."

Jeff stared at the other faces around the table. Terence, Willow, and Delia would not look at him. They were taking their cue from Uncle Giles. He could expect no help from them.

"My mother and I will appeal the board vote."

"You are assuming that you know what that vote will be. However, you certainly have the right to appeal. Of course, such appeals tend to take a long time to be heard." Giles's smile for a moment took on a little genuine humor. "Now, until Uncle Fairborn arrives the board has other business. So if you would be kind enough to wait outside. . . ."

Jeff saw no choice. He left the conference room feeling shaky, and found Simon Macafee outside. He was leaning, eyes closed, against the wall.

"Did you hear that?" Jeff closed the conference-room doors.

"I did. Every word." Simon slowly shook his downturned head. "This is all a damnable nuisance. But it's my own fault if I was surprised. I should have known." He opened his eyes. "I need a bathroom."

"Right along there, on the left."

"And for the next fifteen minutes, I want you some place where your aunts and uncles are not likely to look for you."

"Why?"

"You'll see before too long. Don't go to your mother's suite; she will be gone by now, but that's where they might expect to find you."

"I could go to the old library. No one but me ever seemed to go there."

"Fine. If I don't come for you, meet me back here in a quarter of an hour."

"What's all this about?"

"It's about doing what I don't want to do. What I hate doing. Fifteen minutes more, and you'll understand."

Simon was walking away. He did not look back. Jeff stared after him, longing to follow and demand more information. Then he fancied he heard movement from inside the conference room.

He hurried at once in the opposite direction and headed upstairs for the safety of the old library.

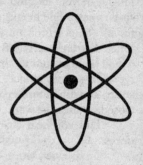

CHAPTER TWENTY-FIVE

NOTHING had changed in the months since Jeff last sat in the quiet, vaulted room. The fireplace contained the same charred remnant of a massive old log; the shelves bore undisturbed their arrays of leather- and cloth-bound books.

He was too excited and worried to sit down this time. Instead he prowled the aisles, every two minutes looking out of a window that faced the front of the house. He ought to see any car approaching along the drive, but nothing moved in the deepening darkness. There was still no sign of Uncle Fairborn.

Jeff returned to his wandering along the shelves. What was going on? Giles was orchestrating his takeover of the family business, that was certain. Jeff couldn't stop that, nor could his mother. But Simon Macafee's response was to tell Jeff to hide away, while he retired to the bathroom for a quarter of an hour.

And did what? Threw up?

That's what Jeff felt like doing.

When ten minutes had passed, he decided that roaming the library with a head full of useless speculations was a good way to go crazy. *Do something*. He switched on the overhead lights, went across to one of the shelves, and pulled an atlas from the section of oversized books. He took it to a gnarled table in one corner and leaned over it.

The volume was as huge and as old as he remembered, thirty pounds of smooth, heavy paper sheets inside the thick cardboard covers. For as long as he could remember, he had loved to turn the great pages and look at the multicolored maps of countries and colonies with names long vanished into history. What had happened to Tanganyika and Transylvania, Aquitaine and Arcadia, Siam and Serendip, Burgundy and Burma?

Today he turned instead to the first pages of the atlas. Here were maps that in the past he had glanced at briefly, then skipped over. They showed the face not of Earth, but of the sky. The stars displayed on the celestial sphere of the atlas had a permanence that mocked human dynasties and empires. And since the constellations remained the same for centuries, Jeff had argued, why look at drawings? You could go outside on any clear evening, gaze upward, and see the real thing.

The book that he held was an antique volume, so old that the constellations were still identified by their ancient names. The Swan was called Cygnus; the Big Dipper, which his mother referred to as the Great Bear, was Ursa Major; the Bull was Taurus; the Eagle, Aquila. Only a few constellations, like Orion and Hercules and Perseus, had the same names.

He did not see the word that he was looking for, but chances were the atlas gave the Latin version. If he was to find the Dragon, he would have to do it from the configuration of the stars themselves. It was a harder job than it sounded—he worked from memory, and a lot had happened since his last look at the little plastic card.

The minutes sped by. Five and more passed, and he was ready to give up and leave when the pattern seemed to jump off the page at him. It was a constellation in the northern hemisphere. There was no mistaking the long, curling tail that arched downward and then back up to the right. He saw the name written beside the pattern, gasped, and understood.

With understanding came sudden and surprising anger—at his own stupidity, at Simon, at Lilah, at Hooglich, at anyone who had been in on the conspiracy to keep him ignorant. But as he rushed for the door he realized that everyone was probably innocent except Simon and Connie Cheever. Lilah, he was sure, had had no idea. She would have told him.

And now he was late. He had been told fifteen minutes, and he had surely been away for twenty and more.

The double doors to the conference room were closed. He ran toward the unfamiliar person standing by them, and said, "I know! I understand about the Dragon and everything. Why didn't you tell me? It wasn't fair."

"Maybe not. But I thought you'd rather work it out for yourself. Anyway, this isn't the time to discuss it. And keep your voice down!"

The stranger was Simon, transformed. His beard had gone, and his hair was cut short. He looked ten years younger and much paler. Jeff recognized him only by his uniform, faded and wrinkled, and those unforgettable deep-set eyes.

"Fairborn arrived two minutes ago," Simon went on. "If you weren't here in one minute, I was going in without you. Come on. Let me do the talking."

It was an unnecessary instruction. Jeff's brain was so brimming with questions, accusations, and guesses that he didn't know where to start. He followed as Simon pushed open the doors and stepped forward into the conference room.

The tableau was as before, augmented by the presence of

Fairborn Lazenby: Willow and Terence were on the left, Giles sat at the head of the table, and Delia and Fairborn flanked him on the right.

Jeff saw them turn their heads, stare, and stare again. Anger changed to bewilderment, and then to shock—for Giles and Delia—and open disbelief on the part of Aunt Willow and Uncle Terence. Uncle Fairborn, pale-faced and dark under the eyes, made a gobbling noise like a turkey and said, "Drake? Is that you? It can't be."

"Even if it can't be, it is." Simon stepped forward. He slid a small packet the length of the polished table; it came to rest in front of Delia Lazenby. "Take a look at that. You may not believe me when I say this, but I'm no happier to be here than you are to see me here."

Delia picked up the packet and felt inside it. She pulled out three objects: a tiny glass tube, a folded slip of paper, and a little card of plastic that Jeff knew at once. Willow turned to Giles. "First he says he's Simon Macafee, and you grovel to him and tell me I'm an idiot. Now he says he's Cousin Drake, back from the dead, and he gives us a packet of rubbish. Is he mad, or are you?"

"Neither one of us is mad." Simon/Drake walked along the left side of the table, moving past Willow and Terence until he stood beside Giles Lazenby. "What Delia is holding represents a few credentials. I don't think you really need them in order to be convinced, but I'll save you time by explaining what they are. In the glass tube is a certified tissue sample. You'll find its DNA profile will match exactly the DNA profile of Drake Kopal, taken at the time of my birth and in storage at Midvale Hospital. The plastic card, one of you knows well. It's my old school ID. Recognize it?"

He spoke to Giles, who had taken the card from Delia and was studying it, holding the plastic carefully by the edges.

"I do, I do." Alone of the five Lazenbys, Giles seemed close to his usual self. His facial expression could not be seen as he stared down at the card. "Yes, I remember this. *Draco*, that was it. Your favorite constellation, you said, the one that had your name. Drake, Draco, the Dragon. And they gave you hell for erasing your picture ID and putting the constellation in its place. Why did you do that, Drake?"

"If I told you I knew, today, why I did everything I did then, I'd be lying. Maybe I *wanted* to get hell. I know I hated being a Kopal worse than anything in the world. All I wanted to do was escape. I think you understood that, Giles, even back when we were children. You were always the smart one, the one with an instinct for what was really going on. When I came in here today, I was convinced that you had recognized me."

"No." Giles raised his head to look at Drake. "That's not true. I had a funny feeling about you, but I couldn't put a name to it." He stood up and held out his hand. "Anyway, enough of all that. Welcome home. You've been away too long, and we'll have lots to talk about. I assume you'll join us for dinner? But first, if you'll excuse us, we have to get this meeting out of the way."

Drake—still Simon Macafee in Jeff's mind—ignored the outstretched hand. "Giles, I just told you that you were smart. Don't pretend you're not. Do you believe that I'd leave the Cloud, where I felt at home and was doing work that I love, to come twenty-seven light-years just for social chitchat?"

"We are your family, Drake." Giles didn't seem to mind the refused handshake. He was smiling, apparently delighted to be with his long-lost cousin. "Your only family."

"Sure—the family I ran away from. It was an accident that took me to the Cloud, and it almost killed me."

"You can't blame us for that, Cousin."

"I don't. But once I recovered and realized that no one knew where I was and I didn't have to come back here, I never felt such relief in my life."

"You can go back there anytime, Drake. All I was trying to do was welcome you home."

"I'll accept your welcome in good faith. I was even hoping

for it, in a strange way, all the time on the journey from the Messina Dust Cloud. But that's not why I came back. Do you want to know why I did?"

No one at the other end of the table responded. Finally Drake went on, "That's what brought me."

He pointed to where Jeff stood watching and listening in silence. "He did. Not because of what he said about you and the family business. That was bad enough, but I could have guessed it for myself. The thing that made the difference was Jeff's determination to come home and face the charges against him, even though he dislikes the military life as much as I do. He taught me that it takes a lot more guts to stay and face a problem than it does to run away from it."

The other Lazenbys, after a few minutes of shock, were coming back to life. Aunt Willow was the first to recover. She turned to Giles.

"How much of this nonsense do I have to sit and listen to? You were right earlier, when you said that this was a private meeting, in a private house. I don't see that anything has changed."

To Drake, she said, "I don't care if you are my cousin, or some stupid impostor. I never liked Drake Kopal. It meant nothing to me when he disappeared, and I don't see why it should mean any more if he pops up again. When you presented yourself to us as Simon Macafee, I said you were a disgusting person. I have no reason to modify that opinion."

"You say you came back to Earth to follow Jefferson's example," Delia chimed in. "Well, you've come, and you're here. Now you can go. We managed fine without you all these years, we'll manage just as well without you in the future."

"Go, before I come over there and throw you out." Uncle Terence, who to Jeff's knowledge took no form of exercise and could not walk five steps without wheezing, blew out his fat cheeks and shook a fist threateningly in the air. "Go, or you'll be out on your bloody neck. Eh, Giles? What do you say?"

Giles Lazenby seemed to have lost interest in the whole matter. He was staring down at the tabletop, his brow furrowed. At Terence's question he roused himself and rose to his feet.

"In a way they're right, you know," he said to Drake. "You are certainly our cousin, and I'm delighted to see you. But we didn't ask you here. You came barging in on a private board meeting, without permission, and interrupted our work. As Terence says, there is no reason on earth why you should not be made to leave. On the other hand, if it were my decision alone I would invite you to stay."

Drake nodded, but rather than leaving he sat down at the table. "You haven't changed, Giles, not since you were twelve years old. I was watching you while the others were speaking, and I could almost see the wheels turning in your head. You had to think it through before you spoke. Now you've decided. There's no way that I can cause problems, so why not be nice to me? Whether I am here or not, you can carry on with your agenda."

"You assume malice where there is none." Giles also sat down, swiveling in his chair to face Drake. "But I don't mind telling you what is going to happen next—whether you are here to observe it or not. We are going to propose and pass a resolution. Once that is done, I will be responsible for running Kopal Transportation. I don't see why you should object to that. I've certainly earned the right. You made it clear when you left that you had little interest in the fate of the company. But I've worked for it, all my life. I wasn't like you, born a Kopal and never realizing what you had. You were handed on a plate what anyone else would kill to get."

"Not anyone, Giles."

"Anyone who deserves it." Giles Lazenby was so concentrated on Drake, the rest of the people around the long table did not exist for him. "I deserve it, and I'll get it. I'm over all the hurdles now. Nelson Kopal is dead. Jeff is tainted. Go and read the bylaws for Kopal Transportation. A person who fails entry into the Space Navy, or is dishonorably discharged from the navy, cannot be involved in running the company. He can hold stock, but it's nonvoting stock. A resolution to bar Jeff from management has already been prepared. As soon as you leave— or even if you don't—we will vote on it. Do you want to know what the outcome will be?"

"Giles!" Delia said. "It's none of his business. You shouldn't be telling him this."

"It doesn't matter. He can't stop us voting any way we want. Can you, Drake?"

"I cannot. I have no power to influence your votes." Drake stood up and started back along the table to where Jeff was waiting. At the end, he turned. "You know, I'm a fool. I've changed over the years, and I really hoped that you might have. But you haven't. Same old Giles. Methodical, cold, and ruthless. When we were eight years old, I was the one who wondered why insects needed six legs to walk, and mammals managed well with only four. But you were the one who cut a pair of legs off ants and ladybugs, to see what happened."

"And you were the sissy who started to cry when he saw what I was doing." Giles stood at the other end of the table, radiating benevolence. "It's been a long time, Drake, but I guess you are right. Neither of us has changed. You're still the same gutless weakling."

"I'm sure I am. So go ahead, hold your meeting. I don't want to see it. Come on, Jeff, let's get out of here." Drake walked toward the door of the conference room. Halfway there, he halted and turned.

"You know, Giles, talking about the old days like this reminds me of one other thing. Remember when we used to play chess together? I always beat you. I wasn't a specially good player, but you had a fatal flaw. You became so absorbed in your own strategy to win, you didn't take enough interest in what I was doing. Right at the moment when you thought you were closing in for checkmate, I'd spring a trap on you. It happened dozens of times."

Giles scowled. "I was never much interested in chess. I didn't care a bit who won."

"Not true. You'd be angry for days."

"Anyway, that's ancient history. I've not played chess for decades."

"Nor have I." Drake nodded to the group at the table. "Go ahead, have your vote, finish your meeting."

He walked to the door, but paused with his hand on the doorknob. Again he turned.

"The strange thing, Willow, is that although you say you never did like me, I was always fond of you. I was sorry for you, too. You struck me as a sad young woman, always a bit out of it. You were like me in a way; you never seemed to know quite what was going on."

"Rubbish. And I neither need nor want your damnable sympathy."

"Of course not. But I wonder if all of you may not be a bit out of it. I suspect that you're all overlooking one little thing."

"I think you should leave now." The speaker was Giles, but from their expressions he spoke for everyone.

"Going, this very minute. I just want to point out that I was in the Space Navy, too. Of course, I was there for only a few months before I was stupid enough to put myself through a network node and disappear. But I was accepted into the navy, and I was not dishonorably discharged. So according to the by-laws, I am an eligible voting stockholder in Kopal Transportation. In fact, with Nelson dead, I think you'll find that I'm the *major* voting stockholder. Which means I get to appoint the board of directors."

He passed one final glance over the people sitting at the table, ushered Jeff ahead of him out of the conference room, and said over his shoulder as he was leaving, "So go ahead, pass as many resolutions as you like. But you know what? Without my stockholder consent, they won't mean a thing."

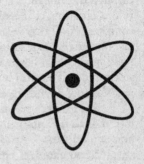

CHAPTER TWENTY-SIX

AS Drake closed the door of the conference room, Jeff heard a buzz of rising voices sounding through it. All his aunts and uncles seemed to be shouting at once.

"Were you saying what I thought you were saying?" Jeff could see that his uncle was trembling, and his face was white. "You control Kopal Transportation?"

"For the moment I do. But it's not giving me any pleasure." Drake took a long, deep breath. "My God, Jeff, I hated that. I'd forgotten what Giles can be like when things don't go his way. So civilized on the surface, and so vicious underneath."

"Are you all right?"

"Not yet. Give me a few minutes." Drake started forward through the antechambers that led out to the stone-paved corridor. "It's strange," he said softly. "I've never wanted to run the company, and I don't want to do it now. But when I saw Giles and the others ready to steal control, I just had to do something. As soon as I can, I'll halt all board actions. I can do that as major stockholder. That will hold things until you get the navy hearing behind you and are old enough to vote your own stock."

"But I don't want to run the company! I'd be no good at it. I'm not a military man, or a businessman. I want to be a jinner, or a scientist."

"Good choices. That's the awful thing. The only people you can trust to run the biggest transportation company in the solar system are people who won't misuse power. And they don't *want* the job. While people like Giles, who want the position so much they'd die for it, mustn't be allowed to have it."

They had reached the corridor and were hurrying toward the front doors. The whole house seemed unnaturally quiet. The staff would all be down in the basement levels or in the manor kitchens.

"So what happens next?" Jeff asked. The confrontation was over, but Drake still seemed awfully nervous and depressed.

"I'm having second thoughts about coming here at all. I wouldn't have, except I knew Giles. I suspected he was planning some sneaky move. I told Connie, and she said to be careful, it might get nasty. I didn't really believe her. I thought, after all, it's our own family. But now I do."

"We have to leave?"

"Fast."

"Why? Giles and the others know they don't have a chance. They lost, and you control Kopal Transportation."

"True, and that fact must be sinking into them. But it won't take Giles more than ten minutes to draw another conclusion: If I were dead, which he thought I was until half an hour ago, he'd be back in the game."

"You don't honestly think he'd try something like that?"

But Jeff did not need an answer from Drake. It was provided by a memory of the dark face with its knotted jaw muscles, and the soft voice saying: "You were handed on a plate what anyone else would kill to get."

"I don't know what he'll do. He might try anything. Giles likes to win." Drake spoke jerkily. After his slow start he was running, so fast that Jeff could scarcely keep up. "We have to get away from here. And I ought to be locked up for allowing you into a situation like this."

They were approaching the front doors, where a man lounged against one of the flanking pillars. Jeff felt a tingle of horror. They were too late, the way out was blocked, Giles had been too smart and too fast for them. Then he realized that the man was Uncle Lory.

His uncle nodded pleasantly and said to Drake, "I thought I saw you earlier, but I wasn't sure. You were away for a long time, weren't you?"

"I was indeed." Drake was trying to sound normal, but Jeff could hear the tremor in his voice. "How are you, Lory?"

"I am fine. Drake, were you in space? They said you went there."

"Yes, I was in space. And I have to go there again."

"That must be wonderful."

"Lory, we will talk about it some other time, as much as you want." Drake's voice was gentle, masking his tension. "Right now, Jeff and I have to leave. Quickly."

"Florence left in a hurry, too. She said she was going to space."

"We are in even more of a hurry than Florence."

"It's nighttime now."

"I know. But we can't wait for morning, we have to be on our way at once. Jeff and I will start running, but we will need an aircar to come and pick us up. We have to call a service."

"I can do that," Jeff said quickly. He wasn't sure that Uncle

Lory was up to making such a call, and at last he had something to do other than stand around and gape. "The service numbers are in the data bank."

But Lory was frowning at them, standing in their way as they tried to get to the front door. "I suppose if you don't want to take one of the family cars, out back. . . ."

Drake glanced at Lory, then gave Jeff a strange look. Jeff was convinced that it meant, What sort of an idiot are you, Jeff Kopal, who doesn't know what's in his own house? until Drake said, "I could say it's my nerves, but it's actually my stupidity. I live here for eighteen years, and I don't remember a thing about the place."

They had all three turned and were hurrying toward the rear door of the manor. "Do you think we'll find one ready to fly?" Drake asked.

"Mine," Lory said promptly. "It will be ready, it always is."

"Lory's right," Jeff added. "His car is kept in tip-top shape, and it's always ready. The car's your pride and joy, isn't it, Uncle Lory?"

"It is." Lory beamed for a moment, then he shook his head. "Of course, they won't let me fly it. I think I know how, but they won't let me."

As they left the house and started toward the garage hanger, Jeff felt an irresistible urge to turn and look back. The whole rear of the house was quiet, with not a light showing. Would Giles come after them in darkness, trying to stop them leaving? Surely not.

The hangar door was open. Jeff, hurrying toward Lory's gleaming aircar, decided that he had too much imagination. Not even Uncle Giles would attempt something so direct.

He followed Drake into the car. Lory climbed in after them. Jeff, about to tell him to get out, saw his uncle's excited face and changed his mind. This was Lory's aircar, his most cherished possession. He at least ought to get a ride in it.

"Ready?" Drake was in the pilot's seat, and the motor was already humming.

"Ready." Jeff closed the sliding door and settled in the rear seat next to Lory.

"Hold tight then. We're not going to hang about."

The car left the hanger, turned, and shot forward with a great burst of acceleration. Within forty yards it was close to airborne, wheels skimming along the smooth lawn. Jeff took one last look at the house. There was a light now, shining from the open back door. He thought he saw a man's shape, outlined in the doorway. A flash of violet light across the ground came and went almost too quickly to see.

The car lurched and dipped for a moment to one side.

"Left wheel of the undercarriage gone," Drake said. Now that he had something physical to do, he seemed totally calm. "Good thing we have plenty of lift. We're going straight up—I hope."

The car was clear of the ground, rushing nose-high into the night sky. Jeff saw another flash of pale violet, but it passed far beneath them.

"One thing you have to say for Giles." Drake was taking them up in a steep, banking curve, away from the dark bulk of Kopal Manor. "When he chases something, he chases it all the way."

"What did he chase?" Lory asked.

"I meant that he wants to run Kopal Transportation."

"Oh. What a dull thing to want."

"I agree with you. Hey." Drake was examining the controls of the aircar. "This shows a second set of engines, and they're not for an air-breathing mode. Can this car go orbital?"

"It's supposed to be able to," Lory said.

"It must have cost a fortune."

"Not by Kopal standards." Jeff felt his spirits rising as the car soared and Kopal Manor vanished far behind. "You were away for too long, Drake. You've forgotten what it's like. When you're a Kopal and it comes to transportation systems, you have nothing but the best."

"Then orbital it will be. With Giles on the warpath, we

don't want to mess around on Earth longer than we have to. I'll feel a lot safer when we are outside the atmosphere."

He touched the control board, and the nose of the aircar tilted further. Jeff felt himself pressed back harder into his seat.

"Do you mean it?" Lory turned to Jeff. "You're going to space, and you're taking me with you?"

"That's right, Uncle Lory." Under Drake's guidance the car was moving faster and faster. The sun was visible, rising again around the curve of the earth.

"I can't wait to get there." Lory's face glowed in the light of a new dawn. "You've been to space. Is it really as good and exciting as people tell you it is?"

"No, it's not."

For the past few hours Jeff had been controlled by others, with no more say in where he went or what he did than a wasp trapped inside a jar. But finally he had a question that he could answer, without consulting Drake or anyone else.

He thought of the network nodes, glimmering opalescent bubbles providing transfer points to distant parts of the universe; he remembered Hooglich and Russo, speaking of Diabelli Omnivore drives and Anadem fields in tones normally reserved for a religious experience; he recalled the eight-armed, bottle-bodied Logans, perpetually frustrated by and patient with human frailties and failures of logic; he saw in his mind the Messina Dust Cloud, that vast tapestry woven by twisting rivers of dust and glowing gas, with the space sounders coming and going as they chose, moving in mysterious ways across the Cloud's broad face; he recalled the monstrous wheel of the Galaxy, seen from so far away that a hundred billion suns merged into a single bright image. Last of all he remembered Lilah, hanging in free fall, babbling relentlessly of horses, and making Jeff swear that he would one day return to the Cloud.

"Space isn't as good as people tell you," Jeff said. "Uncle Lory, it's much, much better."

TOR
BOOKS The Best in Science Fiction

LIEGE-KILLER • Christopher Hinz
"*Liege-Killer* is a genuine page-turner, beautifully written and exciting from start to finish....Don't miss it."—*Locus*

HARVEST OF STARS • Poul Anderson
"A true masterpiece. An important work—not just of science fiction but of contemporary literature. Visionary and beautifully written, elegaic and transcendent, *Harvest of Stars* is the brightest star in Poul Anderson's constellation."
—Keith Ferrell, editor, *Omni*

FIREDANCE • Steven Barnes
SF adventure in 21st century California—by the co-author of *Beowulf's Children*.

ASH OCK • Christopher Hinz
"A well-handled science fiction thriller."—*Kirkus Reviews*

CALDÉ OF THE LONG SUN • Gene Wolfe
The third volume in the critically-acclaimed Book of the Long Sun.
"Dazzling."—*The New York Times*

OF TANGIBLE GHOSTS • L.E. Modesitt, Jr.
Ingenious alternate universe SF from the author of the *Recluce* fantasy series.

THE SHATTERED SPHERE • Roger MacBride Allen
The second book of the Hunted Earth continues the thrilling story that began in *The Ring of Charon*, a daringly original hard science fiction novel.

THE PRICE OF THE STARS • Debra Doyle and James D. Macdonald
Book One of the Mageworlds—the breakneck SF epic of the most brawling family in the human galaxy!